The Wolves of Whitebark Stand

Serenity's Gift

M.L. Cook

Thanks for your Support!
Mary L. Cook

Serenity's Gift

ISBN: Paperback: 9798840373576
ASIN: B0B6B89CM5

Contact Information: Lynndaniels1986@gmail.com
Cover and editing by: Lisa Miller @ Got You Covered

Also by M.L. Cook

The Adventures of Lok'Toria

The Princess Finds a Pet

The Pet Finds a Boy

The Boy Finds a Crown

Username Unknown

Felidian Warriors:

New Dawn

Dawn of Inception

Forging an Alliance

Relentless Pursuit

Souls United

Tomorrow's Hope

Dark Star Warriors:

Dark Star

Star Captives (coming soon)

Before you begin…

If you're interested in becoming a part of my Facebook group, just hop on over.

https://www.facebook.com/groups/320682151933041

Before you get started, I would also like to invite you to visit my website where you can get updates on upcoming books, plus links to my other books.

https://www.marycooknovels.com

Please sign up for my newsletter. In it you will find information on new and upcoming books, plus much more!

https://mailchi.mp/c94b61528cd5/marys-books

Chapter One

A dark wolf stood on the hill overlooking the quiet community of Whitebark Stand. The cool breeze ruffling his fur was a welcome respite from the sweltering July heat. In the distance, cars could be heard on the highway. His ears pricked; movement stilled. He waited…ready. Minutes ticked by as the cars passed. His pack was safe. All was quiet.

He relaxed and turned his attention to the house below.

He'd stalled long enough. Winter was coming and he wasn't ready. As much as he wished he could spend the afternoon running through the forest, he had responsibilities. As the wolf stepped out of the woods, his form shimmered and changed.

The grass, still damp from the morning dew, was cold on his bare feet. Marcus climbed the stairs, crossed the deck, went into the bathroom, and turned on the shower.

In his office, the phone rang.

Marcus stepped under the hot spray and allowed the tension to melt away.

He didn't hear the answering machine kick on. Nor did he hear the shouted words of his beta. It was something that would haunt him for years to come.

Marcus stepped out of the shower, wrapped a towel around his hips and moved into his office. That was when he noticed the blinking red light. He pressed the button, walked over to the bank of windows, then stepped through the slider and onto the deck. He smiled, admiring the breathtaking view of Mount Rainier in the distance. From there he could see every house and road that wove into and through the small, quiet community that comprised his packmates.

The activity below pulled his attention away from the message that began playing.

Gun wielding men poured from trucks. The wolves—his pack—caught unaware, were attempting to stave off the threat. He watched one leap toward a man then fall, rigid to the ground, unmoving. Others were gunned down while fleeing the sorcerers.

Men, women, and children, whether they'd shifted into their beasts or remained human, fell to the Dämonejäger's evil.

A young girl watched men she'd known her entire life brought down by strangers. Some were shot, others were mysteriously frozen in place. Her baby brother, ignorant of the danger he was in, toddled across the yard. She knew he didn't stand a chance against grown men. It was up to her to protect him, even if she died doing it. Without hesitation, she shifted into a small grey wolf, snarled, and leapt toward one of the men.

The man, unimpressed and unafraid, waved his arms and murmured a few words. She was caught by his magic, tumbling harmlessly to the ground.

Behind her, the wide-eyed stare of a boy who'd learned to walk the week before watched. The man was standing over his sister, laughing. He giggled and toddled closer. He looked from his sister to the stranger. An instant later, he heard a loud boom.

Horrified, Marcus watched crimson blossom across the toddler's back.

With a howl of rage, he surrendered his humanity. His vision sharpened. A low growl rumbled up from deep in his throat. The man was gone. In his place stood an enraged dark wolf. His people, his pack, were under attack. As their alpha, it was his job to protect them.

Snarling, muscles bunched, the huge wolf tore through the meadow. With his gaze centered on the enemy, he crouched to pounce.

Oskar Jäger was the leader of the Dämonejäger. Each of his men had been sired by him, or his kin. And each had sworn their loyalty to him. They'd dedicated their lives to find and rid the world of the demons who'd come in the guise of wolves.

He turned from his clansmen when he sensed the magic radiating from the dark wolf, who was quickly narrowing the gap between them. Nodding in approval, he murmured, "The alpha."

The sorcerer raised his hands and began an incantation that had been passed down through generations. With each repetition, it gained volume, until the roar of his voice thundered through the village. “I call on the powers of darkness. Flow through me. Heed my words. Capture this beast. Bone and sinew. All that is within, and all that is without. No breath shall it take, no movement make, never again to wake.”

Chapter Two

As the pack's second in command, Chance Fridolf's house stood just below Marcus's huge cabin. There were many times he'd stumbled in from late nights trying to convince Marcus to modernize their community. However, as hard as he argued for change, Marcus argued just as much against it.

Today, he'd watched Marcus spend most of the day chopping wood for the coming winter. Chance decided it was the perfect opportunity to bring up a more efficient way to keep their houses warm. Just as he was preparing to step off the porch, he heard the rumble of several large trucks rolling into Whitebark Stand.

He rushed back and grabbed the binoculars by the door and peered through the trees. Chance was a big man, an even bigger wolf, and not much got to him. But this…this made his blood run cold. His first instinct was to save his family, but as the pack's beta, it was his job to alert the alpha first. He ran into the house and grabbed the cordless phone. While staring out the window, he silently prayed for Marcus to answer.

When the machine clicked on, he bellowed, "Marcus, pick up! Marcus! Man, where are you? A caravan of pickups and box trucks just rolled in.

Marc, I think it's them. Riding shotgun in the lead truck…it's old man Jäger, himself."

Chance couldn't wait another second; he tossed the phone and exploded through the door. Through the meadow, he ran toward a cabin on the outskirts of their community.

Chance stopped on the threshold of his brother's house and stared into the darkened rooms. Nothing moved. Was he too late? He ran through the cabin, searching for his younger brother. Cupping his mouth, he yelled, "Henry! Where are you?"

As he ran by an open door, someone grabbed his arm. He spun around and saw his brother. Henry was drenched from shoulder to knee and in his arms, he held his freshly bathed four-year-old daughter.

Henry stared at Chance; never had he seen his brother in such a state. Windblown hair. Torn clothes. His eyes were locked between human and wolf. He knew Chance was keeping the change at bay, but just barely.

Doubled over panting, with his hands on his knees, Chance waved an arm toward the kitchen. Between heaving breaths, he shouted, "Out the back…head for the woods. They're here. Dämonejägers."

With those parting words, Chance surrendered his humanity. A moment later, a large grey wolf leapt through the back door and ran toward the forest beyond.

Henry glanced toward the front of the house; only then did the shouts in the streets register. The howls of his packmates, cut short by those who hunted them, were coupled with blasts from shotguns.

Looking down at his baby girl, he spoke softly, pleading, "Celeste, sweetheart, I need you to concentrate on your wolf. You must shift. Do it now, baby girl, and run. Follow your uncle."

Henry set his daughter on the floor, while silently praying for her to do as he asked. His daughter's form shimmered a moment before a white pup with silver tips took her place. Not waiting for her father, the pup raced after her uncle. All the way, Henry nipped at her heels, urging her to go faster. After a quick backwards glance, he leapt through the door behind Celeste.

Chance stood at the edge of the dark forest, waiting for his brother. Earlier that day, Jonas, the youngest of the three, had volunteered to take Henry's mate to the obstetrician. Henry needed to stay behind with Celeste, who was still learning to control her shift. The last thing anyone needed was for a wolf pup to suddenly appear in the doctor's waiting room.

Chance prayed they stayed away long enough to escape the Dämonejäger.

Panic raced through him when he saw a three-wheeler cutting through the brush hot on the heels of his brother and niece. He mentally urged his brother on, crouched, and prepared to pounce when the moment came.

With Celeste behind them, Chance and Henry stood shoulder to shoulder.

The Dämonejäger leapt from the bike and landed a few yards away. He lifted his hands and began chanting.

Time slowed. Celeste whined and cowered behind the formidable wolves standing protectively over her.

A moment later, the forest sounds faded and the air around them stilled.

***

In the quiet community of Whitebark Stand, rumbling tires could be heard rolling across the highway in the distance. A gust of wind blew leaves and debris across empty streets.

An elderly man, lying in a pool of blood, was experiencing the final moments of his life. A dried maple leaf tumbled across the yard of a house he'd called home for more than forty years. Although age had taken so much from him, including many memories, he still had dignity. He'd never been treated as less by any member of the pack, not even the alpha. For that, he'd been grateful.

Closing his eyes, the pain faded. He was ready. He knew everybody else was either gone or dead. Including his mate. He was helpless to do more than watch while a stranger lifted his rifle. One loud blast, and it was over. Without her, he was nothing.

Although his death wouldn't be as swift, he smiled, knowing he would soon join her in the next world.

The rough blacktop beneath him rumbled with an approaching vehicle. Perhaps they'd come back to finish what they'd started. He could only hope. After sucking in a deep breath, he coughed, then rolled onto his back to face his attackers. A dark shape knelt beside him.

"What happened here?"

A familiar voice. He blinked once and a face came into focus. Jonas. How could that be? His pack was gone. He blinked again. What was the man asking? Was this a test? A single word came to mind. Licking his dry lips, he murmured, "Dämonejägers."

Chapter Three

Thirty years later

Erika Jäger laid still in her bed and listened to the party below. Mixed voices, laughter, and good-natured shouting, along with the softly playing music, drifted up the stairs. With her gaze focused on the ceiling above her bed, her hands fisted at her sides, she grumbled. Hours.

That's how long she'd been laying here waiting for sleep to claim her. Well, it may not have been hours, but to her six-year-old mind, it felt like hours. She threw the blankets off, sat on the side of the bed, and glared at the narrow shaft of light beneath her bedroom door. This wasn't her first party. She knew it would continue until the sun sent colorful streaks across the eastern sky. Too many nights, she'd sat beside her window and watched stars blinking out while light overtook the night. One by one, the party goers eventually ambled out to their cars while waving and calling their goodbyes.

Tonight, like every night for the past week, the little sleep she'd gotten was filled with vivid dreams. In each nightmare, she ran through the forest while attempting to get away. And every night the enemy came a little closer. His pounding footsteps ate up the ground between them, narrowing the gap. Even in her young mind, she knew if caught, she would be doomed to a fate worse than death. She'd be punished for some imagined wrongs, innocently accused of crimes she'd had nothing to do with.

Again, as with every night, someone spoke to her from the realm of dreams. She didn't know if he was real. But each time he'd called her, his plea was more frantic than the last. His name was Chance Fridolf, and she knew she must find him before it was too late. Too late for what, she could only guess. But more than anything, she needed him to explain his whispered plea, "Find the alpha."

Erika whispered into the darkness. "But I'm just a little girl. I don't even know what alpha is."

Erika slid her feet into soft pink slippers then padded toward the door. Inching it open, she listened for a moment. When she only heard the same party sounds as before, she stepped into the hall. On tiptoes, with one hand brushing the wall, her wide-eyed gaze drifted over the railing to the room below. She reasoned if she could only see the tops of their heads, then they couldn't see her.

Erika paused at the dark door at the end of the corridor. Glancing over her shoulder one more time, little fingers gripped the cold brass and twisted. She inched the door open but winced at the loud creaky hinges. Too loud, according to her little ears. With her heart racing, she paused. With a hand on the doorknob, she glanced over her shoulder. Nothing.

The party raged on, undisturbed by her attempted escape.

One hand on the railing, she stepped down. The dark stairwell had always scared her. Momma told her since this was for the servants, there was no need to put in a light. But when she asked if the servants could see in the dark, her mother got mad and told her to go play.

Erika slipped from the staircase into the narrow passage between kitchen, dining room, and back door. A headful of blonde curls twisted first one way, then the other. She noticed the party was even louder down here. At the sound of approaching footsteps, she hurried through the back door and down the steps.

She ducked around the corner, sucked in a breath, and waited. A moment later, the silence was interrupted by one of the women scolding another for not shutting the door.

After the door slammed, she sank to the ground and the breath she'd been holding exploded with a loud whoosh. By the light of the full moon, she could see she was alone.

Erika turned and ran. She didn't stop until she reached the forest.

Tall trees loomed overhead as she stepped from the dewy grass and onto the soft bed of pine needles. The forest was thick with trees and brush, allowing only a little moonlight to penetrate. She was safe from the party goers. She knew it with absolute certainty. Not even her white-blonde hair, or her pale pink nighty could be seen from the house. She'd become one with the forest and all its creatures.

As she walked, her small hands brushed against rough bark. While winding her way around trees, she hissed, "Chance?"

Nobody answered.

She tried again. A little louder this time, she whispered, "Chance? Where are you?"

Erika clamped a hand over her mouth after a startled yelp. She'd come around a tree and came face to face with a huge beast. Laughing nervously, she muttered, "It's just a dog." Stepping closer, she held a hand under its muzzle and waited, like her parents had taught her. When the dog didn't react, she brushed a hand down his silky neck a few times. Cocking her head, she squealed, and murmured, "It's you! I found you!"

Erika buried her face in his fur and wrapped her arms around his thick neck. "I just knew I would find you, Chance," she murmured into his fur.

After hearing another name whispered into her mind, she stepped back. She leaned away while trying to see where he wanted her to go. She said, "Henry, right. I don't see anything…"

She walked around him, then gasped. Beside her new friend, she found tufts of light grey fur beside a few, scattered, old bones.

Erika stumbled, then rushed back to Chance. She didn't know what to say or do; she wasn't even sure what she was looking at. But she suspected it was Henry. “I’m so sorry. Henry…he…I think he’s dead.”

Her chest ached with the pain of knowing he’d died out here, and that he’d been all alone in his last moments. More than that, her heart broke for her friend. She didn’t know how she knew, but she did with absolute certainty, that Chance had been unaware he’d lost someone he loved.

Nodding her understanding of his unspoken words, she ran a hand down his back while slipping around behind him. Gasping, she whispered, “Well, hello. Who is this? Why, you’re just adorable.”

Erika plopped to the ground and scooped the tiny pup into her arms. She kissed her nose, murmured words of comfort, and stroked her soft fur.

Finally, exhaustion caught up. With the pup cradled in her arms, she yawned and scooted closer to Chance, then fell into a peaceful sleep.

***

Sounds filtered through her sleep muddled mind. Voices overlaid with the sounds of birds and creatures of the forest invaded her sleep. Running a hand through her hair, she screamed after something crawled across her arm.

Shouted words got her attention. “Over here!”

Erika leapt from the ground. She brushed her hands down her filthy gown and stomped her feet. Shuddering her revulsion, she finally looked around. Through the trees, she could see someone running toward her. Blinking away sleep, she mumbled, "Poppa?"

"Baby girl! I can't tell you how scared I was," her father exclaimed while scattering kisses on her face and in her hair.

A second later, her father stiffened.

Erika shuddered. She knew what was coming. And it wouldn't be pleasant. At the very least there would be yelling. But at the most…

She trembled. There were only a few times she could remember her father's anger reaching a point where rage overtook reason.

After it was over, he always offered his heartfelt apologies. But it never really wiped away the fear and pain that accompanied this level of fury.

And Erika had a feeling this would be one of those times.

Chapter Four

After that night, Erika's father had forbidden her to step foot into the woods. To emphasize his point, he'd followed through with a very severe reprimand that continued to ache for days afterwards.

However, once she'd recovered sufficiently to put on her thick jeans, she snuck out again. This time, she'd make sure she didn't fall asleep. Father was at work, and Mother was busy with the boys. As always.

It was *always* about the boys. There was *always* more training for them. When she was younger, Erika had begged to come, to get whatever training her brothers received. Her request was refused. Instead, her mother told her the boys needed more training before it was too late. When she asked her mother to explain, she'd received a backhand for her troubles.

After a few times of getting the same results, she'd learned to stop asking.

Erika wasn't sure if what she felt was jealousy, or sympathy. From her earliest memories, her brothers hadn't been allowed to enjoy the same things she had. While she was playing with dolls, the boys were taken to a secret location for some kind of mysterious training.

She knew better than to question her mother, so she went to her father instead. Before he'd had a chance to respond, her grandfather backhanded her, sending her across the room. That was the day she learned the truth.

Unless you were male, you didn't matter. The only purpose they had for females was to serve and support the men.

Pushing her feet into boots and donning a long-sleeved sweatshirt and thick pants, she was ready. Her mother left the house thirty minutes ago and wouldn't return until dusk. Erika ran down the stairs and into the kitchen.

Five minutes later, with a sloppy peanut butter sandwich and a bottle of juice, she was out the door and running toward the tree line. Today, she intended to explore the woods. Well, just as soon as she visited Chance and the baby.

Several minutes into her walk, she paused to get her bearings. Everything looked so different in the light of day. Better, but different. The trees didn't look so scary. She also didn't need to be afraid of monsters lurking in the shadows, ready to pounce and gobble her up. She stopped, closed her eyes, and waited. A moment later, she twisted to her right and stared up at a tall pine tree and whispered, "Okay."

Erika moved closer to the tree and studied the trunk. She closed her eyes and traced a pattern while imagining the outline of her fingers brushing against the bark. She slipped around the tree and came face to face with a snarling wolf.

In the light of day, she could see that's exactly what it was. Not a dog at all, but a wolf. Still, she wasn't afraid. The only thing she felt when she was near Chance was warmth, acceptance, and the love she'd always been denied. But there was also a sadness. Not just for himself, but for the loss of someone close to him. She stepped closer and whispered, "I'm sorry, Chance."

After wrapping her arms around his neck, she buried her face in his soft fur. Then she stepped back, peered around his huge body, and asked, "What's the baby's name?"

Although no words were spoken, nor did she hear them whispered into her mind, she just knew. After nodding her understanding, she knelt beside the pup, then said, "Celeste, don't be afraid. You're not alone. I'm here with you."

Then she looked over her shoulder at the wolf, who was unable to return her gaze, and added, "Chance is here too."

She walked back to her friend and asked, "Are there more? Do you want me to find them?"

She nodded again then turned away. After one more glance at Chance, she realized she could get hopelessly lost in a short time.

After gathering an armful of sticks, she carefully laid them on the ground like an arrow pointing the way back. Then, turning to Chance, she smiled and said, "That was a good idea. Thanks, Chance!"

After walking far enough that she could no longer see so much as a tuft of Chance's fur, she stepped around a tree and came face to face with another wolf. She ran her hands down his soft fur, then sat beside him and chatted for a few minutes before gathering more sticks and continuing her search.

"Well, hello, big fellow. And what's your name?"

Erika paused before the largest member of the pack and waited. So far, every wolf she'd seen welcomed her with warmth and kindness, even if they did so without word or deed. She'd felt it just as strongly as she felt the warm afternoon breeze whipping her blonde curls around her face.

But this one, this one was different. He was more closed off. Angry. If it weren't for the love for him radiating from the others, she would've left him there.

Erika sat on a fallen log and waited. She opened her mind and searched for the path that led to this wolf. A wave of dizziness knocked her from the log. Her head spun with swirling darkness. Feelings of hatred, remorse, and sadness overwhelmed her.

She gripped her temples and screamed. The agony of his thoughts, memories, and feelings, invading her mind was too much. Especially for someone as young as her. This wolf, every part of him, every thought, was tinged with a sharp edge of insanity that crept closer and closer with each passing moment.

There was bone chilling darkness and terrifying loneliness.

Those were his only companions. There was no sound. He felt nothing. Time rolled on. How much? He didn't know. Hours? Days? Years? There was no morning sun to mark the beginning of a new day, and sleep refused to come. For all he could tell, a hundred years had passed. Day after day. Always the same.

For this wolf, it was an eternity trapped in an inescapable nightmare. Memories. That's what he had. And every moment was filled with a remembrance of a day he would never forget.

With an effort that belied her youth, Erika struggled to separate herself from this wolf. She knew, with absolute certainty, he would unknowingly drag her into the nightmarish world holding him captive.

While rolling on the leaf strewn ground, she fought. Knees drawn up, she cried and begged for him to release her. Fighting her way onto her knees, one hand still gripping her temple, she inched her way closer to the dark wolf. She fell to the ground between his front legs then brushed the palm of one hand across his snarling muzzle.

Agony, unlike any she'd ever felt, filled her. It was coupled with pity for the wolf who shouldered all the blame for something he'd been helpless to prevent. Tears flowed down dirty cheeks to wet the rotting leaves beneath her while Erika begged, "Please. You have to let me go."

Marcus's thoughts once again returned to that day. It was what haunted him day in and day out. How many times had the scenes replayed in his head? Thousands? Millions? It didn't matter, there was nothing that could take its place. His conscience wouldn't let him put it to rest. Nor would it allow him to replace it with happier memories. The hatred he felt for the Dämonejäger burned, a grim reminder of why happy memories refused to come. With so much anger and animosity in his heart, there was little room for anything else.

All at once, thoughts, memories, rage, and remorse, ceased. In their place an awareness fell over him. Featherlight, something brushed against his subconscious. It was so fleeting; it would have been easy for him to play it off as another slip into his ever-increasing insanity. But then it came again.

A thought.

A softly spoken whisper pervaded his mind.

For the first time in more years than he could imagine, he was able to escape the total emptiness consuming him day and night since the Dämonejägers came. Although blind in every sense of the word, there was a sensation that embraced him.

A presence. He wasn't alone. He could feel it. Love. Trust. Awe.

Erika was finally relieved of the agony imposed by this beautiful dark wolf. She stood and brushed dirt and twigs from her clothes. Then she curled her arms around his neck, buried her face in his thick fur and whispered, "I have to go back now, before they discover I'm gone. The next time I come, you'll have to tell me your name. Goodnight, dark wolf."

Chapter Five

Present Day

Erika's hand brushed against the railing. After one final glance over her shoulder, she was ready. She stepped off the porch, her heart was racing, emotions raging.

She was torn, terrified, yet exhilarated. Was she really going to do this? Could she walk away from everything and everyone she'd ever known? Away from her old life and toward a new one.

The answer was a resounding yes.

With grim determination, she clenched her teeth and narrowed her eyes. She refused to allow herself to see the past as anything more than it was. It was time to look toward a brighter future; time to change her life.

In the distance, over mountains and into valleys, her family's forested estate spanned as far as the eye could see. In the farthest reaches of the densely wooded property stood silent sentinels. Far enough off the main road to remain invisible to the casual passersby, but close enough for unsuspecting trespassers to stumble upon. Even with notices posted along the fence, the occasional hitchhiker or mushroom hunter would wander onto their property, only to be shocked by what they found. She'd heard her father's grumbles about it often enough, along with her grandfather's dire threats of shooting the intruders.

Erika thought back on her many forays into the forest. She couldn't help wondering how her grandfather had been able to pose each one of the lifelike residents in such a way as to invoke terror. Some appeared poised to pounce, while others were crouched with a vicious snarl forever etched on their muzzles.

The animals, motionless guardians of the dark woods, were the ones she'd come to think of as her pack. When it happened, the day, the moment, she wasn't sure. But over the years, that's exactly what they'd become.

She was so very young the first time she'd snuck out of the house, and the punishment was severe. But when it was over, their intended lesson had the opposite effect. After that day, more than ever she knew she had to continue her visits. She just needed to make sure she never got caught.

Erika stopped where the grass led into layers of decaying leaves and pine needles. The same place she'd paused nearly every day for the past fifteen years. After saying a silent prayer, she glanced at the house one last time.

The house was quiet.

Free from spying eyes, Erika ran north toward the only wolf she'd not said her goodbyes to. Fifteen minutes later, she stepped around the towering oak. Slowing her steps, she brushed a hand down the silky fur of a huge wolf who was as dark as the night.

Many afternoons found her sitting beside him watching the sun set, and then staying by his side long after the moon had passed its zenith. Most nights were spent in quiet one-sided conversation while she brushed his thick fur. Other times, she was content to lay beside him. Visions of what life would be like if he were real played out in her mind. She'd imagined an evil wizard had cast a spell that locked him in this form. One that could only be broken by true love's kiss. A blush spread across her cheeks, remembering her multiple attempts to break that same curse. Then sadness took embarrassment's place when she recalled how heartbroken she'd been when he didn't turn into a handsome prince.

Erika dropped to the damp ground beside him. With her fingers buried in his thick fur, she leaned closer and breathed in his scent. Even after all these years, nothing changed. His fur was still just as lustrous as the first day she'd seen him, and his eyes as bright. Sitting back, touching foreheads, she closed her eyes and murmured, "Marcus."

Her fingers curled into his thick fur while her heart raced in anticipation of what she was about to do.

Rising to her knees, she explained her plans, "I'm sorry about last night. I had to go see all the others…even the ones they thought were hidden from me." She shook her head and fought back tears, whispering, "The babies."

Erika cocked her head and narrowed her gaze. Harumphing, she growled, "Are you even listening to me?"

She rolled her eyes, slapped her forehead, and mumbled, "Oh my goodness, listen to what I'm saying. What's wrong with me? Of course, you're not listening. If you were ever alive, you're certainly not now."

She leaned closer. Studying his eyes, she whispered, "Although, sometimes…"

Shaking her head, she went on, "Sometimes, I swear it looks like your gaze follows me. Like now, if I didn't know better, I'd say you're mocking me."

Slapping her legs, she continued, "Okay, pay attention. I've already said goodbye to the others…"

Marcus's senses were on high alert; this wasn't the first time she'd mentioned there were others hidden away. Thanks to Erika's continued visits, he'd awakened…in a sense. With each visit, he'd become more aware of things around him. Although she'd vowed to visit daily, over time, the visits had become sporadic.

But because of her, he now understood the cruel sorcerers had positioned his pack far enough apart to ensure their continued loneliness but close enough to know they weren't alone. All the time he'd been here, he'd been under the impression that only one pup had survived. The hope he felt for the knowledge that the most vulnerable lived, was also shadowed by the knowledge that they were still forever locked in their silent forms. It wasn't difficult to imagine the terror and grief each felt, believing they were alone.

Then Marcus realized Erika suspected his attention had wandered. He did a mental smirk, along with a snorted thought. If he could speak, he'd tell her that indeed, he was mocking her.

Then her last statement hit him. She'd said her goodbyes to his pack. His blood ran cold. Was she leaving him? No. She couldn't. She was the only reason he maintained any semblance of sanity. Through her, every member of his pack knew they weren't alone, even if they couldn't communicate. In addition, with each member she'd visited, she'd carried their scent to the next. Because of her they were able to feel each other on a psychic level.

"Marcus! I swear…I feel like an old married couple, begging you to listen," she chuckled. Leaning closer, she lowered her voice, "I'm leaving. Obviously, right?"

She shook her head and mumbled, "Stop stalling, Erika."

While stroking his fur, she continued, "After the sun sets, I'll be back. I'm taking you with me. Well, you and Celeste. I promised Chance I would look after her. I bought a cabin. It's a long drive, but it's far enough away from *them*," she said, knocking her head toward the house. "At least I hope it is. I'll come back for the others; I promise. For now, I only have a little bit of room, so it's just you and Celeste."

After dropping a kiss on his nose, she walked away. Away from her pack. Away from the family she'd adopted after she learned just how evil her real, human family was.

It was several minutes before it registered that he was alone. Erika was leaving, but he wouldn't be left behind. Wherever she was going, she was taking him. Not only that, but one of the pack's youngest members. A part of him wanted to stay and do everything he could to protect the others. But he knew it for the lie it was. No matter how hard he'd wanted to protect them before, he'd failed. Now he was once again left in a position of complete helplessness. Would this be what was needed to break the spell that bound him to this torturous existence? Or was that only wishful thinking and he'd be forever doomed to this stillness of only existing but not really living.

Chapter Six

Erika sat beside her window and stared down at the sedan that should have already left. Her parents had begged her to come with them to visit her brother, Dieter, and his wife, Bailey. It seemed they had some happy news to share. It didn't take a genius to figure out what their news might be. Dieter was, if not worse than her father, he was at least in the same jerk category. He was also well on his way to surpassing their grandfather. She couldn't imagine why anyone would want to carry on the jerk gene, but evidently, it was cause for celebration.

Footsteps in the hall alerted her that her mother hadn't given up on coaxing her to come along. Kicking off her shoes, she dipped her fingers into a glass of water and flicked it across her face then rushed toward the bed, yanked the covers up to her chin, and closed her eyes. She waited.

The door creaked open. Her mother's tsk was followed by soft footfalls ending beside her bed. Her cheeks burned, knowing her mother stood above her, but not missing a single thing. Cool fingers pressed against flushed cheeks, followed by a gasp. "Oh, my word! You're burning up!" Her mother's weight settled on the bed. A moment later she crooned, "That does it, Erika. I'm not going to leave you like this. We'll just have to visit your brother after you're feeling better."

Because of her burning anger, Erika knew her cheeks would be even hotter. Not only was she upset with her mother but with her own inability to follow through with a plan that should've worked. Cracking an eye open, she gazed up at the feigned concern on her mother's face and almost felt bad. Almost. Licking her lips, she struggled to produce the croaked words that floated around in her head. "Mother…" She cleared her throat, then in a stronger voice, she continued, "It's okay, I'm fine. Just let me—"

"—You'll do no such thing, young lady," her mother scolded. "If what I believe is true, the last thing poor Bailey needs is for you to bring whatever germs you have to their doorstep."

Her mother stood and walked over to the door, mumbling, "Why do I even care?"

After slamming the door shut behind her, she yelled, "Luca! I'll be down as soon as I wash my hands. Your daughter has some sort of nasty germ, and I don't want to spread it to our son's growing family."

Erika winced at her mother's calloused words. Echoing her mother's sentiment, she whispered, "And why should *I* care?"

Lying still, she waited until she heard the engine roar to life beneath her window. Then counting off the seconds in her head, she stayed still. Five minutes later, the front door banged against the wall, followed by her mother's shouted words, "Got it!"

Erika sat up then snorted a laugh at her mother's feigned sympathy. It was a good act. But an act it was. There was no way Sabine would miss the announcement of yet another Jäger coming into the world.

She slid out of bed and peeked through the curtains. If there was one thing she could count on, it was Sabine's inability to remember some little something that she couldn't live without. Usually, it was her purse, but not always. She remembered the day they'd been forced to go back home because her mother forgot, of all things, her favorite handkerchief.

Erika's heart raced while watching the fading taillights and contemplated her next move. If she slipped away and they came back home for whatever else her mother may have forgotten, then her cover would be blown. But if she waited too long, she wouldn't have time to get both Celeste and Marcus into the car.

Even though he was nothing more than sawdust and cotton, he was still very heavy. Only once had she tried to move him closer to the house. When that plan failed, she was content with visiting him where he stood.

Five agonizing minutes of indecision later, Erika dragged her suitcases out of the closet and down the stairs. After wedging them behind her seat, she leaned against the car and stared up at the house.

For twenty-three years, this had been all she'd ever known. Childhood memories danced in her head. Visions of her brothers carrying her while they helped find the Easter eggs they'd hidden. And memories of Christmas mornings while she stared in awe at all the packages under the tree.

Her smile faded.

Those same memories were replaced with her brothers unwrapping gift after gift while she sat on the floor all alone, with a dime store doll in one hand and a package of plain white socks in the other.

Giving a jerky nod, she knew leaving was the right thing to do. It was also something she'd never regret. And she prayed they'd never find her.

***

On one of Erika's many forays into the woods, she'd stumbled upon a one-lane dirt trail. Ironically, every single wolf was positioned within a few yards of the path. She'd been certain it would make loading Marcus into her car that much easier. She was mistaken. She hadn't considered just how much room she'd need to put the few things she'd decided to bring. Not only that, but he looked so much smaller standing in the woods than he did once she began trying to fit him between boxes and suitcases.

Now, here she stood with both hands fisted on her hips. She was hot, sweaty, and quickly running out of time.

What was she going to do now? After a quick glance at her phone, she knew she'd better find a solution, and soon. Her family would be getting home before too much longer. The last thing she wanted was to get caught just before she made her escape. Their only daughter wasn't just sneaking off…nor was she leaving alone.

But surely, they wouldn't miss the wolves. They'd been here for as long as she could remember, and not once had anyone from her family visited or mentioned their silent residents. However, she'd been forbidden long ago to come back into the woods. Finding her here now, it wouldn't be hard for them to figure out that she'd been coming here all along. And that wouldn't bode well for her, or the wolves.

Cocking her head, she stared at the wolf that now looked more like a dog that had gotten stuck trying to climb inside a compact car. Except it wasn't a small car; it was a full-sized SUV. Erika shook her head, threw her hands up, and began rearranging everything.

Thirty minutes and a clean shirt later, Erika drove away from her family home for the last time. If luck was on her side, she wouldn't pass her parents on the way. She glanced skyward and pleaded, "Just this once, please don't let them catch me."

With every approaching set of headlights, she shrank down. She knew she wouldn't be able to relax until she'd passed the turnoff leading to her brother's house. It was the longest fifteen minutes of her life. When she got closer to his driveway, she slowed just enough to peer through the darkness toward his house.

Unlike the rest of the people who lived in this community, Dieter refused to allow the dark forest to encroach upon his domain. His large house spoke of his pretentiousness more than anything else. As the oldest, he stood to inherit the top position in the hierarchy of their clan, not to mention the fortune that everyone believed her grandfather had bequeathed to his oldest son.

However, at the reading of the will, Oskar's three sons were shocked to learn that the only thing they'd received was the land upon which their homes had been built. They'd argued amongst themselves, eventually hiring attorneys, all to no avail. One of the conditions of his will was that the name of the recipient must be withheld until such a time as the beneficiary came of age.

It was all she could do to persuade the attorney to hold off this long. It was amazing what you could get people to do with a little extra incentive.

She'd been told by her grandfather's attorney that in just a few days, a letter would come to her parents. As per her grandfather's wishes, it would inform them that the entire Jäger fortune had gone to his favorite granddaughter. Erika refused to analyze it, instead accepting it as the blessing it was. If she were to guess? Perhaps the bitter old fool was overcome with remorse for the things he'd done to her over the years. More than once, he'd called her a spoiled, ungrateful, useless member of this family. The day she was born, instead of feeling joy for the miracle of another child, he'd joined her parents as they lamented the birth of a girl, instead of another cherished son.

Thinking about the old man, she snorted. Erika was sure her grandfather was spinning in his grave. The day she'd turned twenty-one, she'd gotten a short text from a stranger, requesting she respond to the message. Immediately after she pressed send, her phone rang. Years before his death, Oskar Jäger had set up a secret account in her name, withholding only enough to live for the rest of his miserable life. It was the only good thing any member of her family had ever done.

After learning how much money she'd inherited, she'd scanned the web, looking for the ideal place to start her new life. The small house she'd found was dwarfed by the rise of the majestic Cascades behind it.

She learned that starting over was expensive. She'd had to pay someone to give her a whole new identity. New name, social security number, and a history to go with it.

However, the real irony came when she'd decided what to do with what was left of the vast fortune. Reserving only enough to get by for a few years, the remainder was donated to a local wolf preserve. Her most cherished memory was the day she'd anonymously visited that same sanctuary. Sitting alongside the driveway was a huge sign.

"In loving memory of our most generous benefactor: Oscar Jäger."

She'd only been gone a few hours when her family started calling. She wasn't sure if they could track her phone, but she wasn't about to take any chances. After tossing it out the window, she knew it would soon be nothing more than indistinguishable chunks of plastic rolling down the interstate.

"Goodbye, Erika Jäger, hello Serenity Chase."

Chapter Seven

Serenity was filled with excitement. She was almost there. The turnoff was just half a mile up the road. The realtor warned that if you didn't know what you were looking for, it would be easy to pass. But he'd also told her specifically how to find it. The entrance to the small town wasn't marked, as if they wished for it to remain hidden from the world.

He'd explained that once you turn onto the main highway leading into the mountains, reset your tachometer. At exactly 22.3 miles into the drive there would be a narrow, single lane road on the right. If she wasn't careful, she would pass it. Should that happen, it would be impossible to find coming from the other direction. When she suggested that she just turn around again, he shook his head, handed her the keys and walked away.

Returning her attention to the road, she spotted her turn off. Humming in delight, she pulled into the secluded community. After checking for traffic, she stopped just long enough to snap a picture of the sign welcoming her to Willow Run. While driving, she slowed to take in her new neighborhood. When the realtor showed her the pictures, she'd fallen in love with the house. The quaint neighborhood just made it better. She glanced down at her notes for the hundredth time since driving into the mountains.

Mumbling to herself, she rattled off the directions as she drove, “Left on Cedar Bend. Then right on…” Distracted by the large houses she passed, she cheerfully waved at a few people she’d seen working in their yards. Each person stopped what they were doing. But not one single person waved back, choosing instead to continue staring long after she’d passed. Shrugging, she murmured, “Must not get a lot of new faces around here.” Smiling, she waved to a large man washing his car and said to herself, “Might as well get used to it, honey, because I’m here to stay.” When her smile faded, she muttered, “I hope so, anyway,”

She was so distracted by the neighbors, she nearly missed her turn, “Aspen Boulevard… Wow! Look at these houses. They’re huge compared to the one I bought. I hope nobody hates me for being the oddball living in a normal sized house.” She laughed at the thought.

She passed what she at first thought was another street. Slowing her car, she stared up the long double wide driveway to an enormous chalet. Shaking her head, she said, “That’s just vulgar. Why would anybody need such a big house?” Slapping a hand over her mouth, she chastised herself, “Now you sound like *them*. Don’t be so judgmental. It’s none of my business. Maybe they just have a really big family.” Nodding, she decided she liked that idea. "Yeah, mom, dad, and all the little ones."

There it was. The last house on the block, smack dab in the middle of a cul-de-sac. Pulling up to the curb, she sat in the car and stared at the house. Her house. Her home.

The pictures on the internet had been taken in the winter, giving it a warm, Christmassy feel. This was early June, though, and the charm still held. It was surrounded by huge oaks and lofty pine trees, which left the house in perpetual shade.

When the mower across the street finally quieted, she turned to wave. Instead of the friendly greeting she expected, her new neighbor sent her a scathing glare before turning and walking away. Shrugging it off, she mumbled, "Can't win them all…or any…"

Serenity turned back toward the house. The movers had already taken in the loveseat and were now bringing in the rest of her living room furniture. She knew that if she didn't get in there, she'd be forced to move everything by herself.

The unfriendly neighbor forgotten, she ran past the moving truck and into the house. She watched one of the men set a chair in front of the picture window before heading for the door. Rushing toward him, she grabbed his arm and said, "Excuse me, would you mind moving the loveseat over therc?" Shc pointed toward the fireplace then said, "I think it would be perfect about…Oh, what do you think? About eight feet from the hearth?"

The man snorted a laugh then said, "Listen, babe, we just haul it in. We're movers, not interior decorators. The only thing guaranteed is putting your furniture in the house. After that, you're on your own."

A few hours later, Serenity stood on the porch and watched the huge moving truck drive away. It'd taken more time to drive here than it had to unload. She'd told them she believed the truck was overkill, but they'd said it was the only one they had. Since they were the cheapest in town, she couldn't argue.

Serenity shrugged off the cold reception she'd gotten from everyone since arriving. She'd come from an isolated community herself. Not only were strangers not welcome, but she'd overheard her father on more than one occasion talking about running them off. It was just her luck that she'd left one crazy paranoid place only to find another. At least here, nobody knew who she was. And if she had her way, nobody ever would.

Giving the quiet houses one last glance, she stepped inside. While closing the door, she noticed a car pulling up across the street. Tugging the door open a few inches, she watched a heated exchange between two men. The largest of the two grabbed the other and dragged him into the house. Before shutting them inside, he turned toward her. When his gaze locked on hers, she felt a shiver of fear inch up her spine. She had the distinct feeling that the man could sense her fear when he nodded then closed the door.

Heart racing, she slammed the door. Serenity stumbled back, leaned against the door, and waited for her breathing to even out. The longer she stood there thinking about it, the more foolish she felt. Really, what were the chances that she'd stumbled upon another place like the one she'd just left? No. She decided she was being paranoid.

Determined not to let nerves get the better of her, she inched the door open. The car was still there, but there was no sign of the driver or her grumpy neighbor. It was time, past time in fact, to move her car. The last thing she needed was for her strange neighbors to get curious and peek in the windows. Although, she knew they would probably just think it odd for driving her taxidermy wolves here instead of putting them on the truck. One way or the other, for some reason, she wanted—no needed—to keep them hidden.

Driving over the curb, she pulled the SUV around back. Serenity felt silly opening all the windows, but she did it, nonetheless. Standing at the back door, she stared at her truck. Even though she kept telling herself they weren't really alive, she just couldn't seem to get the thought to move from her brain to her heart. For Serenity, they'd always been alive. Real. And because of that, she knew there was no way, after all these years, she'd ever see them as anything else.

Shaking it off, she walked into the kitchen to pull a sandwich and cola out of the cooler. Stepping back onto the porch, she sat on the swing. While eating her dinner, she continued to watch the house across the street. Every few minutes, the curtains were pushed aside just long enough for someone to stare at her house. Finally, the door was pulled open, and big guy was hauling grumpy guy out to his car. She watched them squeal out of the driveway, around the corner, then on to the mansion that she'd been giving the evil eye to just a few hours ago.

***

Behind the house in the SUV, the cool mountain air blew across the fur of a large black wolf. Through the course of time, awareness had slowly come to Marcus. Although he had no way of marking the days, much less years, he'd been given hope. After all this time, not only was he aware, but he could also hear, see, and scent what was happening around him. Most of his pack still lived. Erika carried their scent on her. He gave his head a mental shake…Serenity. He must remember she'd changed her name. He didn't know from whom she ran, but he knew the moment he was able, he would rip them apart.

Before they'd left, she'd buried him beneath blankets and pillows. Now he could finally scent clean, crisp air. He was in a new place, far from his pack, but still near Serenity. His hope was, given enough time with Serenity, he would once again be free from the binding spell cast on him by the Dämonejäger.

***

Serenity stuffed the last of her sandwich into her mouth. With one more glance toward the house across the street, she decided it was time to go back to work. While pushing the door shut, she shook her head then mumbled, "Great. I've moved into a neighborhood full of jerks and weirdos." Laughing at herself, she said, "Look who's talking. Aren't I the one with a giant stuffed wolf hidden in the back of my car? Oh, and let's not forget the cute little pup that sat beside me all the way here."

Kicking crumpled newspapers out of her way, she headed toward the back yard. After yanking the hatch open, she grinned and announced, "Welcome to your new home. Sorry, Marcus, but there's really only one way for someone as small as me to get a guy as big as you out of the truck."

Sweating and panting, Serenity grunted under the weight of the heavy wolf. Clawing her way out, she huffed then set the wolf to rights. Looking around at the darkening forest, she decided he would be safe enough where he stood. At least for tonight. When she got her errands done tomorrow, she'd come back and drag him further into the woods.

Serenity reached into the front seat and scooped the tiny body of her white pup into her arms and headed inside. After a quick shower, she had no doubt that sleep would come quickly tonight.

Toweling off, she looked past the door and into the bedroom. There, in the center of the bed, sat the ever-cowering pup she'd rescued. Memories returned of rushing into the woods during the harshest weather. Crinkling her nose, she decided she really didn't want to climb into bed with something so dirty.

Stepping into her room, she scooped up her silver-tipped pup. Returning to the bathroom, she announced, "Well, little girl, let's get you cleaned up before bed. How's that sound?" Serenity laughed, then added, "I don't know what I'd do if you suddenly answered me."

Freshly bathed, brushed, and dried, Serenity swept a hand down the soft fur of her precious Celeste. Kissing the top of her head, Serenity whispered, "Goodnight, sweet baby."

Chapter Eight

Luke was still standing in the same place he was when the moving van backed into the driveway of a house that should've been vacant. When he first saw the van, he thought nothing of it.

There were a few rare occasions when someone accidently stumbled into their little community. But they never stayed long. There were still others who'd stopped for directions. Each had the same things in common. They were jittery, always checking over their shoulders, sometimes with an involuntary shudder.

But this time, the men got out and began unloading. He'd seen both suddenly stop and look around more than once. So, he knew, like most people, they were uncomfortable. When the SUV pulled up to the curb, that's when he knew there was something wrong—very wrong.

He'd heard her coming as soon as she turned off the highway. All four windows were open, and her music was cranked to maximum volume. When she stepped out of the car, the short hairs on the back of his neck stood on end.

There was something about her. Not only did she *not* feel uncomfortable, but she was elated. Releasing the handle of his lawn mower, he reached for his phone. The sudden silence caught the attention of the blonde across the street and she whipped around. When she turned her dazzling smile on him, his knees buckled. She was stunning.

He knew at once, there was no way he could talk while looking at her. There was something almost hypnotic about her gaze that captured and held him. He didn't scare easily, but this pushed his boundaries. It was all he could do to turn away and call Gage, his alpha.

Gage ran out of his house and jumped in his car. He slammed the door, turned the key, and fishtailed out of the driveway. At the end of the block, he slammed on the breaks, twisted the steering wheel, and sped toward the last house on the right. It was the first one he looked for every morning from his balcony. The two-story house belonged to his best friend and second in command, Luke. Rolling over the curb and past the driveway, he surged out of the car.

Seeing his beta staring across the street, Gage shoulder bumped him then said, "Talk to me."

After he turned toward his house, Luke cleared his throat then said, "I saw the truck. I figured they'd just turn around and leave like usual. When they backed into the driveway, I knew something was up." He nodded toward the SUV parked in front of the house and added, "The car was only a few minutes behind the moving van."

Gage knocked his head toward the house. He didn't know what was up with the female, but he wasn't about to take any chances. When Luke once again looked back toward the house, jaw locked, feet planted, he knew he had to do something. Catching the other man by surprise, he dragged him out of the yard and through the door.

Luke paced back and forth, alternating between clenching and unclenching his fists. Gage suspected he was losing control. When Luke stopped, his suspicions were confirmed. His wild golden eyes were the first sign that his beast wasn't just knocking but was about to burst through. Gage stepped away from his casual lean against the door.

Then, while speaking in a low, commanding voice, he stalked toward his beta. After a low, snarling, growl, he demanded, "Get it under control. You can't lose it now. There's a human across the street. Take deep breaths—"

Luke bellowed, "Why do you think I'm like this?" Somewhere in the back of his mind he knew he was very close to having his throat ripped out. No one, not even him, spoke to the alpha in such a manner and lived. But his emotions were out of control. Seeing Gage's glowing silver eyes and his elongated canines should have been all he needed to calm. Should have.

But control wasn't coming. It wasn't even close. He walked over to the refrigerator and grabbed a beer. Twisting the cap, he chugged the entire bottle. After taking a few deep breaths, he turned to his alpha and explained, "When I caught her scent, I knew I had to get away from her.

There's something about her that speaks to my wolf."

Gage pulled the curtains aside and watched the beautiful woman who was busy giving directions to the movers. Then stepping away from the window, he turned to his friend and grinned. Leaning against the door again, he said, "She's a beauty, that's for sure. Do you think she could be your mate?"

Looking down, Luke squinted his eyes shut. After taking a few calming breaths, he mumbled, "She's gorgeous, no doubt about it. But it's not her beauty that got my wolf's attention." After striding over to the door, he glanced out the window. He shook his head, then growled, "No. It's all I can do to keep my wolf from crossing the street to tear her throat out."

Snarling, Gage grabbed Luke and dragged him out to his car. With one last glance at the woman who shouldn't be here, he sped away from Luke's house. After turning onto his driveway, he drove straight into his garage.

When Luke began fighting against his lap restraints, a low growl sounded in the back of Gage's throat. He wouldn't kill his friend, but he wasn't above bringing him a hair's breadth from it. Fighting to stay in control, Gage's voice came out as a deep snarl, "Don't push me."

Even though it was only a two-minute drive, it was fifteen minutes before they were both able to rein in their wolves. Although he didn't understand Luke's rage, he was sympathetic.

Luke had come to them when he was still a pup. It was right after his entire pack was slaughtered, including his father and baby sister. His mother had been driven to Willow Run by his uncle with a brand-new baby sleeping in the backseat.

They'd been away when it happened. Later, they'd returned to discover most of their pack was missing. They'd found one member on the brink of death. He'd told them humans had come and somehow crossed the borders into their community. Those who hadn't shifted were shot where they stood. The others were spelled, loaded onto trucks, then driven away. Before the man took his last breath, he muttered a single word, "Dämonejäger."

Devastated by the loss of her mate and pack, Bethany had gone into labor. Refusing to leave her home, she'd birthed Luke in the comfort of her own bed. They'd come that same day with nothing but the clothes on their backs, along with what they could fit into the trunk. Separated from her mate, Luke's mother lost the will to live. Three years after arriving, she walked into the woods and never returned.

After stepping into the house, Gage said, "Call a meeting." He pulled out his phone, checked the time, then added, "I want everybody here in ten minutes." He walked into the den, closed himself in, then poured a drink. It was much too early, but judging by the way the afternoon started, he knew he'd be falling down drunk long before dark. At least that was the plan.

He leaned against the bar then spun toward the door after hearing his brother's voice. Noah and his twin, Scarlett, walked in. His younger brother stood only a few inches shorter than his own six-foot-six. However, the biggest difference between the brothers was their build. Gage had a runner's body, tall, lean, and built for speed. Noah was tall, but he was broad chested, a powerhouse. Gage was quiet, watchful, and always mindful of his surroundings. But when Noah got quiet, you knew it was time to run and hide. Their sister, more than a foot shorter, was all smiles. She was as opposite from her brothers as one could get. She was always happy and the first one to lend a hand where needed.

Stepping into the room, Noah was still talking to Scarlett, arguing, "All I'm saying is that he's going to be pissed."

"What am I going to be pissed about?" Gage demanded after the twins walked in, leaving the door open behind them.

Scarlett glared at Noah, then mumbled, "Why can't you leave things alone?"

Noah shrugged. "He knew what he was doing when he did it. Why should we cover for him?"

Gage rubbed his temples. His morning had started amazingly great. He'd had a few friends over last night. Then, after the frantic call from Luke, he had to kick them out of his bed so he could see what the problem was. From there, it just kept getting worse. Judging by his sibling's disagreement, something was up with Allister. Again. Not bothering to look up, he growled, "What did he do this time?"

Noah and Scarlett spoke at the same time.

Scarlett cheerfully announced, "Nothing."

But her words were drowned out by Noah's snarled, "You're not going to believe this…"

Holding a hand up, Gage just shook his head.

Before anything else could be discussed, Luke joined them. "Jonas isn't happy, but he said he'd be here in about thirty minutes." Before Gage could argue, Luke held up a hand, "It's dinner time. You can't honestly expect him to leave right in the middle of his busiest time of day."

As people began filing in, Gage wore a path between the window overlooking Willow Run and the fireplace. Every time someone stepped through the door, he stopped only long enough to glare at them.

After Jonas and Ariana finally arrived, he walked back to sit on the corner of a table beside the windows. Looking each person in the eye, he waited until they submitted before moving his gaze to the next. After the last person, he nodded. "Am I right in assuming that none of you want to challenge me?" When he was met with silence, he bellowed, "Ten minutes!" He glanced back at Luke and snarled, "You did tell them ten minutes?"

Luke nodded before turning his gaze away.

Gage scooted back then addressed the leaders of his pack. "Unless you want to find out what happens when you keep your alpha waiting, I suggest this not happen again." He gave them all time for any rebuttal they might wish to voice. When he was met with silence again, he nodded, then said, "The reason I called you here—"

Jonas's son, Hunter, stood and shouted, "There's a human here! I was washing my car when I saw her. I want to know what happened to our wards."

Gage slid off the table and leapt across the room. With a hand around the man's throat, he held Hunter suspended above the floor several inches. His canines dropped; his eyes shifted from grey to a glowing silver. Gage was struggling to hold his shift at bay. Breathing through the rage, he knew he was seconds from ripping out the boy's throat.

With a downcast gaze, Hunter didn't fight back. Judging by the blue tinge of his skin, he was close to passing out…still he didn't struggle. With a snarl, Gage released him and stepped back.

Looking around the room, he bellowed, "Is there anyone else who wishes to challenge me?"

The sound of weeping brought his attention back to the pup's tearful mother. Looking down at the male lying on the floor, he sighed and said, "Ali, please see to your pup. Your mate can explain everything later."

He watched while the grown pup, leaning on his mother, limped out of the room. Then turning his attention back to his packmates, he began, "I know you're all upset about the human that moved in, but we need to be careful."

Chapter Nine

Stretching and yawning, Serenity's hand bumped the tiny pup lying on the pillow beside her. Smiling, she turned to face her silver tipped guest. Running a hand down her back, she said, "Good morning, Celeste." Giggling, she asked, "And how did you sleep last night?" Frowning, she stared at the small wolf beside her. She could swear the word cold, was whispered into her thoughts. Sitting up, she tucked the blankets around Celeste, then cooed, "I have to go into town today." She snorted a laugh then added, "Make yourself at home."

She grabbed her clothes then left the room. If she'd bothered to glance back, she might have noticed the slow blinking from the now shivering pup tucked into the plush quilt. Instead, she went straight into the bathroom. Thirty minutes later, after a quick shower, she was ready to begin her day.

Serenity had several stops planned, beginning with a job search. She'd tried to find an online application for the local eatery, but they didn't even have a website. Then after picking up an application, she planned to run to the store and grab something for breakfast.

After stepping onto the porch, she noticed movement from the window across the street. She shook her head then got in and started her car. Shifting into gear, she muttered, "Oh great. The hot neighbor across the street is a weirdo."

The center of the small town held everything a person could need. A grocery store with a pharmacy sat on one corner. Down the street from that was a police and fire station all in one. On the other side of the street was a building that housed every grade from kindergarten through high school. And beside the school was a large park with a variety of things to amuse both young and old. Then a little further down was a large pond with a walking path and benches all around it. She couldn't help wondering if it froze over in the winter to double as a skating rink. At the end of the block sat her destination. It was just a wannabe restaurant.

Serenity pulled into the parking lot, shut off the car, and stared at the cafe. She needed this job. Going home wasn't an option, not after the way she'd left. Not only that, but she knew there wasn't one person in her family she could trust. They were crazy. But not in a fun way. No, her family was more of the axe wielding kind. She'd never be welcomed back, especially now that the family fortune everybody wanted was gone. There'd just be a small mound of dirt somewhere on the acres and acres of forest. And she'd be nothing more than a distant memory.

Thinking about home also reminded her of what she'd left behind. Each wolf was dear to her, but none so much as Chance. Although she was very young, she remembered the overwhelming sorrow she felt after telling him about the other wolf. Whether it was real was anybody's guess, but she'd felt like she understood him. She knew Henry was important to Chance; there was a familiar feeling about him. Son? Brother? She didn't know, she just knew she never wanted another wolf to go through that.

There were many times she'd had nightmares about the wolves. In them, she'd run outside and find nothing but dried bones and fur. Each time, after waking up in tears, she'd rushed from the house to check, only to discover nothing had changed. More than once, she'd collapsed beside Marcus, sobbing.

Movement in the dark interior caught her attention. A man was standing in the door watching her. When he noticed her looking back, he waved for her to come in. He then unlocked the door and walked away.

Serenity was determined not to let anything keep her from getting this job. Not her past, and certainly not her own crazy thinking. Squaring her shoulders, she glanced once more in the mirror. After blotting her still wet lashes, she smiled, then with a nod, she said, "You got this Serenity. Don't let the ghosts of your past haunt your present."

Pushing through the door, Serenity stepped into what she hoped would soon be her place of employment. Looking around, she was impressed. It had a down home feel to it. The shades were still pulled over darkly tinted windows. Above each table hung an old-fashioned lantern. Instead of the occasional booth, she noticed they had tables covered with gingham tablecloths. All the chairs, seat down, were sitting on top. Nodding her approval, she smiled. When she looked up, she saw someone walking toward her. The closer he got, the bigger he appeared. And the look on his face was anything but welcoming.

Serenity took a step back then glanced toward the door. Could she get there before he got to her? After looking him up and down, she realized the futility of it. If the man wanted to hurt her, there was nothing she could do to stop him. She suddenly wondered why she'd chosen this town. Willow Run looked so peaceful when she saw it. After everything that happened today, she realized just how wrong first impressions could be. She tried to appear smaller by curling into herself. She tucked her chin into her chest and whispered, "Please don't hurt me."

The last thing she expected was the full belly laugh that filled the room. She looked up. Instead of seeing an intimidating beast of a man, she saw a big teddy bear. The full beard and wild hair only added to the impression, but when he spoke, there was no doubt in her mind. His rumbling deep voice put her at ease immediately. Cocking her head, she felt a catch in her throat. For reasons she could only guess, he reminded her of Chance.

Chance was one of the largest of all the wolves, second only to Marcus. His fur reminded her very much of this man's thick and wild hair. The first time she saw Chance, she ran and threw her arms around his neck. The memory of her beloved wolf brought with it the burn of tears. After blinking them away, she cleared her throat. She had to land this job. She had to save her wolves. And the first step in doing that was to appear as normal as possible. A young woman who didn't need to work would certainly arouse suspicion. Then add to that, the many trips she would need to sneak the wolves out of her family's forest and into her own yard. Which introduced yet another problem. How was she going to hide hundreds of stuffed wolves?

"Well, out with it. As you can see, it's too early for lunch. If you're hungry, then the only thing I have to offer is a sandwich and a bowl of soup." The big man crossed his arms and waited.

Serenity straightened. She gave him what she hoped passed for a self-assured smile and said, "Thank you. But that's not why I'm here. I just moved into the neighborhood, and I'd hoped you're hiring."

The big man leaned against the counter and looked her up and down then said, "You're just a little thing, aren't you? The customers I have coming in here are all nearly as big as I am. Don't think I didn't notice your reaction to seeing me. Imagine this dining room filled with men just as big. Are you still sure you want to work here?"

Serenity's thoughts drifted to what she'd left behind. There was more back there to fear than the scary wolves that surrounded their property. She knew her dad was completely unaware that she'd been in the barn. If it weren't for that old oak, she might never have found them. The floor was filled with wolf pups of varying ages. However, there was one thing they had in common…they all looked terrified. The thought cemented her hatred for her family, for the monsters who could do such terrible things to such young animals. Even if they were wolves, it was like killing puppies. No matter what happened, anything would be better than going back to that.

Determination leading her, she squared her shoulders, nodded and said, "I have to."

The man cocked his head, studied her a moment, then nodded. He waved for her to follow then announced, "You can fill out the application in my office. You brought your identification, I take it? I'll run your license while you fill out the paperwork."

Serenity stopped short. When she'd gotten the fake ID, she'd taken them at their word. Then a few days before leaving, she'd decided to check and see if everything was as it should be. Nope. Not even close. The driver's license looked like it'd been pasted together by a four-year-old. And the detailed past she'd paid for? It only went back a few months. Even then it was sketchy at best. Taking a step back, she whispered, "This was a mistake." She shook her head then mumbled, "Why did I ever think I could escape them?" Raising her voice, she turned back toward the door and called out, "I'm sorry to have wasted your time."

When a beefy hand settled on her shoulder, she spun around to face the man. Her mouth went dry after looking up. Did she say big? The man was huge. He was well over a foot taller than her with his broad chest and arms that reminded her more of the thick limbs of her favorite oak. He was an intimidating sight, especially this close.

He leaned in and said, "Why don't you tell me what you're running from?"

Swallowing hard, she nodded then followed him back to his office. He led her through a door in the back, past the kitchen, and then outside. She stopped a few feet away from the restaurant and watched him approach the back door of a house. Apprehension filled her. Where was he taking her and why? Also, why in the world had she believed she could trust him?

Before he had a chance to do anything, a woman nearly as large as him pushed the door open. She took one look at Serenity then exclaimed, "Oh, you poor girl! Jonas! What did you do?"

Serenity held her hands up; the man had done nothing to her. In fact, he'd gone out of his way to be kind. She stepped forward and said, "Please, no. He didn't do anything."

The woman waved off her remark and scoffed. "Don't be afraid of him. Why, he wouldn't hurt a fly. Come on in here…" When Serenity got closer, the woman stumbled back.

Serenity swore that for just a moment, the woman's eyes glowed. Then she heard a low rumbling growl a second before the older woman was yanked back into the house. Not a full minute later, Jonas stepped out. In a soft, soothing voice, he said, "Come on in, darlin'. Ariana is starting a pot of coffee."

Serenity was shaking her head while backing away. Holding her hands up, she murmured, "No. That's okay." She glanced back to make sure no one was sneaking up on her. She had the sudden urge to get in her car, drive away, and forget this town ever existed. When Jonas took a step closer, she turned to run back to her car. That's when she noticed the six-foot privacy fences that separated her from the outside world.

Serenity yelped when a hand clamped around her bicep. The same woman who'd just been pulled into the house was now standing in front of her. Before she knew what was happening, she was pulled into the woman's embrace. The moment she felt the arms come around her, the tears she'd successfully kept at bay gushed in a storm of emotions. The fear she'd felt for these huge strangers was wiped away by a sense of love and acceptance. They were things she'd not felt since…

Unbidden, the image of Chance came to mind. Humming her joy, she allowed the fears she'd been running from for the past two days to melt away. It was like he was here. She'd always imagined him as a favorite uncle, or perhaps even a brother. Well, a better brother than the ones she had, anyway.

After sitting her down at the table with a fresh cup of coffee and a muffin, Ariana patted her arm and said, "I'm going to go get Jonas. You just drink your coffee." She pointed at the muffin then added, "That's one of my famous apple cinnamon muffins, fresh out of the oven." She pushed a small clear bowl toward her. "It's really good if you drizzle the cream cheese topping over it. Oh! And some butter. The real stuff, too." She made a face and muttered, "Not that crap they try to pass off as butter."

Ariana pulled the door closed while she stepped out of the room. Whipping around, she ran toward the den where Jonas was talking to Gage. She ripped the phone out of her husband's hand and put it on speaker. She leaned over her mate, lowered her voice, then asked, "Can you hear me?"

Chapter Ten

Silence met her question. She rolled her eyes, feeling like an idiot. Of course, he heard her. He could probably hear her racing heart as well. If it was one thing the wolves were known for, it was their keen hearing. "Never mind. Listen. I know you and Jonas have been talking about the human…that is if she's human."

That got Gage's attention, "What do you mean if she's human? What else could she be?"

"Please, before you get upset, let me explain first. I know you told us to let the newcomer believe there was nothing unusual about our community."

"Exactly," Gage said. "The last thing we want is for her to start searching the internet, looking for answers. Act normal. Give her a wide berth. Be friendly, but not her friend. We can't take the chance that someone might screw up. Stay calm. If you do nothing, nothing will happen that could arouse suspicion. Above all, remember, human eyes don't glow. Ever."

Jonas cleared his throat. "Yeah, about that…"

Gage snarled, "What happened?"

Ariana spoke up, "When I met her, there was something about her scent that enraged me. If it weren't for Jonas…"

Gage sighed. "Thank you, Jonas. I don't know what it is about this woman. But like I said, you need to stay calm. If you feel your wolf trying to push through, walk away. You know what would happen if she decided to search for answers as to what would make a person's eyes glow."

Jonas felt the blood drain from his face. Visions of what happened long ago came rushing back. Memories returned of him driving into the deadly silent town he'd called home. Of him finding dead and dying packmates, only to discover the rest had been taken. Taken where, and to what end, he could only speculate. When he stepped out of the car, the air still reeked with the stench of magic. Tales passed down from generation to generation of the horrors their ancestors had experienced at the hands of evil. Mixed with myth and legend were the answers of their origins. He shook his head and told himself that there was no such thing as magic. Whatever he'd scented all those long years ago had grown into something more. Something sinister. But it couldn't be. His mate's voice interrupted his thoughts.

"Yes, Gage. I realize how quickly it could turn ugly."

Ariana's statement was met with silence. Then the sound of fist meeting plaster was followed by Gage's growled response. "Ugly? Things turning ugly would be the least of our worries. It could lead the Dämonejäger right to our front door. Ugly? No.

How about dying? How about suffering a fate worse than death?"

Both Ariana and Jonas stayed quiet, wondering what could possibly be worse than death.

Jonas was the first to speak, saying, "I thought all of that was just a myth passed down from our superstitious ancestors."

Gage snorted. "Myth? What would ever make you think it was a myth? I have journals from pack alphas dating back to the early 1300's. Journals. Where the original Lycans recorded how they'd been created and enslaved by the ones who'd made them. At one time, they were all human."

Gage walked away, grabbed a stool, and reached for a thin leather-bound book on a top shelf. After opening the book, he returned to his desk. Then dropping it on the smokey grey glass, he began reading,

"This will probably be my last entry. It's been fifty years since my pack was set free from the Dämonejäger. Yesterday, my beloved mate passed from this world to the next. I fear I cannot go on without her. My children have begged me to share her secrets with them. I could not. I gave Sabrina my oath. Even though she's no longer here, I can't break that promise. It would serve no purpose, neither aiding nor the furthering of our kind. Just beware of the men from the Dämonejäger clan. Their grudges run deep. They have vowed to hunt us to the ends of the earth. I've sent my oldest son to the new world in hopes they won't find him there."

Gage picked his phone up and continued, "It goes on with instructions to all future alphas. The journal was copied word for word then passed from one alpha to the next. Just as every generation has kept a record then passed it down. Each pack has one from their own line, plus the original, translated from German to English." Gage turned to stare out his window, finding the roof of the diner, he said, "Myth? Absolutely not."

Ariana spoke up, "Perhaps she'll think it's just a trick of the light." She saw Jonas shaking his head. "What? Did you…"

"I'm sorry. You didn't see her face. She knew it for what it was. Perhaps since it only happened once—"

Gage asked, "Is there anything else?"

Ariana swayed then dropped into a chair. She turned her pale face toward her husband then muttered, "I felt bad about scaring her…Well, you know sometimes I just feel like a mom to all the kids around here."

Gage's loud sigh came through the line. He chuckled then said, "Yes, we all know how you take everybody under your wing. I'll bet she's enjoying a cup of cocoa and a muffin right about now."

"Coffee," Ariana corrected. "I felt bad about scaring her, so I…well, I threw my arms around her…and…," she swallowed, "Gage…She said a name I'd never thought to hear again." A sob that refused to be denied escaped, "Chance."

The silence was deafening. A moment later, Jonas burst from his seat and roared, "I knew it! She's one of them! They've come to finish what they started in Washington! Gage, you need to—"

Ariana placed her hand on his arm and said, "I don't think she even knows she said it."

In the background, they heard the heavy footfalls of Gage's pacing. Then in a low, measured voice, he said, "Hire her. We need to know where she is and what she's doing at all times."

***

Scarlett's attention was on her phone while skipping down the stairs. A text from Alistair had just popped up.

"So, what was the big emergency this time? And thanks for covering for me. I know I can always count on you. Unlike your evil twin." The last statement was followed by a grinning emoji.

Not expecting to reach the last step so soon, Scarlett stumbled. If it weren't for Noah grabbing her arm, she would have fallen.

Noah frowned and nodded toward her phone. After peeking over her shoulder, he asked, "That from our brother?"

Tucking the phone in a pocket, she sidled around him. Then leaving him there, she turned toward the kitchen and called over her shoulder, "Nope."

Noah's deep voice followed close behind her shouting, "Liar. Why didn't he come home last night? Oh wait…He had an important meeting to attend, right? Maybe at the college? Could it be something involving women maybe? He needs to start putting his pack first. Screwing around with human women is going to end badly. He needs to start looking either here, or in one of the other packs for a mate."

Scarlett ignored her twin and grabbed a bagel while pouring herself a cup of coffee.

Again, Noah stepped into her path. In a low voice, he said, "You know I'm right."

She stabbed a finger into his chest and countered, "I don't know that you're right. In fact, I think you're just jealous because of the way women fall all over him." When he opened his mouth to speak, she stepped past him and mumbled, "I don't have time for this, Noah. I'm already late. You know Jonas's big sale starts today, and we're going to be packed for lunch. If I'm late, he's going to be upset, to say the least."

She pushed through the front door then jogged down the winding steps toward her car. She raced toward town then cranked the music up and the windows down. When she blew through a stop sign, she didn't hear the siren over her music. It wasn't until she pulled into the diner's parking lot, she realized what happened. She stepped out of her car, held a hand up, then said, "Sorry, Griff. I'm late."

After shutting off the siren, Griffin, one of two of the town's police officers, rushed after her. "I don't care who you are, Scarlett. You can't just do whatever you want."

Scarlett stopped so suddenly, Griffin stumbled to keep from running into her. After spinning around, she leaned into him. She cocked her head, then stared up at his surprised expression. She smirked and decided it was only fair to use what she had to her advantage. And it wasn't being the only sister of the pack's alpha. No, it was so much simpler than that. Unfair as it was, she knew Griffin had had a crush on her since first grade. Raising her hand, she tapped his chest. Then running one red, manicured nail from the top of his shirt all the way down to his belt buckle, she crooned, "I'm sorry, Griff." She stood on her toes and inched closer, murmuring, "I didn't mean to run the stop sign. You're not going to give me a ticket, are you?"

Deputy Griffin Long gripped Scarlett's arms, pulling her closer. Dipping his mouth down to her ear, he whispered, "I wouldn't dream of it, Scarlett." His lips brushed against the shell of her ear as he whispered, "I'm just going to tell Gage."

Scarlett's body sizzled. Panting, she closed her eyes while her imagination whisked her away to somewhere more intimate. His words faded when she felt his lips against her ear. Scarlett tilted her head, silently begging for more. When the more didn't come, she opened her eyes only to find that he was gone.

Griffin was standing beside his car. After opening the door, he shouted, “Two can play your game.” He slid one foot into the car then looked back. “I wasn’t kidding. I’m on my way to your house now.”

It took a couple of seconds for her to recover. Never in a million years would she have believed she’d be attracted to Griffin like this. He’d always only been that weird, awkward kid that followed her around all the time. When had he grown into the big piece of muscle-bound meat he was now? She licked her lips then decided she could be just a little late for work. It was long past time to take Griff out for a spin. She’d only taken a few steps when his words sank in. Mouth gaping, she stammered, “But…no. Wait. Griff. No. Please don’t tell Gage!”

Instead of answering, he winked then drove away.

Scarlett growled. Kicking at the gravel from a small pothole, she stared back toward the restaurant. That’s when she noticed the other car. She walked around it, frowning. As a member of the alpha’s family, it was part of her job to know every person in town. This car. It didn’t belong. Where had it come from? After the fifth pass, she stopped. She gasped, stumbled back, and stared at it blankly. “Of course.”

It had to be her. The human Gage had warned her about. What was she doing here? She took out her phone while rushing toward the door. She was just about to click on her brother's name when Jonas stepped into her path.

He looked down at his watch and growled, "It's about time you got here. We open in fifteen. And nothing's ready."

She stared up at her boss and mumbled, "Sorry. I just have to—"

"—Scarlett, meet Serenity. She's starting tomorrow morning. You're training her. So, you will be here on time tomorrow. Right?" Jonas dwarfed even Gage. He was known for his gentle nature. Still, nobody was foolish enough to cross him. Well, except for his mate and Gage.

She looked behind him. There, standing in his shadow, was the smallest woman she'd ever seen. She couldn't have been much over five feet tall. She was gorgeous, with a cute, upturned nose, and the brightest blue eyes she'd ever seen. Long blonde hair hung in waves past her waist. No matter how jealous she wanted to be of this beautiful woman, she couldn't. An aura of peace and love surrounded her…but there was more. The bitter scent of fear hung in the air around her. Turning a glare on the only target she could see, she felt her wolf pushing to be set free.

Jonas stepped between Serenity and Scarlett. His large hands gripped her arms in a bruising hold. In a voice so low, she knew human ears would never detect it, he whispered, "Hold."

Calling over his shoulder, he said, "Serenity, you go ahead and get busy with everything you need to do today. I expect you here by eight tomorrow morning. Oh, and don't worry about eating. Ariana will have breakfast waiting when you get here."

Scarlett kept her gaze locked with his until she heard the car pulling out of the parking lot. Then, jerking back, she paced away. She glared at him, then opened her mouth, only to shut it again and continue her pacing. Finally, she stopped. After throwing her arms up, she bellowed, "What was that? Why did she have that effect on me?" She shook her head, then squeaked, "And what do you mean, Ariana will have breakfast waiting? Since when does she cook for your employees?"

Knowing how close to dying he was, Jonas stumbled back. He grabbed a chair, slid into it, and took a deep breath. "That's—"

"—I know who it was. Again…" she waved her hands for him to continue.

"Your brother wants her kept close. He told me to hire her." He didn't say anything else but waited for her to process that information.

"Okay. I get that she's new here. I also understand that she somehow sneaked past our wards. What I don't get is…" Scarlett paced away, then grabbing a chair, she sat next to Jonas. After leaning on the table, she lowered her voice and said, "Jonas… To protect her, I was ready to kill you."

He nodded then murmured, "I know."

Chapter Eleven

Serenity stepped from the restaurant into the sunshine. While walking to her car, she thought about her interview.

Serenity sat in the stifling heat of a car that'd been closed up for hours. For a few moments, she allowed everything to sink in. Before putting the car in gear, she looked once more into the windows of a diner that would soon be coming to life. What was with this strange town and all it's weird inhabitants? So far, every person she'd met had glowing eyes. Well, maybe not every person. Still, it was strange. Perhaps there was something wrong with her? That had to be it. Maybe she was just tired from everything that had happened in the last few days.

After all, the drive here took over five hours. Plus, she'd stayed up way too late unpacking. Then adding to that, having to heave an extremely heavy stuffed wolf into and out of her car…Yeah, it was her. It had to be. Right?

She didn't bother with opening the windows or turning on the radio. She also didn't realize how slow she was going until some impatient driver laid on the horn. She waved an apology then pressed the accelerator until she'd managed to creep up to an overwhelming twenty miles an hour. Serenity pulled into the driveway and sat in the car for a few more minutes to allow everything to continue sinking in.

She slammed her palms against the steering wheel, squeezed her eyes shut, and screamed. A steady rapping against her window brought her back to earth. When she looked up, she saw Mr. weird, grumpy, paranoid, himself looking back at her.

Serenity bit back a scream. She continued staring at him while she tried to decide what to do. Did she trust him enough to open the door? Or should she just open the window a few inches to see what he wanted? Deciding on the safest route, she chose to leave both door and window shut. Serenity blinked up at him then asked, "What?"

She saw his lips moving but couldn't hear what he was saying. After a full minute of her staring at him, he gripped the handle and jerked the door open. Serenity yelped in surprise then flinched back. Squeezing her eyes closed, she begged, "Please! No, please." It took a few seconds for her to realize she wasn't dead. Or even close to dying. She squinted one eye open and was shocked by what she saw.

With his hands held up in a placating manor, he crouched beside her car and spoke in soothing tones. "I'm sorry if I scared you. I just wanted to make sure you were okay. I noticed how slow you were driving. Then when I heard you scream…" He shrugged.

Blinking back at him, her mind numbed for a second. Then a laugh bubbled out, "Boy do I feel like an idiot. I'm sorry. It's just been…" she paused, trying to think of the right words. After a deep sigh, she continued, "It's just that the past few days have been really weird."

He stepped back, giving her room to get out. He looked away for a second, cleared his throat, then said, "I think you left your television on."

Serenity looked from him to her house, then back. Confused, she said, "My television?"

"Unless you have a kid that you left all alone. I could hear a baby crying from across the street." He continued staring at her while waiting to see what she would do or say.

Serenity gasped. Caught off guard, her head spun toward the house. She had neither a child nor a television. A sudden foreboding came over her. After looking at her neighbor, she smiled then said, "Yes, I'm really sorry. I must have forgotten to turn it off when I left this morning. The radio. I mean. I don't have a television." She laughed nervously. "And well, I certainly don't have a baby. I'll just…" Shrugging, she pointed toward the house while walking backwards.

Her neighbor nodded. "Of course. I'm sorry. Oh, and by the way, I'm Luke. Luke Fridolf. I live right across the street if you need anything."

The familiar name...She remembered. It was Chance's last name...Serenity suddenly felt very lightheaded. Stumbling back, she reached for something to grasp onto. After coming up short, she dropped to the ground.

Luke lunged forward but stopped when she held her hands up.

"I'm okay. I just skipped breakfast. I'll be all right as soon as I get inside and make myself some…something to eat." She grabbed the door then pulled herself up. She didn't know why, but she knew that if this man touched her, something bad was going to happen. She forced a smile. "Please. I appreciate your concern. And thank you for telling me about my television being too loud. But really. I don't know you. So, if you could…" She made a shooing motion with her hands then waited for him to back up.

Serenity lunged toward the porch. After cramming her key in the lock, she spun around. She expected to see him behind her. Instead, he was halfway to his house. At the last second, he turned back. Confusion and doubt lined his face for a moment before it cleared. After waving once more, he closed himself inside. Again, peeking through the curtains.

She shook her head, then mused, "What is it with him? He could at least be a little less obvious." She reached for the doorknob, only to stop short. Panic threatened to make a return visit. She breathlessly whispered, "Television." Freezing in place, she cringed, remembering she'd told him she didn't own a television. She glanced back at the dark windows across the street then mumbled, "Maybe he didn't notice."

Just then a loud wailing came from inside. Eyes rounded, she twisted the knob then threw the door open. At the sound of it slamming through drywall, she glanced over her shoulder, cursing her luck.

After slipping into the hallway, she paused in front of her bedroom. She stared at the door, hesitating to reach for the knob. The sound of whimpering on the other side broke her resolve. She twisted the handle then inched it open. The door caught on something heavy on the other side for a second before whatever had blocked it moved. Slowly pushing the door open, she stared down at something that shouldn't be there.

Serenity knelt beside a little girl who looked to be somewhere between three and four, leaning more toward four. Long, straight black hair tangled around her shoulders. Her nearly black eyes were swollen and red. Tears continued to flow down chubby little cheeks. Red-faced, she hiccupped before a heartbreaking sob was sucked back in. Sniffling, she struggled to her feet, then with little hands flexing open and shut, she reached toward Serenity.

After wiping a hand across her suddenly damp cheeks, Serenity picked up the child. While hugging her tightly, she found herself sobbing in sympathy. Which for some crazy reason, the toddler found extremely hilarious.

She knew that she knew. But she still had to verify it. Serenity glanced at the bed. Other than a few silver-tipped wiry white hairs, there was no sign of the pup that had been there only a few hours ago. After dropping to her knees, she held the girl at arm's length. Then biting her lip, she shook her head and whispered, "No. It can't be." She glanced back at the bed, to the girl again, then murmured, "Celeste?"

Chapter Twelve

With bated breath, Serenity waited to see if the child responded to the name that she somehow knew was right. With her thoughts racing, she stared at the bed and told herself that it couldn't be true. For seventeen years, she'd seen the wolf pup in the forest. The pup was simply a taxidermy project from one of her grandfather's many hunting trips. What he'd done was sick, for sure. Nonetheless, it was a wolf he'd shot a very long time ago. She'd overheard them talking about the day they'd brought their prizes home. In her mind, she went over the details again.

She felt her blood run cold. Not once in the many retellings had anyone mentioned shooting the wolves. If they hadn't shot them…

That's when she realized the truth. The child she suspected was, in some crazy way, her pup.

Long, straight black hair in matted clumps bobbed with an exaggerated nod. Tiny fists rubbed circles on swollen, red eyes. After a sob, she finally spoke, murmuring "The…The bad mans came. They hurt my daddy and Uncle Chance, then they made me take a nap." She scrunched her brows together. "I didn't like my nap. I had bad dreams. My daddy…" She sobbed then collapsed in a heap of tears.

Serenity scooped the toddler up then carried her into the bathroom. After setting her on the floor, she began filling the tub. With her back to the child, she murmured, "I know baby girl. I'm very sorry. We're going to go get Chance. I promise."

She felt a weight on her back then little arms came around to encircle her neck. Celeste murmured into her hair, "When?"

Serenity wrapped her hand around the thin wrist then pulled the young girl into her lap. While fighting tears, she whispered, "Soon."

Bath over, her heart felt lighter hearing Celeste's tinkling laughter. She kept an arm locked around her waist while she continued to towel dry Celeste's hair. Serenity then grabbed her brush and carried her charge into the bedroom and began untangling her matted hair. Starting at the bottom, she worked her way up.

"Ow!" Celeste slapped a hand down on the brush then turned her glowing black eyes toward Serenity. In an instant, the toddler vanished, and in her place stood Serenity's silver-tipped wolf pup.

In that instant, any lingering doubt she may have had, vanished.

The pup twisted around then nipped at the hairbrush and growled. She leapt off the bed and began sniffing around the bedroom before nosing the door open.

With a startled shout, Serenity leapt from the bed and gave chase. Celeste was fast, that was for sure. With hands grasping at air, Serenity watched while the pup made a beeline for the front door. After halting at the barrier, her little snout frantically sniffled along the base of the closed door. With her tail swishing side to side, she raised her head and let out an ear-piercing howl. Then sitting in front of the door, the small pup continued to bay at the boundary that sat between her and the rest of the world.

Luke slammed the door shut then jerked the drapery back. He glared at the mysterious woman then released the curtain and pulled out his phone. While pacing away from the door, he called Gage. Once again fighting his wolf, he was ready to get in the car and drive to Gage's house when he finally answered.

He stepped onto the patio then turned toward the house on the hill. While facing his alpha, who was now staring down at him, he took a few deep breaths. With grim determination, he pushed his wolf down and hissed, "She's hiding something. I know she is."

"Just calm down and tell me what happened." Gage disappeared for a moment before reappearing gripping the neck of a brown bottle.

Luke walked back into his house and grabbed a beer of his own. After downing half, he began telling Gage what had transpired between him and their newest resident.

Gage leaned against the banister and listened before responding. "So, what do you think she's hiding? I mean you can't go with just her saying, thanks for telling me about my television. Maybe was being sarcastic. You do know people sometimes do that? Right?"

Luke slammed his bottle down on a table. He looked from Gage to the house across the street, then snarled, "But what about the baby? And Gage, you didn't see her face when I told her my name."

He watched Gage straighten with his attention riveted on Luke's house. "What did you say?"

Luke shook his head, blinked then queried, "You mean…what about the baby?"

Gage fought the sudden need to shift. He gripped the railing while his long sharp claws dug into the wood. His voice deepened and with his eyes glowing, he growled, "No! Your name. What did you say about her reaction to your name?"

Luke took another draw off the bottle. Then turning his gaze to the male who was more brother than friend, he said, "She reacted to my name. I thought it was weird, but since it's an unusual name…" He shrugged. "More importantly, what do you expect me to do? I can't just sit here and do nothing."

Gage growled into the phone, "It's exactly what I told you to do. Nothing. Is that so hard, Luke? Do nothing. We need to learn everything we can about this woman. Meet me at the diner in an hour. Something happened during her interview with Jonas. I think it's something you should know about."

While gripping the phone hard enough to crack the screen, Luke asked, "Why in an hour. If it affects me, I need to know now." He gazed up at his alpha and knew he was pushing the boundaries again. Then he heard the clatter of Gage's phone meeting the deck, followed at once by a huge grey wolf leaping toward the winding stairs. After pocketing his phone, he cursed under his breath then mumbled, "When will I learn to keep my mouth shut?" He rubbed a hand down his face then stepped through the slider and walked toward the front door. He peered through the curtain, searching for the mysterious woman across the street. After seeing nothing, he returned to his deck to wait for Gage.

Luke pondered what it was about her that made him do things he normally wouldn't? Before he had a chance to roll the idea around in his mind, he heard the pleading howl of a very young pup. He ran back inside and jerked the door open.

Nothing would stop him from reaching the female this time. Everything made sense now. He understood why he wanted to rip her throat out. If what he suspected was true, nothing would stop him from doing exactly that. Not even his alpha.

Serenity's gaze flew to the large picture window. If Luke heard the soft weeping from a baby, he'd certainly hear the loud wails of the wolf pup. Her gaze shot around the small living room. For the first time in her life, she regretted not buying a television. While looking across the street, she watched when the front door was jerked open. Luke stood on the stoop, staring daggers in her direction. Before he could take a step off the porch, she ran into her bedroom. Dropping to her knees beside her nightstand, she switched her alarm clock to FM and cranked the volume. Then rushing toward the front door, she scooped up the pup and ran back into her room. After depositing the pup in the middle of her unmade bed, she spoke through gritted teeth. "No. You need to stay quiet. Do you understand me, young lady?"

The wolf shimmered and the small child was back. In wide-eyed terror, Celeste clamped both hands over her mouth and nodded. Serenity's heart broke for the little girl when she saw tears streaming down her cheeks.

Serenity stepped back. Hands on her hips, she felt guilty for making the girl cry again. But she knew the child needed to understand. After a quick nod, she said, "Okay. You stay here. Not a peep. Do you hear me?" When Celeste nodded again, Serenity left the room, shutting the bedroom door behind her. While trying to look nonchalant, she headed toward the kitchen. Heart racing, it was all she could do to not glance out the window. In the background, she heard a commercial loudly proclaiming the benefits of refinancing your home.

When the front door was thrown open then slammed shut, Serenity couldn't hold back a terrified scream. After looking into the eyes of a very angry Luke, she reversed directions. Instinct took over. Her only thought…Protect the child.

His eyes took on an eerie golden glow. Then a low growl rumbled up from deep inside. In a voice that sounded more growl than human, Luke demanded, "What are you hiding? Tell me." The glowing ceased. His head rose. Then his eyes closed while he inhaled deeply.

The familiar scent that he'd picked up both confused and enraged him. It was home. It was a combination of his uncle and the long-forgotten scent of his own mother. He stumbled, then suddenly stopped. Eyes wide, mouth gaping, his gaze shot past her to the door at the end of the short hall. How could it be? His family was dead. Long dead. They'd been killed by the Jägers just before he was born. At least that's what he'd been told. Had he been lied to? Could his uncle have been mistaken, or did he purposely deceive him? Now, more than he wanted to take his next breath, he wanted to sink his teeth into this woman's throat. He wanted to taste her blood, to bathe in it.

Serenity braced her feet. She was determined to protect Celeste. First, she glanced down the hall then back to Luke as she attempted to shore up a small amount of courage. Instead, all she succeeded in doing was stammering, "I don't…I'm sorry. I had no idea my radio…"

Luke's attention veered away from the mystery down the hall. Then he focused a rage filled glower on this strange woman. Once again, a low growl rumbled up from deep inside, sounding impossibly loud in the quiet room.

With his intention clear, Serenity saw her own death in his piercing gaze.

However, before he could close the distance, the front door burst open. The huge man Serenity had previously seen dragging Luke out of his house, now stood in her living room. And of course, like everyone else, his silver eyes were glowing.

Right after the man came in the front door, she heard a loud crash in the kitchen. She didn't have to wait long to figure out what happened.

Serenity's shocked gaze switched from the immediate danger of the two strangers in her living room to the large black wolf standing between her and the other men. Gasping, she whispered, "Marcus?"

Chapter Thirteen

Awake. It was a slow awakening. But at long last, he was awake. When they'd arrived, he could only hope that the days of being trapped inside the body of his wolf would soon be over. For every mile that passed between them and the forest that had been his home for so many years, he'd felt his body respond. When Serenity reached for his rigid legs then jerked him toward her, he knew it was only a matter of time before the rest of him came alive.

When his body met the cold hard dirt of his new home, for the first time in a very long time, he felt something. Even given that his first sensation was pain, it was more than he'd experienced since that day so long ago when the Dämonejäger first came to his home. If it was to be pain, so be it. He would take it and be glad.

After Serenity set him on the ground, yet another sensation returned. A gentle wind ruffled his fur. That in itself was an amazing feeling. Even greater than the feeling was the scent carried on the breeze. His nostrils flared, pulling in the scent of the female. Her scent reminded him of a mixture between the first snow and freshly cut pine. A single word whispered through his mind. Mate.

A shiver began deep inside. It rolled through him, ending with a full body shake. At last. He was awake. Completely. He decided for his first order of business, he would claim his mate. Then he would see about finding the rest of his pack. Once they were united again, they could go home and plan their revenge.

Then an instant later, familiar, yet unfamiliar odors came, causing a low growl to rumble through him. Another pack. They were close. Too close to his mate.

His head whipped toward the house after he heard a loud crash. Inhaling deeply, he picked up two unfamiliar scents. Two different males were in there. With his mate. His ears twitched. He then picked up two separate growls coming from the same house. They were followed at once by the sickly-sweet aroma of fear. Her fear. His mate was afraid. Terrified. She was in danger. Added to that, he realized unfamiliar wolves were stalking her. A single thought screamed through his mind. Protect his mate.

He leapt toward the house and his massive paws connected with both screen and a solid wooden door. He slid into the kitchen. Then he noticed the male standing beside the broken front door. He didn't see the other male, but he knew he had to be close to his mate. If he touched her, he would die. For his offence of scaring her, he would simply suffer a beat down. It would be severe. But he would live.

He charged into the living room and saw his mate slowly backing down the short hall toward another room. She would find no refuge there. What she didn't know was there was no barrier capable of holding a wolf that was determined to get his prey. Unless, of course, that barrier was an alpha protecting his mate.

Marcus crouched. He leapt past both males, landing between them and Serenity. The form of his dark wolf shimmered, leaving behind a furious man.

A very tall, very naked man. Serenity found herself staring at what could only be described as the absolute perfect backside. Her gaze roamed from thickly muscled shoulders down his wide back. Her mouth gone dry, she wasn't sure if she should wait for him to turn around…or run.

Did she think the man standing beside the shattered front door was huge? No. Compared to the man standing between them, hands down, it was easy to see exactly what huge meant.

Saying he was surprised, was putting it mildly. Gage blinked. Who was this newcomer? He wasn't part of his pack. Plus, he knew most of the members of every pack along the west coast, and this guy wasn't one of them. Still, there was something familiar about him.

A truck rolled over the curb and into the front yard, stopping just a few feet in front of the porch. The driver's side door flew open, spilling out Serenity's new boss.

Serenity pried her gaze from the naked man to the truck in the front yard. "Great. Just great. Anybody else want to show up uninvited?"

Still poised to attack, Marcus said, "Don't worry. They're about to leave." He shrugged. "Or die. The choice is theirs." After looking back at the two men, his gaze swept past them to see what new threat had arrived.

Serenity's cheeks flushed when the man she now knew was Marcus, turned around. After slapping a hand over her eyes, she said, "Where's your clothes?"

Looking down, Marcus opened his mouth to answer, but before he got a chance, Serenity spoke again.

"I know losing your clothes isn't a thing when you shift. When my little pup..." Her hands fell away and her eyes widened then she sputtered, "I mean...Um...Never mind."

Marcus stared at Serenity and waited for her to elaborate. When she didn't, he realized at once she didn't feel safe enough to tell these males about Celeste. He returned his attention to the two males, then took a step closer. That's when familiar scents hit him.

He gasped, stopping mid step. The male closest to him was familiar, yet not. There was something about him that reminded him of his pack. However, this male wasn't a member of his pack. He knew that all of them were still imprisoned in the forest.

When a figure appeared in the doorway, he relaxed his stance, now understanding how this young male could be familiar and yet remain unknown to him.

From the front yard, Jonas's gaze swept from the door that was hanging by one hinge to the picture window. He walked to the threshold then staggered back a step. His breath caught, and under his breath he mumbled, "No. It can't be." He shoved past Gage then stumbled across the living room. Stopping between his nephew and the newcomer, he dropped to his knees. Tears streaming down his face, he sobbed, "Alpha."

Gage took a moment for everything to sink in. He'd told his pack to watch her. To do nothing more. Then to report back to him.

This female, the one Gage had ordered his packmates to leave alone, was now surrounded by wolves. Each of them only seconds away from shifting and attempting to either kill each other. Or worse, her.

Now, not only did he have to deal with what happened at the diner, he had this.

Jonas, who'd come to him thirty years ago and sworn his loyalty, was now prostrate in front of another man. A male he'd called alpha.

Luke staggered, his legs giving out as he fell in a heap on the carpet, confused beyond words. He stared past his uncle, past the newcomer, then beyond the female. Standing in the hall, he saw something…someone who shouldn't be here. Someone he'd thought long dead. Although he'd only seen pictures, he knew it was her.

Serenity noticed where her neighbor's gaze had gone and gasped. Then walking backwards, never taking her eyes off the man sobbing just a few feet away, she reached for Celeste. She looked away just long enough to pick the child up then heard a snarl. Whipping her head around, with her back to the threat, she watched a snarling grey wolf spring from where the man had been sitting only seconds ago. Before he reached her, both Jonas and Marcus tackled him to the ground.

One second later, another wolf leapt into the mix. Tables snapped. Chairs flew across the room. Then something crashed through the picture window.

Serenity turned around and whispered to her precious Celeste. "Honey, go hide." Not waiting to see if her instructions were followed, she held her hands out and bellowed, "Stop! All of you. Back to men. On the floor. Do not speak. Do not move."

The room quieted. Four men sat on the floor in front of her. Shocked expressions lined their faces but none spoke.

Serenity looked around the room then felt like crying. There was nothing left. They'd destroyed every piece of furniture, every fixture. Everything right down to a potted plant on the fireplace. She fell to her knees then allowed the tears to flow. She was broke. She'd used every penny she had to move here and furnish her house. All she had left was enough to make it through the next month. Certainly not enough to replace everything that had been destroyed…

By them.

After slamming a fist against the wall, she screamed, “What is wrong with you? You came into my home.” She pounded her chest and sobbed, “My home. Nobody invited you here. Then you de…destroyed…” stammering, she couldn’t go on. While cupping her face, she continued crying. After a few minutes, she glared at the men. “Nothing? Really? Not even a gee, I’m sorry Sav…” Slapping a hand over her mouth, she watched for any kind of reaction. When none came, she threw her hands in the air then bellowed, “Speak! Say something.”

All at once the men started talking. She heard phrases like, “We couldn’t.” Along with angry shouted questions, “What did you do to us?” But one single word captured her attention above all the others. Dämonejäger. After narrowing her gaze on the man who’d busted her front door, she asked, “What did you say?”

Chapter Fourteen

While waiting for the light to change, Lena shivered. Goosebumps peppered her arms. The same arm that rested in the eighty-degree heat, which felt more like one-twenty, while sitting in bumper-to-bumper traffic in the heart of downtown Seattle. She flicked on her turn signal but didn't wait for the other cars to move or for the light to change. She checked once to make sure it was safe, then flipped around and headed out of town.

While slamming her foot down on the accelerator, she reached for her phone. Flashing red lights reflected in her mirror told her that at least one person noticed what she'd done. After mouthing a curse, she wished that just once she could wave a hand and her problems would be erased. But that would go against everything that had been taught to her since before she could walk.

She let up on the gas and coasted to a stop. After pulling up every sad memory she had, she opened the top three buttons on her blouse. By the time the officer got there she was a blubbering mess. She glanced out the window and saw that her current state of dress, or should she say, undress, hadn't gone unnoticed. When the silence stretched on, she felt the ire raise. She looked up and saw the officer standing in the sun. With his pen still poised above his ticket book, his gaze was riveted on her cleavage. Using her left arm, she reached for her purse, blocking his view of her lacy bra. It was the distraction needed to bring his attention back to her.

A deep red blush bloomed across his cheeks. He stumbled away, muttering, "Yes. Thank you, Ma'am. Drive safe."

She watched his departure in the rearview mirror and laughed. She decided she wasn't about to wait until he remembered why he'd stopped her in the first place. After shifting into gear, she eased away from the shoulder. Inching her way toward a hair over the posted speed limit, which wasn't eighty, she turned onto the freeway then headed toward I90. Cocking her head as if listening, she exited the interstate then reentered heading south instead of north. She also knew it would take a good hour before she would get out of this mess of downtown traffic.

After finally hitting Interstate 5, she again reached for her phone. Then, scrolling through her contacts, she tapped her cousin's smiling face. Immediately, it went to voicemail. She held her phone closer then shouted above the wind noise. "Erika, I don't know what's going on, but you need to call me as soon as you get this message."

She crossed the Columbia River then stopped in Portland to grab dinner. Once again at a complete standstill, she cursed the seven other cars who'd also decided on fast food tonight. She tossed a twenty at the boy in the window, waved off her change, and drove away. Rotating between fries, burger, and sips of her drink, she headed back to the interstate.

She slowed every few minutes, cocked her head, then sped on. Lena prayed she'd get there before anything happened. She glanced at her phone then mumbled under her breath, "Erika, where are you, and what have you done?"

She almost turned onto interstate 84. Instead, she kept driving. She was finally sure of her next move. She exited the interstate then continued toward the mountains, murmuring, "I hope you appreciate what I'm doing for you, cuz. I've been driving for hours in complete silence, listening for the next sign telling me what to do next."

Lena steered onto the shoulder then stared up at the mountain in front of her. She was close. She could feel it. She prayed she didn't lose the connection she shared with her cousin. Well, she had other cousins. Cousins galore. It was the rare female cousin that was missing from her clan. Lena shrugged off her apprehension and started up the mountain. After fifteen minutes, she was overcome with an overwhelming need to stop. She closed her eyes. While sitting on the shoulder, she muttered a simple revealing spell and at once noticed a narrow lane winding through the trees. Luckily, the dark highway was deserted this time of night. A moment later, she was cruising down the path. Her eyes widened when the road led into a small community.

She stopped in the middle of the road, realizing where she was. She expected at any moment to be set upon by the residents. Gasping for breath, she whispered, "Oh, Erika. What have you done?" More than that, she was amazed that her cousin still lived.

After switching off her headlights, she steered into the forest surrounding the village. She muttered a concealing spell as she stepped out of her car, but it failed immediately. Which told her the magic here was very strong.

She ducked her head and strove for nonchalance. As she passed each house, a porch light came on. The sound of screen doors opening on rusty hinges was followed by growls and angry curses. There was no way she'd be able to reach her cousin unnoticed and immediately regretted ditching the car. Then she felt the first man stepping onto the sidewalk.

Without looking back, Lena raced toward the next block, knowing that's where she'd find her cousin.

Chapter Fifteen

The sound of an angry mob coming their way had everyone rushing out of the house.

Serenity glanced toward the back of the house, praying Celeste would still be safe. She had a feeling this was a neighborhood filled with werewolves. Even though her sweet little pup was one of them, she didn't trust the others to not hurt her.

Under the light of the moon, she could see someone was being chased by at least twenty big burly men. Judging by the size of the pursued, she knew it had to be a woman. Then, as if running full tilt into a brick wall, Serenity stumbled back before landing on the porch. She didn't know how she knew, but she knew with absolute certainty it was Lena. It had to be. She stood and pushed her way through four huge bodies toward the woman who'd always been like a sister to her.

Anger boiled inside. She lifted her hands above her head ready to scream at the crowd to leave Lena alone. However, before she could speak, Lena shouted, "No! Erika, stop."

Lena rushed toward her but stopped just short of mowing her over. With hands on her knees, she panted. Lifting one arm, she waved a finger around, breathing, "Just…Just a… minute."

Two men leapt between Serenity, Lena, and the oncoming crowd. Landing in a crouch, snarls warned the newcomers to stay back.

Lena collapsed in the grass then turned her astonished gaze back to her cousin. Her eyes darted between the angry mob, the men protecting her, and her cousin. She said, “Erika—”

Kneeling beside her, Serenity gripped Lena’s shoulder then sternly said, “Serenity Chase. I don’t know who this Erika is. But my name is *Serenity*.”

Nodding her understanding, Lena whispered, “Smart.” Then waving a hand to encompass everything, in a whisper, she asked, “What have you done? Do you even know…” She set a hand in the dirt preparing to stand. Before she could, a large hand was shoved into her face. Looking up at the tall dark form, she knocked the hand away then arose to stand beside her cousin.

With dawning realization, she whispered, “You don’t know. Nobody ever told you. Did they?” Shaking her head, she added, “Of course they didn’t. Why would they tell you?” While muttering under her breath, she walked into the house. Looking around the room, she commented, “But I’ll bet you’re starting to get at least a little idea.” Turning back to Serenity, she leaned closer and asked, “And what’s up with the naked Lycan?”

Gage never took his gaze from the small female who’d wandered into his town. Mate. He had a mate. With a crooked grin he walked toward the house.

Gage shoved his hand toward the man he had yet to meet. Shaking his hand, he said, "Gage, pack alpha."

Marcus grabbed his hand like it was a lifeline. Introducing himself, he said, "Marcus…and I have no idea where I stand anymore." Then giving Gage a sidelong glance, he asked, "Where am I, anyway?"

Gage chuckled. He knocked his head toward the house on the hill. "Come on. I think I might have something that'll fit you."

Marcus stopped and looked from Serenity's house to the one that reminded him very much of his own home. He wasn't sure.

Gage turned around, cupped his mouth, and yelled, "She's under my protection."

After hearing the alpha's orders, the crowd wandered away.

Marcus still didn't move to follow Gage. Instead, he growled and started toward the male who'd threatened his mate.

Gage grabbed his arm. Jerking him to a halt, he asked, "Do you know who that is?" When the male shook his head, Gage continued, "That's Luke, my second. But you might know him as Henry's only son. And that pup in there…she's the only family he has left."

Serenity watched Marcus walk away. She didn't know who the man was, but judging by the reaction of everyone else, he must be important. Then turning back to the only family she really cared about, she threw herself at Lena. After wrapping her arms around the other woman, unable to hold back the tears, she blubbered, "I'm so glad you're here."

Arm in arm, they walked back toward the house. After stepping over the mangled screen door, Lena asked, "What in the world happened here?" She nodded, surveying the living room and the destroyed furniture. "Too many wolves in a small area." The sound of crunching glass and metal had both women turning back to the door.

Luke paused just inside the house. With his eyes downcast, he waited.

When Lena stepped closer, he took a step back. She smirked, cocked her head, and tried again. And again, he stepped away.

After the third time, he growled, "Please stop."

She walked across the room to the only piece of furniture still in one piece, flipped it over, and sat down. Then nodding for Serenity to go ahead, she waited.

Half expecting to back him all the way to the street, Serenity strode toward Luke. As she drew even with him, instead of backing down, he faced her…as well as a man who stood a good foot and a half taller than her could. Determined to show no fear, she squared her shoulders, jutted her chin out, then simply said, "What?"

Luke chuckled, leaning just a few inches closer. Then, taking a deep breath, his nostrils flared. After putting his lips next to the shell of her ear, he whispered, "I can smell your fear."

In seconds, Lena was standing between them. She poked one long manicured nail into his chest and hissed, "Careful, wolf. Don't let her name fool you. Standing before you is the beloved granddaughter of Oskar Jäger himself. With no more than a thought she could turn your entire village to dust. So, what do you suppose she'd do to a low-ranking wolf who threatens her?"

Luke's gaze flew from the stranger to the woman they'd been ordered to watch. He stumbled back a few steps. The edges of his vision darkened. Then, unable to stand, he collapsed.

A gasp behind Lena had her spinning to face her cousin. She stepped closer then reached for the girl she'd always known as Erika Jäger. In a soft voice, she murmured, "I'm sorry…"

She glanced behind her and murmured, "Serenity, I'm sorry you had to find out this way."

Snarling, Luke chose that moment to shift. By the time Serenity got to the door, he was nothing more than a smokey grey shadow heading toward the house at the top of the hill behind hers.

While watching him disappear, Serenity said, "No matter what, I would never…"

After nodding, Lena said, "And you should never. We'd better follow him. The last thing we need for him to do is call our bluff."

Serenity grabbed her cousin's arm and asked, "Our bluff? You mean I couldn't—"

Lena shook her head. “I didn’t say you couldn’t. I said you shouldn’t. Serenity, you’re an immensely powerful sorceress. It’s a wonder you haven’t figured it out by now. The only thing I can guess is that your grandfather recognized your potential and put a dampening spell on either you, or your house…or both. It would take something that strong to prevent you from learning the truth.” Then glancing toward the house overlooking this small community, she said, “Come on. We need to get up there. It’s time to reunite the wolves and Jägers.”

Serenity nodded then went back inside. A moment later, she came out cradling a tiny sleeping, silver-tipped white wolf pup. Tsking, she said, “Poor little thing, the excitement must have worn her out.”

Lena gaped at the pup in Serenity’s arms. “Serenity…where did you get that pup?”

“From the forest near my father’s farm, of course.” She looked away. “That’s also where the naked man came from. It’s crazy, because yesterday, I thought both of them were nothing more than stuffed wolves. I mean, you know…like taxidermy.”

Lena gasped. “You took them away from where your grandfather placed them?” She shook her head, grabbed her cousin’s arm, and began dragging her toward the house on the hill. “I only hope nobody’s missed them. If so, you’ll bring the wrath of the entire Jäger clan down on both of us.”

Serenity stumbled for a moment. Shaking off Lena's hold, she asked, "So, what do you think will happen when they learn that I inherited the entire Jäger fortune?"

Chapter Sixteen

For every step closer to Gage's house she got, the more Serenity wanted to turn and run. Not just to run. But to get in her car and start driving. She didn't care where she ended up, just as long as it was away from here. There were two things preventing her from doing exactly that. The first was the small white pup in her arms. The second was the mysterious man who was once a wolf.

A wolf she'd been sure was nothing more than a cotton stuffed hide. Although she'd tried to convince herself the voices in her head weren't real, she'd never completely believed it. The idea that she wasn't crazy should have made her feel better. Instead, she felt like her head was going to explode. For years she'd, heard their pleas, begging her to help them. At times, it was so overwhelming she'd clamp her hands over her ears and scream. It wasn't until she was sixteen that she'd finally figured out how to block most of it.

She thought about what she'd been feeling while driving away. At the time, she'd played it off as simple homesickness. Now, she realized those feelings of sadness weren't her own. Then when she drove out of the mountains, that sense of being united with her pack faded. By the time she'd crossed the state line, she'd experienced a lightness she'd never imagined possible. Outside of Marcus's quiet influence and Celeste's warm love, all the rest was gone. What was left behind was a gaping hole, something she only now realized.

Panic hit. Stopping short of reaching the door, she fell to her knees. She stared, unseeing, into her memories. Her arms relaxed, releasing the small pup. Her thoughts turned to the wolves she'd left behind, and then to Chance. Tears flooded her eyes: Celeste vanished in a blur. In her place stood Chance. Was he safe? What if he gave up on ever finding his own freedom? And what about the barnful of young pups? Their faces flashed before her eyes. It ended with windblown dark smokey grey fur and a few dried bones lying in the decaying leaves of a final resting place.

***

Marcus stood in the bathroom, staring at his own reflection. He was amazed to see that he looked exactly the same as he did the day the Dämonejäger's came into his community. He'd neither aged, nor had his hair grown, not even an inch. Looking at the clothes Gage had given him, it looked like he was the only thing that hadn't changed. Stepping out of the bathroom, shirt in hand, he went searching for his host.

Marcus followed sounds of conversation and found himself in a den that reminded him very much of his own. Looking past the large desk centered in Gage's office and beyond the bank of windows, an overwhelming sense of déjà vu came over him. Something about this struck a chord. He half expected to hear the voice of Chance telling him the Dämonejäger's were here. He knew that if he stepped onto the deck, he would see one of them looking back. Without thinking, Marcus took a step closer to the window.

"You're dressed. Great. Come on, I want to introduce you to my sister and brothers," Gage called out while standing by the door.

Who was this man? Other than someone he knew absolutely nothing about, other than his status as another alpha shifter.

The feelings that had been so strong a moment ago vanished. After looking around, Marcus realized that this office was as opposite to his own as one could get. Where his desk was a rich dark oak, Gage's was sleek lines of chrome and dark smokey grey glass. Then he noticed that there wasn't a single phone in sight. He walked over to the smooth surface then pointed to something he couldn't even venture a guess as to its purpose. Tapping the corner, he asked, "What's this?"

Gage motioned for him to follow, saying, "We'll get to all that later. For now, let me introduce you to those closest to me." Gage led him down a hallway and continued, "You're in luck. My youngest brother has deigned to grant us with his presence tonight."

"Your youngest brother? How many brothers do you have?" After having grown up an only child,

Marcus couldn't fathom having either a brother or sister. His parents had spent most of the time away on pack business, up until their sudden death right after he turned twenty.

"Well," Gage chuckled. "You're about to find out."

Marcus was shocked to see so many people packed into this one small room. He'd always held gatherings this large in the basement. He had seating set up for two hundred but most of the meetings consisted of only a dozen or so of his closest officers. Judging from the camaraderie between those gathered here tonight, he doubted any were officers.

After closing the door, Gage stepped inside. He whistled to get everyone's attention. "This is Marcus." He looked at the other man. "What's the name of your pack?"

Marcus nodded to the others, then said, "Whitebark Stand."

Gage walked over to one man who resembled him but was nearly twice as big. He slapped him on the back, grinned, and said, "This guy is my little brother, Noah Kenneally. If he makes you uncomfortable, don't worry, he does that to everybody."

Then walking toward two people speaking in low voices, he cleared his throat. "And this is my beautiful sister, Scarlett. She's as sweet as she is pretty. It helps to make up for Noah's difficult personality. You know what they say about twins having opposite personalities. And as far as these two go? It couldn't be closer to the truth. And sitting beside her is our usually absent baby brother, Allister."

Marcus hung back, studying Allister, the youngest member of the alpha's family. Then looking at Gage, he asked, "Are you sure he's not a bear shifter?"

Allister stood, flexed his muscles, and growled. His steely blue eyes glowed for a moment before he broke out in a fit of laughter.

Gage shoved him into his seat. Turning back to Marcus, he said, "Unlike Noah, Allister's pretty easy going."

He walked over to the long sofa. "And you've met this guy."

Marcus stared at the older man before dropping onto the coffee table in front of him. "Jonas. You're…"

Jonas slapped Marcus's shoulder. "Yeah. I know. I'm an old man. Do you know how many years it's been?"

Marcus hung his head "I don't think I want to know. But I have a feeling you're going to tell me anyway."

Gage stood then paced toward the windows. Far below, he watched the two females inching their way closer to his house. Not only were they taking their time, but at one point, Lena stopped and looked up. He didn't think she could see him through the tinted windows, but he knew she could sense him watching her. Then turning away from what he knew would alter his world in ways he couldn't imagine, he walked over to the bar and poured himself a drink. He hesitated with the bottle in one hand, a shot glass in the other. Shrugging, he tilted the glass back then grimaced at the burn. After pouring another, he turned, held the bottle out, and waited. When Marcus nodded, he grabbed another glass.

Jonas stepped behind the bar and began pouring drinks for the rest of the room.

After handing Marcus his drink, Gage nodded.

Marcus tossed the shot back and said, "Tell me."

After a deep sigh, Gage said, "As far as we can guess…thirty years."

Marcus stumbled back. He swept his gaze around the room, shook his head, then stammered, "No. It…It can't…" But looking from Gage to Jonas, he knew. Jonas was Chance's youngest brother, not more than a pup himself when he'd volunteered to take Henry's mate to the doctor. He sighed. "How—?"

The door slammed against the wall. There, standing on the threshold, was the same male who'd threatened Serenity earlier. Marcus walked over to meet him. "You're Henry's son?"

Luke nodded, "At least that's what they tell me. After my mother died, Uncle Jonas and Aunt Ariana raised me."

Marcus studied the male. He was about the right age. His eyes narrowed. "I'm very sorry to hear about your mother. I wish…" It was just too much. All of it. He walked away, shaking his head.

Turning to Jonas, he said, "So you married Ariana? How is she? *Where* is she?"

Gage walked up to him. "You'll have plenty of time to catch up and meet everybody else. For now, we need to know about the rest of your pack."

After walking over to join his uncle, Luke echoed the sentiment, "Please. I need to know. My father?"

He shook his head. "I was trapped inside my body. I was able to learn about only a few members of my pack from Serenity. She spoke of Chance. She also told me there was a barn filled with pups of various ages."

Luke stood. "So, she'll know about my father?"

A voice from the doorway caught him off guard. "If you're Henry's son, you're going to want to meet your sister, Celeste."

Chapter Seventeen

Even though Serenity's brothers weren't going to win any awards for best brother of the year, she still loved them. But she had no desire to see any of them any time soon. She also knew not all families were like hers. Even Lena's family was more loving than her own. Of course, Lena hadn't grown up under the thumb of Oskar Jäger, either.

The house she'd grown up in had been in the family since they'd arrived in this country over four-hundred years ago. Since then, it'd been passed down from father to son. Oskar lived in the house with her family until the day he died, three years ago. She knew one day the house would be passed from her father to Dieter, and she was glad she wouldn't be there to witness it. Oskar was a mean old man, but Dieter was well on his way to surpassing their grandfather.

Luke's welcome hadn't been the warmest, not to mention his attitude toward her. But he still had a right to know his sister. Not to mention, he also deserved to know what happened to his father.

Serenity stepped into the room then stopped in front of Luke. She kissed the top of Celeste's head and whispered, "Don't be afraid sweetheart. I promise, nobody here is going to hurt you."

After setting Celeste on the floor in front of her brother, she knelt beside her. Then brushing a hand down her long black hair, she said, “Concentrate sweetheart. Hold your human form. I know you can do it.”

Celeste looked back at Serenity, nodded, then scrunched her eyes tightly for a moment. When she finally opened them again, she smiled and said, “I’m not scared.”

Serenity gave a sad smile. “I know you’re not, baby girl.”

Luke watched the interaction between them with growing awe. The child called Celeste smelled like him, but not. Plus, he’d seen her wolf, bringing back memories he’d forgotten long ago. His mother’s wolf had also been white with silver tips, although more silver than Celeste. Still, it was the same. Hands fisted, teeth clenched, Luke was fighting with everything he had to remain calm. The last thing he wanted to do was scare this young girl. His sister. *Sister*. He had a sister. When he looked back at Serenity, he was suddenly overcome with emotion.

It was her. Serenity. She’d kept his sister safe. All these years, he hadn’t even known he had a sister. And now there she knelt, inches away from him, ready to become a part of his life.

Little fingers brushed against his cheeks and Celeste whispered, “Don’t cry, little wolf.”

Luke gasped after hearing the same phrase his mother used to say to him when he was just a pup.

He found he could no longer hold back the tears and emotions that fought to be released. All at once, they exploded, pouring from him like a dam that had finally broken. Pulling her into his arms, he wept.

Jonas stood beside his nephew and pulled him and the young girl closer. Then looking at Serenity, he asked, "My brother?"

Tears flowing down her cheeks, Serenity bit back a sob then shook her head.

Jonas bowed his head. He was silent for a moment. then asked, "Both of them?"

Smiling through the tears, Serenity shook her head. A hand filled with tissues appeared in front of her face. She looked up then smiled her thanks to Gage. When she tried to stand, she stumbled.

Marcus was there in an instant, holding her steady. He led her to a chair. "Thank you. For everything. Thank you."

Serenity nodded and asked, "Can I get something to drink?"

Lena sat next to her cousin. "I think we're all going to need a drink after what I have to say."

Allister walked over to the bar and began pouring. "It's going to be a long night. Maybe Ariana can bring something from the diner. It's time for me to tell you what I've been doing, as well."

Gage stood from his perch by the bar and said, "Excellent idea. Scarlett, can you call Ariana. The rest of you, follow me to the dining room. Noah, can you put some coffee on? We'll reserve the drinks for after we have a full belly."

Marcus waited for Serenity. While keeping in step with her, he said, "I mean it, what you've done, even before this..." He shook his head, overcome with emotion. "You know you're going to have to let Celeste go, right?"

Serenity bowed her head, and fighting back the swirling emotions, she nodded. "It's going to be one of the hardest things I've ever done. But I know she belongs with her family." She gave a small laugh. "You know I was only six when I found all of you. Chance, he was the first. Then…then, Henry." She sighed. "But Celeste. I can't tell you how ecstatic I was when I found her. I really wanted her to be real. I'd always wanted a puppy. I guess to my six-year-old self, that's what she was. I slept out there that night, curled around her little body. I wanted... needed to keep her warm and safe."

Marcus stopped walking and asked, "By yourself? Didn't your family miss you?"

She laughed. "Oh, they missed me, all right. I think they called in every cousin, second cousin twice removed, and anyone else they thought might be related. My brother, Kurt, told me later that they discovered I was missing right after midnight. I guess I wasn't found until almost ten the next morning. Boy, was my dad mad. It was a whipping I'll never forget, that's for sure. I don't think I could sit for a week afterward."

Marcus grabbed her arm and swung her around to face him. Bringing his face down to meet hers, he snarled, "He beat you?"

Shocked, Serenity yanked her arm away then turned to catch up with the others. Although her arm hurt from his bruising grip, she wasn't about to tell him. Without looking back, she said, "That's what fathers do. They spank their kids."

Gage, Jonas, and everyone in front of her turned around. Striding back to her, Gage snarled, "No. They don't beat their kids. Especially not the way you described."

Lena stopped beside her, glaring at the others. "That was a very long time ago. Why do you think she's here instead of there? Now leave her alone. Nobody wants to be reminded of their abuse."

Marcus stepped into a dining room large enough to seat several hundred people. Banquet tables filled with coffee urns, punch bowls, and buckets of ice lined the walls. Surely Gage must have an enormous staff, if this was any indication of how his pack was run. Such splendor, it was everything his home hadn't been. After the death of his parents, he'd lived in the large house alone. Outside of the occasional visits from the few who'd insisted on taking care of the upkeep a home that large would require, he stayed to himself. There was a large meeting room in the basement. But nothing like this.

Gage stopped beside him and said, "I could tell by the way you're looking at everything that I've impressed you."

Marcus turned a glare on him. "Impressed?"

Gage laughed, waved an arm around the room, then said, "This…this was all my parent's. They liked to entertain. There are a few stools around the kitchen island. That's where most of us eat if we choose to eat together. But if we have guests, we have a smaller, cozier dining room."

He walked over to an extravagant bar and pulled out an amber bottle. But before he could pour himself a drink, his sister grabbed the glass out of his hand.

She walked over to the sink. "I can't believe you were going to use this. Do you have any idea how long these glasses have been sitting here?" She held it up and peered through the grimy glass. She rolled her eyes, then dropping it in the basin, she filled the sink with soapy water.

Gage followed his sister and grabbed the same dirty glass. Frowning, he picked up a nearby towel and wiped it out. A moment later, he slapped the towel against the counter, creating a billowing cloud of dust. He waved his hands around, blew into the glass, then poured himself a shot. He shrugged. "The alcohol will kill any germs that might still be in there."

After setting the last glass on the drainer, she said, "It wasn't the germs I was concerned with. It wasn't even the dust. But did you see how many spider webs there were? Not to mention how many spiders were inside?"

Waving it off, Gage said, "Did you know…" He held the glass up to the light, revealing a fine layer of dust everywhere except where he'd taken a sip. "The average person eats about six pounds of dirt before they die. So, maybe I'll eat a few extra grams? What is that really when you look at the big picture. Now about spiders—"

Scarlett got in his face. "No. Just don't." She went over to the buffet and poured a cup of coffee. She walked back to Gage, handed it to him, and took his shot. "Just how much have you had to drink?"

Gage snatched the glass from his sister then dumped it in his coffee. "Not enough."

Marcus left the siblings to argue. He walked over to the urns and poured himself a cup of coffee. After looking around the room, he noticed the curtains, billowing along the back wall. Ignoring the others, he strode toward the window. When he got there, instead of a window, he discovered an open door. What he saw when he stepped through the door took his breath away.

An expansive deck faced the snow-capped Sierra Nevada's. Tension he didn't realize was there, dissolved. Taking a deep breath, he filled his lungs with the fresh mountain air. This is what he'd missed.

"It's beautiful, isn't it?" Gage stopped beside him. Resting his arms on the railing, he put one booted foot on the bottom and took another sip of his coffee. While taking in the scene, he said, "I added it after my parents were killed. I come out here when I feel overwhelmed. It never fails to bring me peace."

Marcus set his cup down, leaning forward with his elbows resting on the banister. "I can see how. I would like to…" Dropping his head, he slowly shook it side to side murmuring, "My house. My community…"

Gage patted his back. "I'll take you there, I promise. In the meantime, we have business to take care of." After tossing out what was left of his spiked coffee, he added, "Scarlett is right, I've had enough to drink."

Serenity stopped next to Lena and waited until everyone passed.

When the last person stepped into the dining room, she paced a few more feet away. "He didn't abuse me."

Lena's head snapped back like she'd been slapped. She stomped over to Serenity. She'd never looked as small as she did in that moment. Her arms were wrapped around her waist in a self-hug and she was shaking. Lena put her arms around her cousin and whispered, "Honey, they broke your arms. And it wasn't the first time."

Chapter Eighteen

Ariana walked in with a few shopping bags. She set them on the table, left the room, and returned with two place settings. She put one at the head of the table and the other directly to the right. She glanced at the others. "I brought the food. Get up and wait on yourselves."

Allister rushed over and grabbed a box out of the bag. He returned to the table and sat across from Ariana, grinning. "You don't have to ask me twice."

Conversation ceased. With boxes of food in hand, everybody took a seat around the table.

Marcus paused by the empty chair at the head of the table, solemnly bowed his head, then sat beside Serenity.

Serenity nodded toward the empty chair. "What's up with that?"

Allister spoke before Marcus had a chance to respond. Seeing her surprise, he grinned. "You're in a room full of wolves. Our hearing is very keen. Everybody heard you."

Gage answered her question. "The head of the table was my father's seat. I would imagine Marcus also left it empty."

Without looking up, Marcus raised his glass. "Gone. Never forgotten."

Cups and glasses were raised around the table while everybody repeated the same phrase. "Gone. Never forgotten."

She noticed the other seat was also left empty. A place for both parents.

After a moment of silence, conversation resumed. Once the meal was complete, Ariana removed both place settings. A few minutes later, she returned. After drying her hands on a towel, she wiped down the table in front of the empty seats.

Scarlett had kept quiet throughout the meal. She watched while everyone disposed of their containers, got something to drink, then resumed their seats. After looking at Gage, she said, "Allister has something he wants to say."

Saying nothing, Gage stared at his youngest brother.

Allister's gaze dropped to his lap for a moment. Then he steepled his hands. "I don't think their deaths were an accident."

Noah groaned. "Here we go again."

Gage leaned forward. "Does this have anything to do with why you missed the mandatory pack meeting?"

Clenching his teeth, Allister glared at his oldest brother. "Just hear me out. Yes, that's part of why I was away."

Then, glaring at Noah, he added, "And it had nothing to do with college women, or even the college, for that matter. I decided it was time to do more than speculate as to how our parents would suddenly lose control of their car and drive off a cliff." He turned his attention to Marcus. "I hope you don't mind me asking how your parents died."

Marcus was silent for a moment. Then looking around the table, his gaze landed on Serenity. After a long moment, he looked back at Allister. "They were visiting another pack when they…" He snarled, then looked out the window. Clenching and unclenching his fists, Marcus struggled to keep his wolf at bay. Finally, blue eyes glowing, he returned his gaze to Allister. "They lost control of their car and drove off a cliff."

Lena shoved away from the table and began pacing.

Conversation ceased. All attention was now focused on the stranger.

Lena walked over to the bar, hopped onto the edge, and looked at Gage. "I believe you have some rather old journals. Am I correct?"

Gage nodded. "How did you know?"

Lena explained, "Every alpha was given a copy in the beginning with explicit orders to guard them carefully. They were also told to ensure the journals made it into the hands of their successors. In addition to that, every beta was to learn German so they could interpret the journals."

Gage shook his head and crossed his arms. "The pack beta was with my parents when they died. So, there's nobody here who speaks German."

Luke turned his chair to face her. "This is true."

Gage stared, mouth gaping at Luke.

Luke gave a sad smile and said, "Sorry. I thought you knew. My mother told me before she…" Looking away, his voice faded.

Allister joined Lena on her perch. A low growl from across the room had everyone looking at Gage. Allister grinned and said, "Interesting."

Lena knocked him off center, saying, "No, it isn't. Go get the journal. And don't provoke your brother. While he's gone, I suggest everybody grab something to drink. Maybe something a little stronger than coffee. Especially you, Serenity."

After Allister left, she motioned for everybody to get up. "Help me move these. I think it'd be better if we all sat in a circle."

Gage walked over and picked up one end of the table, while Marcus got the other. A few minutes later, the table was moved and the chairs formed a circle around Lena. Gage sat in the one closest to her and crossed his arms "Why?"

Lena rolled her eyes and muttered, "Must everything be an argument with you?"

Before he got a chance to respond, Allister came in waving an ancient leather-bound book. He glared Gage. "You could've told me it was on the top shelf."

Gage shrugged. "And you could've been at the pack meeting."

Lena snapped, "Give it a rest, Gage. He wasn't there. Move on."

She walked over to Luke and handed him the book before resuming her seat. “Open the book and read what it says.”

Luke scanned the pages for a few minutes. After turning back to the beginning, he said, “Okay, I’ll do my best. It’s been a few years, but I think I can do it.”

Lena crossed her arms. “Think?”

Luke cleared his throat. Clenching his teeth, he glared at her and said, “I can.”

Black Forest. In the year of our Lord, 1312, 12 October.

My beloved Katrin’s birthday was yesterday.

I knew her family had planned a large party, for which I was intentionally left off the guestlist. Having been born poor, her father had hopes of finding a man of good standing for his only daughter. Had I known then the turn of circumstances that was yet to come, I would’ve left her for a better man.

She snuck away from her party to meet me in the forest. The further into the dark woods we wandered, my Katrin began fearing for our very souls. Rumors abounded of demons and evil spirits roaming the dark forest. It was said those who dared wander too far into the woods were driven mad. With a promise of protection, she followed me willingly. What a fool I’d been.

The setting was magical. I’d taken my mother’s finest linen and laid it upon a bed of straw. In the center was a basket filled with freshly baked bread.

I'd also brought along a partial wheel of cheese and some wine that I'd had to sneak past my father.

Of course, she was duly impressed with my efforts, and I was rewarded with one of her sweet kisses. Looking into eyes as blue as the waters of the Baltic Sea, I was smitten. Pulling her onto the blanket, I found myself overcome with feelings I dare not share. Not even in secret. However, before I could indulge in the activities I should never have considered, the forest took on a sinister air.

I vowed I would keep her safe. A vow I truly believed could be fulfilled.

Luke looked up from the thin pages. "So, our ancestors were perves. We don't need to read an ancient journal to know that."

Lena pointed to the book. "Continue."

In the distance, I heard wolves. And they were getting closer. A moment later, I heard an arrow meeting its target. Immediately after, the beast cried its last. Four more wolves lost their lives that night. Relieved that my beloved would be safe from the vicious animals, I poured two goblets of wine.

I heard first, one twig snap, followed by several more. A tall man dressed in dark robes stepped from the shadows. His face, hidden inside the hooded cloak, made his rumbling words more ominous. He said to me, "You have wandered far from your village. You should have listened to the female. Now it's too late."

When his hood fell away, there stood a man with long white hair that framed a face much too young. His blue eyes were so light, they too, appeared nearly as white as his hair. His sleeves fell away while his arms stretched high above his head. What I saw chilled me to the bone. Swirling tattoos that began on the tips of his fingers disappeared far beneath the folds of his robe.

The air stilled. Not so much as a single leaf was disturbed on the forest floor. I heard not a sound. No birdsong. Nor so much as the chirping of crickets disturbed the silence. When he spoke, his voice was but a whisper, but as he continued, his volume grew. Before long, it thundered through the forest. I shall never forget the words he spoke.

"I call on the powers of Darkness. Flow through me. Heed my words. From man to beast, forever our slaves to command, to do as we bid."

In the next instant, my vow to Katrin, as well as her safety, was nothing more than a whispered memory. Pain unlike any I've ever endured enveloped me. It was as if the world itself consisted of nothing but overwhelming agony. I could feel every bone breaking. My body contorted in ways that were impossible. After a mournful howl of pain, darkness brought with it blessed peace at last.

Silence fell over the room. Finally, Marcus said, "My book sat on that top shelf for generations without having ever been opened. Somewhere along the line, the message to share this information with each generation was lost. Keep reading."

Luke turned a page, then another. Finally, he looked up from the book. "The rest of the book is blank."

Gage lunged across the room and grabbed the book. "It can't be…"

He flipped through the pages. Then looking at Lena, he asked, "Do you think he used magic ink, like invisible ink, or something like that? Maybe if we use some special light, or—"

Lena laughed. "Seriously? Do you really think they had that capability in the thirteen hundreds? They were a simple people. You heard what Luke said. He came from a poor family, not a family of wizards. Besides, there wasn't more to his story. If you read the next few journals, you'll only learn how more of your ancestors survived. They were always on the go, running from the Dämonejäger's. The earliest shifters hoped moving to the new world would save them. Instead, they were followed by the same people they were running from. The only difference being, Dämonejägers had money."

Marcus walked over to the banquet table and poured himself another cup of coffee, adding a generous dallop of brandy. After resuming his seat, he said, "Chance also read the journal. Not to me, but he did read it. He speculated there may have been more journals, but for whatever reason, they were never passed down."

Nodding, Lena said, "And he would be right. That was written over many years while trying to stay one step ahead of the Dämonejägers. It was only a brief description of the day the world he'd grown up in ended and a new life began. Everything that happened in Friedrich's life beyond that was never revealed to the Dämonenwolf."

Marcus snarled, "Do not call us that. That's the name the Dämonejägers gave us. We're not monsters or demons."

Lena bowed her head. "I apologize. It's a derogatory name I heard growing up. To me it was no different than calling my family the *Dämonejägers*."

Marcus snarled, "Your family?"

All but Lena and Serenity suddenly stood. Chairs were knocked to the floor. Tension was high. They struggled to hold their forms while fighting against their instincts. The wolves wanted revenge against those who'd wronged them.

It was a standoff between two small women and eight powerful wolves.

Serenity slowly stood while not taking her gaze from the only person who'd ever cared about her.

Suddenly, the air stilled. No longer did the curtains flutter in the breeze blowing in from the mountains. Where the sounds of a forest alive were once heard in the background, now only silence remained. Each of the shifters stopped. Gooseflesh rose and the hair on their arms stood on end while thin wisps of hair lifted and fluttered around their faces.

Chapter Nineteen

Lena surged across the room. She squeezed her cousin's arms then gave her one quick shake. While staring into her eyes, she whispered, "Serenity…"

When she realized her cousin didn't hear her, she tried again. After giving her another hard shake, she shouted the name Serenity was given at birth. "Erika!"

Serenity blinked.

Tension melted. A soft breeze blew through the windows. Once again, the sounds of the forest came alive.

Lena spoke slowly, "Serenity? Honey. You need to relax. Nobody is going to hurt me. Do you understand?"

Serenity stared at Lena a moment. Only then did she notice that she was no longer sitting. Not only that, but every person in the room was staring at her. Serenity pulled away from her cousin. "What happened? I don't understand."

Gage raised his voice and announced, "It's time for a break." He looked at his watch. "Actually, it's almost midnight. Let's call it a night. We'll meet back here tomorrow at three. Plan for a long day. I'll call in a few pack members to prepare snacks and a meal." Glaring at Allister, he added, "A *mandatory* meeting."

He walked over to Marcus. "We have an extra room. Since you obviously don't have anywhere to go, you're welcome here."

Marcus glanced from him to Serenity. He thought about what they'd learned over the last few hours. After everything that happened, he knew that staying away from Serenity was the smartest thing to do. Even if she was his mate. Nodding, he said, "Of course. Thank you."

Gage saw Allister was nearly to the door and shouted, "Allister." When his brother turned around, he said, "Make sure you're here. I want to know everything you found out."

Serenity saw Luke walking toward the back of the room. Celeste had fallen asleep on a bench several hours ago.

Her heart ached when she realized she was about to lose the little pup who'd been so much a part of her life for such a long time. But what right did she have to deny him his family? When her legs would hold her no more, she sank onto a folding chair.

From across the room, she watched the tender moment. Luke lifted the sleepy child into his arms. After kissing her little cheek, she watched him put his lips beside her ear. He then looked down at her and waited. Celeste looked at Serenity, then her brother. Serenity could see that she was saying something to Luke but had no idea what. After he answered, she nodded. Luke smiled, then walked toward Serenity.

Did he give her the choice to go home with him? Was her little Celeste picking her brother over her? Staring down at her empty hands, she allowed the tears to fall. Of course, she would. Serenity was, after all, nothing more than a stranger to the little pup.

A shadow fell over her. She could see the tips of Luke's shoes. Did he come to let her say goodbye? Blinking back tears, Serenity wiped her hands across her face, pasted on a smile, then looked up.

The last thing she expected was to see Celeste holding her arms out. Luke reached down to help Serenity stand. She pulled the tiny child close then turned her tearful eyes toward Luke.

Smiling, he said, "I *am* taking her home with me. But honestly, she was reluctant until I told her that you lived across the street. I promised she could see you whenever she wanted. Or, whenever *you* want." He put his arm around her shoulder then led them toward the door. All while completely ignoring a snarling Marcus. Luke smiled, making it a point to not look at the other man. Then raising his voice, he asked, "Do you mind if we walk together?"

Serenity laid her head on his shoulder, murmuring, "I'd like that."

While walking down the stairs, he called over his shoulder, "I promise I won't hurt her."

Shocked that Marcus had followed them, Serenity stumbled. If it weren't for Marcus pulling her against his chest, she would have fallen. With his arms locked around her waist, he said, "See that you don't. I don't care who you are. I *will* kill you if you so much as make her cry…again." He looked down at her. "And I will see you tomorrow morning."

Serenity shook her head. "I have to be at work at eight. Sorry. But it'll have to wait until tomorrow afternoon."

Shaking off his hold, Serenity skipped down the stairs, ringing laughter from Celeste.

Celeste chatted non-stop all the way down the hill. When they got to Luke's house, she gave Serenity a hard look. With all humor gone, she asked, "He's my brother, right?"

Smiling, Serenity whispered, "Wanna know a secret?"

When Celeste nodded, Serenity added, "He's your *little* brother."

Celeste's eyes rounded in shock. Shaking her head, she frowned then looked at the huge man standing by the curb.

Laughing, Luke reached for her. He nodded at Serenity. "It's true. I wasn't even born when…" He looked away.

Celeste's tiny hands caressed his cheeks. "Don't be sad, little wolf." Grinning, she added, "And you have to listen to me, since I'm the oldest."

Luke threw his head back and laughed. "Is that right? I guess we'll just have to see about that. Even if you are older than me, I'm bigger. A lot bigger."

Celeste's eyes clouded over. Her bottom lip began quivering.

Luke's smile died. When he looked at Serenity, panic was written across his face.

Serenity cocked her head, crossed her arms, and gave Celeste a stern look. Shaking a finger at the child, she said, "That, young lady is called manipulation. We'll have none of that. Do you understand?"

Celeste wiggled until Luke set her on the ground. The moment she was free, she stomped toward the house. Without turning, she shouted, "Fine. But what good is it being the big sister if I can't boss him around?"

Luke's jaw dropped. He looked back at Serenity. "I think I'm in trouble."

Serenity and Lena were both laughing while walking away.

Serenity stopped then looked at the house she'd lived in for only one day. She turned around and called back, "Luke?"

He'd just opened the door when he heard Serenity's shout. Luke turned around and looked from her to the nearly destroyed house across the street. Sighing, he said, "I have a few extra bedrooms. We'll get everything fixed tomorrow. I promise it'll be good as new before you get home from work."

Lena waved her cousin on. While walking away, she said, “I have to get my car. There’s going to be a lot of questions tomorrow. And the answers are in there.” She stopped, looked at her cousin and said, “Serenity, there’s a lot you don’t know.”

***

Marcus stood on the balcony watching his mate go into Luke’s house. Gripping the rails, he considered jumping from the deck. It wasn’t that far down, certainly not enough to injure him. Then he could beat the other male until he knew never to touch his mate again. He’d warned him against hurting her, but he’d failed to warn him against making advances.

Pacing across the deck, he’d almost convinced himself to jump when he noticed someone standing in Luke’s back yard. He leaned closer, then saw it was Serenity. She was looking up at Gage’s house. Could she be searching for him? Did she feel the pull toward him as strongly as he did for her?

“Luke has honor. He would never touch another male’s mate. Especially not an alpha. Your mate is safe. Rest, Marcus. There’s going to be a lot to talk about tomorrow.”

Looking through the open door, he saw Gage watching him.

“I slept for thirty years. I’ve had more than enough sleep.”

Gage tipped his chin toward the stairs. "Then let's go have a drink. It's been a very exciting day for me as well."

After stepping into his office, Gage was surprised to find Allister sitting on a stool staring into the bottom of a shot glass.

Without looking up, Allister said, "You know if they find her, it's all over for us."

Gage poured himself a drink then asked, "Who?"

Allister looked at his brother then finished what was left in his glass. He pushed it across the bar. After it was refilled, he said, "Serenity. Erika. Whatever she's calling herself. She's still a Jäger."

Marcus spun him around and snarled, "What are you saying?"

Smirking, Allister reached for his drink. After tossing it back, he said, "Protect her. Hide her." It's true the Dämonejäger have spent centuries hunting us. However, very few people know about the women behind the men we've come to hate. Legend speaks of the powerful sorcerers. The journal confirmed what I read while visiting a few hole-in-the wall shops from Seattle to San Francisco." Allister turned his gaze to his brother. "That's why I wasn't at your *mandatory* meeting." He went on to explain. "When Scarlett told me what the meeting was about, I figured it was time to bring everything I'd learned back here."

Gage leaned against the bar. "And what did you learn, little brother?"

Sighing, he began, "Not every member of the Jäger clan is human. Not in the way we understand. No one knows where they originated from. They can only speculate. Which, really, what does it matter anyway? It doesn't change anything, and they're here. They used the wolves for hunting. Whenever one managed to escape, the others were forced to track them. The penalty for escape was death."

Marcus asked, "But why would they hunt their own kind?"

From the doorway, Lena answered, "Because the penalty for disobedience was *also* death. I thought we were waiting until tomorrow?"

Gage poured her a drink and waved her to an empty stool seat.

Nodding her thanks, she continued, "They weren't given a choice. If a male refused to do as told, he wasn't the one who suffered. It was his mate who paid the price. Or worse, his children." She reached into her purse and pulled out an old, leather book. Looking at Allister, she asked, "Do you mind?"

When he nodded, she opened the book and began.

12 October 1349

My name is Sabrina Jäger. This will be my final journal entry. I feel it's my duty to warn future generations what'll happen if they choose to follow the path of our ancestors. Therefore, I'm passing this journal down to my daughter. One day, she too will pass it to her own.

Every member of the Jäger clan possesses powerful magic. My father discovered an ancient spell passed down from father to son with an admonition to guard it and to never use its magic on another. Because magic used for evil comes with a heavy price. I watched what the evil did to my father. I tried to tell him, but he refused to listen. In the beginning, our clan only used our magic to help others. That is until the day a human male snuck into our village and slaughtered one of our families. My father was so enraged, he did the very thing he'd been warned against. The man who'd come to our village and did unspeakable acts to the innocent, became the first man to suffer the curse.

After that, every human that happened upon our lands was cursed, enslaved by my father. After a while, whole families had fallen under his spell. Using this to his advantage, the wolves were forced to do his bidding, lest he punish the others. There was more than one male who lost his mate or child after refusing to do my father's bidding.

She slid the journal into her bag. "So you see, they weren't always monsters. The subsequent humans who suffered were mostly innocents. But not all. In addition, each time the spell was cast, the caster lost a piece of their soul."

Lena picked up her glass, tossed it back, then slammed it on the bar. Giggling, she said, "I always wanted to do that. Now. It's extremely late. I've had a very trying day after an extremely long drive. Do you have someplace for me to sleep?"

Gage's heart started pounding. He took in her scent, inhaling deeply. He felt his canines lengthen in anticipation of claiming his mate.

When Lena glanced at him, she smirked and added, "Alone."

Chapter Twenty

Soft music filtered through Serenity's sleep shrouded mind. Lifting her head, she took in the unfamiliar surroundings. Memories of the night before returned. Then, something shifted beside her. Looking down, she smiled. She ran a hand across the downy soft fur of the little wolf and kissed Celeste's head. Careful not to wake the pup, Serenity slid out of bed.

Walking toward the door, her reflection caught her attention. When she saw herself, she curled her lip and groaned. She decided she'd have to brave the wreck across the street in order to deal with the mess staring back at her. She had two hours to get ready for work, but she knew she'd need every minute of it to shower, dress, and get awake.

Serenity tiptoed past Luke's closed door and slipped out of the house.

After crossing the street, Serenity was surprised to discover how many people were already working. After stepping through a brand-new door, she was shocked to find an empty living room.

"Coffee and donuts are in the kitchen. Sorry, but your new furniture won't be here until tomorrow." Luke was standing in the doorway, a long smear of white paint began on one cheek, ran through his hair, and vanished somewhere behind his ears. In one hand he held one of her ceramic mugs, the other held a chocolate iced donut.

Curling her lip in disgust, she said, "Eww. Don't you think you should at least use a napkin for that?" She nodded toward his hand. Not only was it covered in paint, but the paint had also dried in layers of embedded dirt. Eying the donut, she asked, "Is that Bavarian cream?"

Luke snorted, "Of course it is."

Narrowing her eyes, she waited.

"There's more. I'm not a total idiot."

Nodding, she mumbled, "The jury's still out."

She pushed past him and walked toward the table. "You didn't touch any of the others, did you?"

"No. Of course, I didn't." He looked from her to the door. "Did you leave my sister over there alone?"

Coffee and donut forgotten, Serenity ran from the room. Before she could reach the door, Scarlett walked in carrying Celeste. "Thought you might want this."

Luke reached for her, only to have Serenity beat him to it.

Serenity walked toward the bathroom, calling over her shoulder, "She's going to need a bath." She gave him a pointed look. "But more than that, she's going to need more clothes."

Serenity sat on the edge of the tub and began berating herself. "I can't believe I left you there all by yourself. Anything could have happened. And when I saw Luke with that donut…I can't believe I let myself get distracted by a…"

Celeste held her arms up to be lifted into the tub. Smiling, she asked, "Can I have a donut?"

Serenity's mind was racing with everything that could have happened to Celeste. Lathering a cloth, she mumbled, "Maybe after you get dressed."

After a brief knock, Scarlett stepped inside the room with a bundle in her arms. Plopping down on the toilet, she said, "Hey, little wolf, I didn't know if you liked dresses or pants. But I went with pants."

Grinning, Celeste said, "I like pants."

Scarlett nodded. "I agree. You can do more in pants than you can in a dress. Besides, if you're pretty, you're pretty no matter what you have on. Am I right?" When Serenity didn't answer, Scarlett looked toward the sudsy child in the tub.

Celeste's smile fell. She looked from Scarlett to Serenity then dropped her gaze. "She's sad that she forgot about me."

Scarlett scoffed and looked at Serenity. "What did you think would happen to her? Not only do the wards protect her, but she's also surrounded by a pack of very protective wolves."

Serenity spun around so fast, she nearly ended up in the tub with Celeste. Shaking her head, she walked out the door. "I can't."

Scarlett sighed and looked at Celeste. "Honey, why don't you play in the water for a minute. I'll be right back."

Celeste didn't have to be told twice. Her body glimmered for a moment before the wolf pup appeared in her place.

Scarlett left the pup and stepped into the hall, mumbling, "I know I'm going to pay for that later."

Scarlett closed the bathroom door then walked to the end of the hall into Serenity's room. When she got there, Serenity was sitting on the bed with her face in her hands. Her shoulders were shaking with the force of muffled sobs.

Scarlett sat beside her then reached for a box of tissue. Patting her back, she tried to offer a few words of encouragement. It wasn't something she'd grown up with, but she'd watched enough television to realize it was something most humans needed. "It's okay, really. Celeste couldn't be safer here. Luke would've been there long before any harm could come to her."

Serenity turned her tearful gaze to the other woman. Choking back another sob, she asked, "Do you really believe that? You're not there when she wakes up screaming in the night. You've not seen the tiny pup leap from the bed, bashing her head into walls while she tries to run from the forces that will always be able to find her. You didn't see her as a tiny wolf pup alone in the forest with no one to care for her."

She couldn't hold back the sobs or the tears that blinded her to everything but her own memories. "They're monsters. They…my family. They're the ones who did this. I was so blind. All those years, I never knew." Shaking her head, she bellowed, "How could I have not known?"

Scarlett pulled her into her arms. "Serenity, I don't have all the answers. I don't even know how to lend a sympathetic ear. I have three brothers. One of them had to be both mother and father when our parents died. I've had to develop thick skin. Nothing, and I mean absolutely nothing, has ever resulted in the tiniest bit of sympathy from them. It's not that they don't love me. I know they would lay down their lives for me. But what I learned early on was that feeling sorry for yourself never got anything done."

Serenity pushed away and started laughing. "I think I had those same brothers." Glancing at the clock, she gasped. "Oh, no. No. No. No. I can't be late on my first day. I already have the *I'm your enemy* thing going against me."

Scarlett reached for her phone, cursed, then made a call. "Hey, Jonas."

His snarling voice could be heard through the line, "You're late! Do you have any idea…"

She winced then pulled the phone away from her ear. "Sorry. Yes, we're running just a little late. We had a problem." She turned towards Serenity and mouthed *help*.

Serenity grinned then yelled, "Celeste, come back here. You're…Oh, not the bed! Those are my work clothes! Now what am I going to do?"

Winking, Scarlett said, "Your little niece just got out of the tub."

Jonas's voice came over the line again. "Let me guess, she shifted into her wolf?"

Scarlett fist pumped. "Of course, she shifted as soon as my back was turned. Now she's running all over the house. As soon as Serenity finds some dry clothes, we'll head in. I promise."

After tucking the phone into her pocket, Scarlett said, "You get dressed. I'll tell Luke he has to take over. He's going to love that. I wasn't lying when I told Jonas about her shifting as soon as my back was turned. Sorry, but your bathroom is going to be totally wrecked."

Ten minutes later, they were racing toward the diner. Flashing lights and a quick whoop sounded behind them.

She noticed Serenity twist around in her seat, saying, "Um…He wants us to pull over."

Shrugging, Scarlett said, "I don't have time for that. Let him go to Gage. What's he going to do, ground me? He can't, I'm an adult."

She watched the officer turn off his lights, make a U-turn, then drive in the same direction they'd just come from.

Serenity asked, "How did you know he wouldn't pursue us?"

Scarlett pulled into the parking lot. "Bennies of being related to the alpha."

***

Serenity's first day of work was busier than she ever would have believed. Nearly every person from the small community came to this diner for lunch. And Jonas was right…all of them were huge. Even the women, with Scarlett being the exception.

Stepping outside, Serenity said, "I don't think there's anything on me that doesn't hurt."

Scarlett laughed. "Been a while? You'll get used to it. Today was nothing. You should have seen yesterday. Jonas decided to start a two for one Tuesday. By the way, you can forget ever getting a Tuesday off."

They stepped into the parking lot and were shocked to discover Scarlett's car was missing.

Scarlett paced along one side of the building then scanned the packed parking lot again. "No. No. No! Where's my…?" Scarlett slapped her forehead then leaned against the wall.

Serenity ran to her friend and shouted, "Somebody stole your car!"

Scarlett smirked. "Remember what I told you about living here. Nobody in their right mind would steal from any of us. Least of all, the alpha's little sister." After pushing away from the building, she sat on the curb and took her shoes off.

Serenity could only numbly watch Scarlett. When she started walking, she yelled, "Wait. What's going on?"

Without turning around, she shouted, "We're walking!"

Serenity ran to catch up then announced, "I'm not taking off my shoes."

Scarlett shrugged. "Suit yourself. But I thought you told me everything hurt?" She pointed to Serenity's shoes. "You might find some relief if you peel those puppies off."

Serenity kept pace with Scarlett. "Nah. I'm good. I have no desire to add cuts and bruises to my list of aches and pains. So, why are we walking? What happened to your car?"

Scarlett huffed. "Remember when I said that he can't ground me? Well, obviously I was wrong."

"But it's your car—"

Scarlett was shaking her head. "Nope. He owns all the cars in the garage. He just lets us use them. Well, on the condition that we take care of them, of course."

Serenity put an arm around Scarlett's shoulder and laughed "You know, I have a feeling we're going to be great friends. The car I drove here in? Yeah. Not mine at all."

***

Marcus burrowed beneath the crisp sheets then raked his paws down his nose. Two sneezes and a long stretch later, he finally opened his eyes. The world through the eyes of his wolf was sharper. Due to his keen sense of smell and sensitive hearing, at one time he'd felt secure believing that nothing could sneak past his defenses. Now, he wasn't sure if he could ever trust the world again. Certainly, it wouldn't be any time soon.

This was his first night of freedom in thirty years, and he'd shifted in his sleep. As a predator, an alpha predator at that, the slightest change would alert him in an instant. No matter his past, he was determined to never allow himself to be caught unaware again.

Although this wasn't his pack, they needed to be prepared. Today, he'd talk to Gage about putting sentries around their borders. If he'd done the same, perhaps he could've prevented what happened.

Shifting, Marcus sat on the edge of the bed. His unfocused gaze centered on the carpet while memories of what his life had been replayed in his mind. He wondered how many survived. He remembered when Serenity told him about Henry. He wondered how many more had passed through the years.

He needed to know. More than that, he needed his pack. He wanted to go home. But did he even have a home to go to? Thirty years. Had the elements taken what had once been a thriving community? Or had humans moved in? Determined to find answers, he grabbed the borrowed jeans and headed downstairs.

"Well, look at who decided to finally get out of bed," Allister called out. He was sitting at the kitchen island, an open book in front of him with a cup of coffee in his hand.

Noah threw a slice of toast across the counter toward his brother. "Shut up, Allister. Give him a break. He's been awake for less than a day."

"Ah, that's the thing, right? He hasn't been awake for—"

Glaring at his brother, Gage cut in. "Don't push me this morning." Grabbing a large mug, he poured Marcus a cup of coffee then asked, "Cream, sugar?" When Marcus shook his head, he continued, "I don't need to ask how you slept. Let me guess…rough night?"

Marcus slumped onto an empty stool. "You have no idea." He looked around the room. "What time is it?"

While carrying his cup out of the kitchen, Gage said, "Two. There's food in the office. I thought we might meet there. It's a little more intimate. Besides, there won't be as many people here today as last night. Jonas won't leave his restaurant at dinner time. And Ariana won't leave him there alone. I'm not sure if Luke will make it since he's busy overseeing renovations of Serenity's house."

Following Gage, Marcus asked, "What renovations? And what's he doing at her house?"

Gage laughed, "I don't know if you remember what shape we left her house in last night. But he called to tell me he was going to get a crew out there first thing to put everything to right. I figured that's the least we could do since we're the ones who wrecked it in the first place."

Marcus walked past Gage and stepped onto the deck. Feeling the other man's presence behind him, he said, "You know, it reminds me of home." After a quick glance back at the house, he added, "A lot of it does."

Marcus paused, leaned on the railing, and sighed. "Gage, I want to go back. I want to see what's left. Not only that, but I also want to find the rest of my pack."

Gage set his cup on the banister. "It's not a good idea. We don't even know if they've noticed your absence, yet. Obviously, they know Serenity is gone, but they may not realize she didn't leave alone. Besides, do you really want to walk back into that? This time, they may not just put you to sleep. When Lena and Serenity get here, we'll come up with a plan. First, we need to get all the facts."

Chapter Twenty-One

They hadn't walked three blocks when Lena pulled up beside them. She rolled the window down, leaned over, and asked, "Need a ride?"

Serenity got in first. "Thanks. I wasn't sure how much further I was going to get."

Laughing, Scarlett asked, "And just exactly what were you planning to do?"

"That bench in the park was calling my name. I figured I could camp out there. Have a weenie roast and invite a few friends," Serenity explained while taking her shoes off.

Sitting forward, Scarlett's smile fell. "Just how mad is my brother?"

Lena's gaze leapt to the rearview mirror. She remembered the major explosion Gage had after he got the news. She bit her lip. "He was pretty mad when Griffin told him how fast you were going. I'm not going to go into everything he said. You can take that up with him yourself."

Lena steered the car into the long driveway, stopping a few feet away from the walk. She sat inside for a moment. Whatever was going on between Gage and Scarlett was pushed aside. Right now, there was only one thing she could think about.

She sighed and dropped her head against the steering wheel. She knew the consequences of what she was about to do. Not only would it put her life in danger, but her cousin's as well. Still, she knew the time had come to fight.

Serenity paused beside Lena's window. "Hey. Are you okay?"

Smiling, Lena stepped out. She patted her pocket and knew she had everything she needed. Well, except for the courage to finish what she'd started. She impulsively grabbed her cousin's hand then waited until Scarlett was out of sight. She stepped back a few feet, putting more distance between them. She wasn't sure if she was far enough away from the wolves to not be overheard, but she knew she had to prepare Serenity for what was about to come.

Leaning closer, she whispered, "You must stay calm, no matter what happens." When Serenity opened her mouth to speak, Lena placed a finger on her cousin's lips. "I know you don't understand, but you must trust me. First, I want you to know that I can take care of myself. But more importantly, you need to understand that you wield more power than you know. Until you fully understand the situation, you must remain calm. If something happens and you decide you can't handle it, you need to leave. Promise me."

Lena watched her cousin's mouth open, close, then open again before saying, "But—"

Lena shook their joined hands then repeated her demand. “Promise me!”

“Okay. I trust you. I’ll do what you ask. But you’re going to explain this to me, if not now, then very soon.”

Looking at the balcony high above them, Lena said, “Okay. We’re late. I’m not afraid of Gage, but that doesn’t mean I don’t respect him. Let’s go.”

Allister met them at the door then led them to Gage’s office.

Gage leaned into Scarlett. Keeping his voice low, he said, “Do you really understand the gravity of what you did?”

Scarlett pushed him away and shouted, “So I was driving a little over the speed limit. That doesn’t give you the right to take my car!”

Turning toward the bar, she grabbed a bottle of whiskey and reached for a glass.

Gage roared, “A little over the speed limit! You were going sixty. By the park!”

Scarlett’s blood ran cold. Her hand went lax, releasing the bottle she’d been holding. Once it hit the hardwood floor, the bottle shattered. A mix of glass and whiskey spread across the floor. Without turning she asked, “Was anybody…did I…Oh, my sweet Jesus. I’m so sorry.” She flopped onto the stool. Cupping her face with both hands, she wept. She knew there wasn’t a time of day when the park wasn’t filled with young mothers and their children. More than once, she’d watched from the diner while a frantic mother chased a playful pup into the road.

To think that she could have been the cause of the death of one of the most vulnerable was too much. Lurching from her seat, she raced toward the bathroom.

Serenity was right behind her. She reached out and grabbed the door before it could be slammed in her face and walked in. After closing them inside, she grabbed a wet cloth and knelt beside her new friend. She wiped the cool cloth across her forehead and neck. Serenity patted Scarlett's shoulder and waited. She knew there was nothing she could say. It was what it was. If their positions were reversed, she knew how she'd feel.

Scarlett sat back, her sobs turning into hiccups. She laid her head on Serenity's shoulder. Then she took the cloth, gripping it with both hands, she twisted and squeezed until she'd wrung a few drops. Only to smooth it out on her lap a second later. After repeating the process a few more times, she tossed it toward the sink, missing.

Serenity watched it drop to the floor in a wet heap.

After something between a sob and a sigh, Scarlett said, "You're right. We are going to become great friends. Thank you."

When they returned to the office, Serenity noticed Gage was cleaning up the mess left behind by his sister. She glanced from him to the others then saw that they were carrying on as if it were the most natural thing for him to do.

She was shocked. Gage was the alpha, their leader. He could've asked any one of the others to do it, yet he took it upon himself. A moment later, Marcus left the room, returning with a mop while pushing a large bucket of soapy water. When Serenity reached for it, he held a hand up and shook his head. After leaving the bucket beside Gage, Marcus stepped onto the deck and waited. The room was silent while Gage finished cleaning. After the last few drops had been mopped up, he silently pushed the bucket out of the room.

Serenity wasn't sure what was going on so decided to simply follow everyone's lead. Thirty minutes later, Gage still hadn't returned. Needing answers, she joined Marcus on the deck, closing the door behind her.

While keeping his gaze on the horizon, Marcus began, "It's something he had to do. As alpha, every member of the pack is depending on him to keep them safe. He failed them. By cleaning up Scarlett's mess, he absolved her of her crime. Otherwise, he would've been forced to banish her. Or worse."

"But she didn't mean to—"

Snarling, Marcus whipped around. Leaning into her. "And what comfort would that have been to the family of a child that could've been killed in an accident?" He stepped back and took a deep breath. "I'm sorry. There's a lot about us you may never understand. I shouldn't have reacted like that."

Serenity looked toward the horizon, ignoring the tears rolling down her cheeks. She knew he was right. No matter how remorseful Scarlett would feel, there was no going back from something like that. Refusing to look at him, she whispered, "I know you're right. If…if something happened to Celeste…" She shook her head. Looking back toward the house, she saw Gage's arms locked around his sister while they both wept.

After draping an arm around her shoulders, Marcus led her toward the house. Pausing in front of the door, he said, "In this way, she's absolved. But only of this crime. Her position in the pack must now be won back." He turned her to face him then locked his hands around her waist.

While resting his forehead against hers, he closed his eyes and inhaled her scent. He wasn't sure how much longer he could hold back from claiming her, but he knew now wasn't the time. He gazed into her bright blue eyes. "She's going to need a friend now. After today, she will no longer be welcomed here. It'll be up to her to find somewhere else to stay."

Serenity was finding it difficult to breathe with him standing so close, much less think. She murmured, "Friend."

Then his words sank in. She focused her gaze. "She's welcome at my house for as long as it takes."

Kissing her nose, he smiled. "Thank you."

The door was thrown open. Then an arm reached out and yanked them back inside.

Stumbling, Marcus snarled at the offender.

Allister held his hands up, saying, “Sorry. Not that we weren’t enjoying the show, but we’re here for a reason.”

After looking around, Serenity found Scarlett sitting in a chair against the back wall. Her arms were crossed, her eyes red, and her lips were tightly pressed together in a frown. Serenity knew that the anger radiating from Scarlett was all directed back at herself. She also knew that no one would blame Scarlett nearly as much as she blamed herself. If ever she needed a friend, now was the time.

However, before she took more than two steps toward Scarlett, Noah grabbed her arm. Spinning toward Scarlett’s twin, she was ready to lay into him. She’d seen firsthand what kind of a jerk he could be. Instead of seeing the condescending, angry man she’d expected, she saw only his pain.

“I know you don’t understand our ways, but she does. She needs to be alone. Wait for her to come to you. If you’re her friend, she will. Just give her time. I can feel her pain. Scarlett is my sister, my twin. I would die for her. But this is something that I can’t help her with. It’s a road she must travel alone. All I can do is wait for her to come back. When she does, I know you’ll be there for her. Don’t take what’s coming personally.” He nodded toward his sister, who’d moved from the chair to the deck.

When Serenity saw Scarlett shift then leap over the railing, she jerked away from Noah. She yanked the door open then ran through and leaned over the banister. Her heart was racing fast enough that it felt like it might just beat right out of her chest. She was sure she'd just seen her new friend leap to her death. Instead, she saw a sable wolf in warm brown shades. The wolf glanced up at her for only a second then vanished into the woods.

Gage's voice startled her. "If she can forgive herself, she'll be back."

Looking up, Serenity asked, "And if she can't?"

Not bothering to answer, he turned toward the house. "Come inside. We have a lot to discuss and too much time has passed as it is."

Chapter Twenty-Two

Gage motioned for everyone to have a seat. "I hope you're comfortable. This is going to be a long afternoon. Because of the importance of this meeting, even for bathroom breaks, we'll need to stop while you're gone. I don't want anybody coming back later telling me they missed something.

Last night after everybody left, I discovered I wasn't the only one who couldn't sleep. Marcus, Allister, and Lena joined me. At that time, a lot of things were brought to my attention. I think it's time for Serenity to tell us everything. Especially, who she really is."

Serenity's face felt like it was on fire from both shame and embarrassment. She couldn't blame them for wanting to know all her deep, dark secrets. Especially, since they'd been so forthcoming with their own. She'd hoped she'd found someplace where she could disappear. Somewhere her family would never find her. Pausing in her thoughts, she realized that unlike this community, her life at home hadn't been in danger. The worst she'd have to face was a few angry family members. Especially, since she was the one who'd received the family fortune. When she compared her life to these people, her past was nothing. But of course, there was the forest full of what she'd once thought were stuffed wolves. Once she realized that, she knew there were things about her past that even she didn't understand. So, she might as well tell them what little she did know. Maybe then they could help her unravel answers to questions she'd never realized existed.

Serenity took a deep breath and tilted her glass to take another sip, only to realize it was empty. Looking from the cup to the expectant faces around her, she knew a little liquid courage was needed.

Marcus took her glass, filled it, then sat down. With him sitting so close, his thigh brushing against her, she knew she'd never be able to concentrate. She needed to move away. Pacing over to the patio door, her unfocused gaze scanned the horizon while she tried to gather her thoughts.

Serenity turned around and shrugged. "There really isn't much to tell. Of course, you've probably figured out by now my name isn't Serenity Chase. I was born Erika Jäger. The only thing I know about my family is that they're nothing but a bunch of abusive jerks. They never made a secret of how little I mattered to them. Every one of them complained about me being born a girl instead of another son. They hated it so much, my parents refused to have another child on the off chance they might have another girl. As far as who they are, or what…I'm in the dark about it as much as you are. I knew about the wolves, but I just thought my family was weird. I mean, who has a yard full of…" She paused then continued, "I didn't know what they were. If I had, I would've done anything to save them."

Gage spoke up, "Why did you change your name and run away?"

"Oh, that? For some crazy reason, my senile old grandfather left all his money to me. I knew there were going to be a lot of angry people when they figured it out. I just wanted to be as far away as possible before that happened."

Mouths gaping, every head turned toward Serenity. Marcus asked, "Just how much money are we talking about."

Serenity cocked her head and rolled her eyes. "Way more than I could have ever spent. Millions. But before you ask for any…I don't have it."

Gage frowned then asked, "What do you mean, you don't have it?"

She laughed. "I used some of it to buy my house and move here, keeping only a little to live off until I got a job. The rest of it…I gave it away."

When everyone continued to stare at her, she explained, "To a charity. I decided to give it to one that would be guaranteed to make my grandfather roll over in his grave."

Looking at the still questioning gazes, she continued, "Wolves. I mean those poor…" She shook her head. "I knew he didn't want me anywhere near them. I also overheard him threaten to burn every one of them if I ever set foot in the woods again. So, yeah. Wolves." Waving a hand around, she returned to the couch.

She sat beside Marcus. "That's it. That's the only thing I know. Just please…don't call me by that name. I really do want to leave the past in the past."

Gage looked at Lena. "You're up."

She stared into her glass while swirling the amber liquid. Tipping it back, she drained it. Without being asked, Gage went to the bar then grabbed the bottle and held it up. When she nodded, he walked over and filled her glass. Holding the goblet, she watched a single drop weave its way down the side. Then, using the tip of her tongue, she caught it before it fell. She set her drink on the table beside her chair and reached into her pocket to pull out a thin, worn, leather journal. She opened the book, stared at the pages for a moment, then set it on the table by her glass. She sat back, crossed her legs, took a deep breath, then began.

"My name is Lena Jäger, daughter of Oskar Jäger's youngest son, Anton. Of course, you all know I'm Serenity's cousin. There are many, many, family secrets. Most of them I learned through years of research."

She turned her gaze toward Serenity. "As far as why your parents stopped having children…it's not because they were afraid of having another daughter. To each generation one, and only one, girl is born. After her birth, there will be no more. No sons, and certainly no daughters. If they told you anything else, they did it just to be mean. Last night, Allister said we should protect you. You have no idea how important you really are."

Allister held a hand up, stopping her from saying more. "Just how long were you listening to us?"

"Long enough," Lena answered. "You also said besides protecting her, we need to hide her. You may not know how important it is that we do that. What I'm telling you must never leave this room. Not only will it put Serenity in danger, but every other female born to the Jäger clan as well."

After getting nodded affirmations from everyone, she continued. "Katrin Jäger died giving birth to my father, therefore never had a daughter. Petra, his second wife, was drawn to the allure of an extremely wealthy man. She had only one child. A girl she named, Gabriel."

Serenity spoke up, "I have…I mean…*we* have an aunt?"

"Unfortunately, no. Soon after she turned sixteen, she disappeared. I'm sure if anyone were to check, they'd find more than one unmarked grave in the woods on the Jäger property."

Serenity couldn't believe what she was hearing. Standing, she shrieked, "Wait! Are you telling me my grandfather killed his own daughter? Are you serious? I mean, he was a lot of things…but a murderer? His own child, no less."

Shaking her head, Serenity paced away. "How…he…no. No. I just…I just can't…" She begged, "Please tell me this isn't true. If he could kill his own child, then…"

Lena finished her sentence, "Yes, cousin. He wouldn't have any problem killing you. Nor would your father." Looking at the others, she continued, "So, you see, it's vital that you keep her hidden."

Gage interrupted, "I get for her safety why she should be kept hidden. But why is it important to us?"

Lena relaxed into her chair again. "Do we want to take a break before I begin?" Looking around, she said, "You know, we've been here for hours. And I don't know about anyone else, but I'm hungry."

Gage nodded and said, "We'll take a short break." He pulled his phone out. "We'll meet back here in fifteen minutes. I'll have someone bring up some snacks. Dinner won't be ready for another two hours."

Serenity stepped onto the deck. Although she could hear the footsteps, she chose to ignore whoever followed her out. All she cared about was checking on her friend.

"You won't see her. At least not for a few days. She'll stay in her wolf form while she works through everything."

Serenity felt the heat radiating from Marcus's body when he stepped closer. She shivered when his arm brushed against hers. She closed her eyes, inhaled his unique scent, and leaned closer.

His arm came around her. She felt his breath against her neck. Then he turned her to face him. "I don't know how much longer I can wait."

Serenity's breath caught at his words. Staring into his eyes, she saw where they were normally dark smokey grey, but now glowing obsidian. Since arriving, every set of glowing eyes she'd seen frightened her, including his. This time, however, they had a completely different effect. Her breath quickened, her heart raced, and warmth spread through her body. Moving closer, she stood on her toes and whispered, "I don't either."

When his lips met hers, her body exploded. Never had she felt anything like this. An overpowering need shot through her. It was a need to get closer, to hold onto him and never let go. It was primal, but more.

Marcus pulled her closer until every inch of their bodies touched. Never had he known such pleasure. Or such need. So many feelings were coming at once. Overwhelming feelings. He knew, beyond a doubt, he loved her. She was his mate. Nothing would ever separate them once mated. He broke the kiss then he searched for somewhere private to complete their mating. Lifting her into his arms, he kissed her while walking toward the winding stairs that led to the driveway below.

When Marcus broke their kiss to make sure they didn't fall, Serenity grabbed a handful of hair and pulled him back, mumbling, "More."

They were nearly to the stairs when Marcus sensed another male nearby. Setting Serenity down, he shoved her behind him then lunged toward the challenger. He bared his fangs then curled hands that had already begun to shift. He was ready.

"Whoa!" Allister backed away, holding his hands up. Dropping to his knees, Allister looked away, lowered his gaze, and bared his neck.

Serenity screamed. She was certain Marcus was about to rip Allister's throat out. She needed to stop him. She lunged toward Marcus only to be yanked back.

Holding onto Serenity, Gage hissed, "All Marcus's senses are on high alert. The slightest interference will only push him over the edge. If he feels his mate is in danger, there's nothing that will stop him from killing my brother."

Serenity was shocked to find herself suddenly standing alone with Marcus. Only a few seconds ago, everyone who'd been inside, had been on the deck. By the time Marcus turned around, even Allister was gone. When Marcus took a step toward her, she held up her hands then backed toward the door. "I don't know what's the matter with you, but I don't want any part of it. I already escaped one kind of crazy, I'm not about to jump into another."

It took a moment for Marcus to realize Serenity was upset. In no more than a few seconds, he found himself standing alone watching her walk away.

Chapter Twenty-Three

Mouth gaping, Serenity was shocked to see everyone sitting around the circle chatting like nothing ever happened. She glanced through the door at Marcus, who was standing in the same place she'd been standing only moments ago. Stiff shoulders hunched, his clawed fingers were digging into the decorative wooden banister. Glancing at Gage, her eyes rounded, she mumbled, "I'm sorry. I don't…I think he's going to…"

Laughing, Gage said, "It wouldn't be the first time I've had to replace the railing around the deck. When you get a bunch of wolves together, something's bound to get broken."

She nodded absently. "Should I…" She pointed outside.

Gage shook his head. "He'll be in when he's calmed. Besides, he's already heard what Lena has to say. Before you ask, last night when we couldn't sleep, we talked for a while." He nodded to Lena, who was patiently waiting for them to stop so she could continue.

Lena took her book out and read the same entry she had last night. Before anyone could ask questions, she held her hand up. "As soon as Marcus comes back inside, I'll read the first entry from the next journal."

Everybody sat in uncomfortable silence while they waited for Marcus to return. However, nobody was more uncomfortable than Serenity. She felt like she had a banner above her head announcing to the world, not only what happened, but what was about to happen.

The quiet murmurs around her reminded her of the one who wasn't there...Scarlett. With her thoughts focused on her friend, she decided after they finished here, she was going to search for her. Not only did Scarlett need a friend right now, but so did she. Who better to explain what was happening between her and Marcus than another wolf?

The trick, however, would be sneaking away without Marcus figuring out what she was doing. She knew he wanted to take their relationship to the next level. But by her way of thinking, they hadn't even gone further than kissing. One kiss didn't mean they were ready to hop in the sack. It was an amazing kiss. But it still just a kiss. She wasn't ready to take things further, at least not yet. The fact of it being her first kiss certainly played a huge part in her decision. She wanted to make sure she was ready before taking such a huge step. Her first time should be special. She'd always wanted to wait until she found the right man. Since she'd had no experience with men before today, how could she know this was the one? Yes. She definitely needed a friend right now.

Behind her, she heard the door open, followed by approaching footsteps. Marcus settled on the couch beside the chair she'd chosen. She fought against her need to look at him. If she did, she knew she'd be powerless to resist.

Clearing her throat, Lena began.

12 October 1315

Today my life changed forever.

Having reached the age of maturity, I resented my father's demand that I always have someone to protect me, be it wolf or man. A simple short walk to pick a few berries is far from dangerous. However, because I am the daughter of the clan's leader, he refused. For that, I will be eternally grateful. However, I get ahead of myself.

I allowed my temper to get the best of me. After leaving the safety of our village, I stomped into the woods. My only thoughts were of a future spent under the thumb of my father. It wasn't long before I tripped over a vine. Before I realized what was happening, I was slipping down the hill toward a stream. Due to recent rains, the river had begun to overflow its banks. I found myself tumbling through mud toward the raging river. I feared, rightly so, that today would be my last. For I know that in times past, some of our most powerful swimmers lost their lives in smaller, more shallow streams. Since I'd never bothered learning to swim, I knew I stood no chance of surviving.

However, because my father refused the request of an arrogant girl, I still live. My eternal gratitude extends from my father to include the wolf assigned to guard me. A task the wolf did only under the dire threat to his cub. Whatever the reason, I felt it was my duty to repay him.

He had but one desire. He wished for the wolves, enslaved by my father, to be freed from their curse. But once cast, a spell can never be undone. The best I could do for him was to modify my father's spell. It was one that granted the wolves the ability to change from their beast to man at will.

When I learned that the wolf who rescued me had lost his own mate because of my father's cruelty, I pledged myself to Friedrich in her stead. I've taken him and his cub as my own. And now I must flee or suffer my father's wrath.

After closing the book, Lena dropped it in her lap then looked around the room. "There's more. A lot more. But most of it is about life on the run, as well as life with her mate, Friedrich Braun—"

Marcus sat forward. "What did you say his name was?"

Lena furrowed her brows and shrugged. "Friedrich Braun."

Marcus couldn't sit still another minute. Standing, he paced a few times toward the patio and back. Finally, he stopped behind his chair with his hands fisting the back. He studied Gage a moment then thought about the night they'd met. He looked at Gage. "What's the name of your pack?"

"Kenneally, of course."

With his heart racing, Marcus said, "Your pack shares your last name. My last name is Braun."

Lena's head swung from Marcus to Serenity. While staring at her cousin, she muttered, "This is crazy strange."

Allister spoke up, "And with that, I need to tell you about some important information I learned in my research. In a museum, I found a few journals also written by Sabrina. After learning Serenity's true identity, and now Marcus, there are a few things you need to know.

First, just in case anybody was wondering, the shifter gene is dominant. At least when mated with a descendent of the Jäger clan. Friedrich and Savanah had six children together, and all but one was born a shifter. Can you guess which one that was?"

All but one blank stare answered him. When he noticed Gage's glare, he continued. "The sixth child was a girl. She didn't inherit the ability to shift. However, she did inherit her mother's magic. Fascinated by that information, I continued to search for everything I could find.

"I learned that after leaving Europe, the Dämonejägers followed the shifters to the new world and continued to hunt them. To survive, the packs split. Each forming their own, while moving away from the original Braun pack. The first to leave was the alpha's brother. In order to separate his from his brother's, he named his pack after the place they'd called home. Some packs did the same, while others continued the tradition of using the alpha's name. When the original pack found themselves running from the Dämonejägers, they realized because of their name, they were an easy target. After that, it was decided to never use that name for a pack again. To stay hidden, most of them even changed their last names to Brown. I searched for other instances of mating's between shifters and members of the Jäger clan. That's what I was doing when I was called home. If Scarlett hadn't told me the reason for returning, I never would've come. But it was time."

Gage laughed. "No offence, Marcus, but when you told me the name of your pack, I thought you had a really weird last name. All right, if there's nothing else, we'll break for dinner and call it a night." Gage was halfway to his feet when Lena spoke.

"Actually, there is more. Sabrina was the oldest daughter, but not the only one. When she betrayed her father, he realized the danger his other daughters posed. Like the men in their clan, all the females possessed magic. However, unlike the men, they were much more powerful. Fearing his other daughters would betray him as well, he killed them. He began with the youngest, who was only three years old. There was a total of five girls, with Sabrina being the oldest at fifteen. After the death of the first, Sabrina felt a surge in her magic. At the time, she thought nothing of it. But when it happened again a few minutes later, she realized what was happening.

Sabrina returned just in time to watch her father murder her twelve-year-old sister. As her sister's life faded, Sabrina's magic swelled. She told her father because of what he'd done that day, she would curse his line. There would be no more than one daughter born to each generation. Once the girl was born, there would be no other children. That child would be born possessing the same magic Sabrina received after the death of her sisters. Her magic, fueled by rage, encompassed the entire camp.

The members of the Jäger clan began dying. Sabrina's magic killed only the members that were present that day. Others returned later to find their families slaughtered. Fearing her return, they left, taking nothing with them. Just as Sabrina couldn't completely remove the curse placed upon the wolves, her father couldn't remove the curse she'd bestowed upon his descendants. But like her, he could alter it."

She paused, looked at Serenity. "Every ten generations, only the daughter of the oldest male child would inherit the same powerful magic that Sabrina possessed." She looked at Allister. "I know you researched the Jäger clan's history. Would you like to tell everyone what you learned?"

Allister was silent a moment, paling as her words sank in. He stared at Serenity, both awed and terrified, unable to speak.

Gage snapped, "Allister!"

Hearing his name, Allister cleared his throat. "I found the Jäger genealogy online. I wanted to know how many generations had been born since the first shifter was recorded." He walked over to the bar and grabbed a bottle of bourbon then poured himself a shot. After tossing it back, he poured another. Then, setting the bottle down, he picked it up again, and returned to his seat. His gaze swept the expectant faces before landing on the two women who'd wandered into their hidden community only days before. With his hands shaking, he finished his drink. But before he could pour another, Gage grabbed the bottle.

Allister stared at his brother a moment then nodded. "Thirty. Serenity is the daughter of the oldest son in the *third* tenth generation."

Gage sucked in a deep breath. "With that. I think it's time to go eat. After dinner, I suggest all of us take some time to think about what we've learned. We'll meet again tomorrow. At that time, we'll need to come up with a plan."

Everybody wandered into the dining room. But Serenity couldn't wrap her head around the idea that there was magic in the world. Much less that she possessed it. Not only did she possess it, but she was also more powerful than anyone else. "No. It can't be. I…I would know if I was magic. Right? I mean, how could someone be magic and not even know it? Besides, that doesn't explain Marcus, Chance, and all the other wolves."

Standing back, Marcus waited until Serenity sat before taking his seat. He wasn't about to let her put more distance between them. "Actually, it does. If you remember, Lena said that spells couldn't be reversed but they could be altered. What better revenge is there than to imprison those you hate inside their own bodies? Until you began visiting me, I felt nothing. It was like my mind was stuck in a loop, reliving the same day over and over. It might've been different for others, but that was my own personal torment. All I could think about was how I couldn't protect my pack. If I'd only known what was going to happen, I never would have shifted—"

"—That wouldn't have worked," Jonas interrupted.

Gage explained, "When Jonas and Beth came, they told us what happened. I'm sorry I neglected to tell you sooner. They found a man who'd been shot. He told them that every member that shifted was taken. Those who didn't were shot, regardless of age."

Serenity cried out, "No! Please. No!"

Marcus looked from Gage to Serenity. Putting a comforting hand on her shoulder, he said, "It's okay. It was a very long time ago. Long before you were even born."

Shoving his hand away, she yelled, "No, it's not okay!"

Marcus looked from her to Gage. Then he noticed everybody suddenly found their plates very interesting. But not enough to eat. Ariana, weeping uncontrollably, fell into Jonas's arms.

Looking at Serenity, he saw that she was also crying. He looked around the room again. Everybody at the table had pushed their plates away. Gage turned his face away, but not before Marcus saw the tears. Allister didn't bother hiding his. Noah's red face bespoke of the simmering rage that he was struggling to hold back. Lena had already run out of the room in hysterics.

Shaking his head, he muttered, "No."

He felt panic threatening to overtake him. Looking from the others to Serenity, he said, "But you told me…the cubs in the barn…"

The horror of what had really happened sank in. He whispered, "Newborn cubs can't shift."

Twenty-Four

Marcus, lost in memories of a long ago past, stood on the balcony. Sleep refused to come. The only thing he could think about was the pack he'd lost. Not even his previous plans of claiming his mate distracted him.

Although it'd been long ago, for him it was still fresh. As though it'd only been a few days…not thirty long years.

Images of the smiling faces of new parents faded. They were replaced by horrifically imagined scenes of infants murdered in their cribs. No matter how hard he tried, he couldn't get them out of his mind. Nor could he wrap his brain around the idea of how anyone could do such a terrible thing. All his life he'd been told humans saw them as nothing more than fairy tale monsters. He'd learned to live with their ignorance. But now he knew the truth. They weren't the monsters. The real monsters hid behind a human mask.

Rage and fear overwhelmed him. He slammed his hands against the rail. He pushed off then went in search of the man who'd held him off too long. Stepping into the hallway, Marcus pounded a fist against a door and bellowed, "Gage!"

The door opened to reveal a disheveled Gage. The rumpled bed behind him reminded Marcus of the late hour. Suddenly, what he had to say didn't seem quite so urgent. "I'm sorry. I guess…"

Gage waved it off. "It's okay. I couldn't sleep." When he noticed Marcus looking at his bed, he added, "That doesn't mean I didn't try." Gage turned around and looked at the clock by his bed. "Well, it's for sure that's not going to happen now. Come on, I'll go make us some coffee."

Marcus followed Gage down to the kitchen then began pacing back and forth. He waited until Gage sat down at the breakfast bar to talk to him. Or rather, to make his demands. Bypassing the stool, he leaned on the bar. "I need to go get my pack. I can't just leave them there. Especially now that I know what they did to…"

He looked away, unable to go on.

After a moment, Marcus murmured, "How could anyone do something like that?"

Gage sighed then glanced at the coffee maker that hadn't even finished brewing one cup. If this was any indication of how his day was going to go, he knew it would be a long one. Drumming his fingers on the counter, he thought about how to put into words what he was thinking. Finally, he said, "There isn't a nice way to put this, so I'll just say it. I don't think they, the Dämonejägers, see us as human."

Shaking his head, Marcus argued, "Even so…if they only see us as animals, it would be like killing puppies."

Unwilling to wait longer, Gage walked over to the coffee maker. With his mug in one hand, he yanked the pot out and pushed his cup under the steady black stream. Satisfied with not quite half a cup, he switched them back. He walked over to the island and sat down. "I don't know, Marcus. *They* aren't human. Isn't that what Lena said last night?"

Gritting his teeth, Marcus sneered, "They're baby killers. I need to get back to…"

He suddenly realized he had no idea where he'd spent the last thirty years.

Nodding, Gage said, "Exactly. If you don't know where it is, how are you going to go back there? Besides, let's say you somehow find it. How do you know they won't do the same thing they did before? With Serenity gone, there'll be nobody there to save you."

Marcus began pacing again. "I can get Serenity to take me back."

Gage didn't look up. Instead, he asked, "Are you sure you want to do that? I mean she came here to get away from them. She even went so far as to change her name." Shaking his head, he continued, "No. I just can't see her going back there for any reason."

The coffee maker beeped, announcing the coffee was ready. Marcus grabbed Gage's cup and one for himself. After filling both, he sat down. "Lena, then. I'm sure since they're related, she knows where to go."

Gage choked on his coffee, then growled, "No."

Smirking, Marcus asked, "Oh? And why not? She's just as capable as Serenity. Plus, they're not looking for her."

"He's right, you know."

Both men jumped when they heard a voice coming from the doorway. Lena walked over to the pot and grabbed herself a cup. She inhaled the aroma of the freshly brewed coffee then scowled at the pot. She scrunched up her nose and set her empty cup down. "Do you even put any coffee in there? Or do you just wave the can over a pot of hot water?"

"Instants in the cupboard above the pot if you want stronger coffee," Gage offered. Watching Lena he asked, "How do you keep sneaking up on us?"

Smirking, she answered, "Wolves aren't the only ones who can be stealthy. I have two older brothers. Jaxon is six years older than me; Keith is five years older. I spent a lot of time sneaking around, trying to get them in trouble." Shuddering, she added, "You'd think I'd have learned the first time I did it. There are so many things I'll never be able to unsee."

She shrugged. "They never figured out how Mom and Dad knew everything they did."

"I want to know what we're going to do about rescuing my pack?" Marcus slammed his cup down hard enough to break it. Still holding the handle, he got up and began cleaning the mess. Giving Gage a sheepish smile, he mumbled, "Sorry."

Lena walked back to the coffee pot. "Marcus, do you want more of this? Or would you like for me to make it a bit stronger."

Not looking up from what he was doing, he said, “Stronger, please.”

Marcus gave Gage a sidelong glance and mumbled, “Sorry. I didn’t want to seem ungrateful, but that’s the worst coffee I’ve ever had.”

Walking in, Allister said, “Thank you. I’ve been telling him that for years.” After dumping the coffee, he began another pot. “So, what are we doing?”

Gage rolled his eyes. “What makes you think we’re doing anything?”

Allister’s hand hovered over the basket with an overflowing scoop of coffee. Then glancing over his shoulder, he said, “Seriously? Baby killers?”

Sitting on one of the vacant stools, Lena replied, “I’m going to go see what’s going on.”

Allister crossed his arms and leaned against the counter. “I’m in.”

Gage surged out of his seat and bellowed, “Absolutely not! If I thought Marcus going was a bad idea, what makes you think I would approve of you going?”

Allister frowned. “I don’t need—”

In an instant, Gage was on his feet with one hand clamped around his brother’s throat. With his silver eyes glowing, he snarled, “Do not push me.”

Still calm, Allister croaked out, “I don’t need your approval. Never have. Never will. I’ll continue to do what I can to help this pack.”

Gage dropped him then stalked across the room.

Allister was right behind him. "Let me help you. Ever since we lost Mom and Dad, you've had to do it all. I know I'm not your beta, but since he's busy with his baby sister right now—"

Gage spun around and glared at his brother's hand. "Fine. But you check in every day. No. Twice a day. And if anything happens…and I mean, anything, you get out of there."

Allister turned away from his brother, grinned and exclaimed, "Road trip."

Grabbing her cup, Lena got up to follow Allister out of the kitchen. She paused in the door then looked back and said, "Don't tell Serenity. Please. She'll just worry. My family, I mean my immediate family, isn't the greatest. But they're nothing compared to hers. To give you an idea, my dad quit speaking to his brother long before I was born. I'm not sure, but I think it had something to do with Gabriel's disappearance."

Gage stormed toward the back door.

Marcus called after him, "Where are you going?"

Gripping the door, he snarled, "Chopping wood."

Leaving his cup on the counter, Marcus followed him. "Sounds good."

***

Serenity's phone woke her up. She glanced at the number, frowned, then answered. "Jonas, I thought it was my day off."

She could hear the nervousness in his voice. "I know. And I'm sorry for bothering you on your day off…" He was silent for a moment, before continuing, "Scarlett didn't come into work this morning. Not that I expected her to, of course. Please, could you come in and cover her shift?"

"Sure. I'll be there as soon as I can." She rolled out of bed then headed for the shower.

Twenty minutes later, she twisted her hair into a bun while walking out the door. She smiled and waved at her haggard neighbor. But she didn't bother stopping to chat. She knew what he was going through. While in her care, Celeste woke up screaming several times a night. Sometimes, it took hours to calm her down enough to get her back to sleep. She didn't envy Luke, but she was in a hurry.

She pulled into her usual parking spot then rushed through the door. A frantic Ariana was rushing from table to table. She looked up from taking a large order then rushed toward Serenity. She pulled the younger woman into her arms and gave her a quick squeeze. After slapping the order book into Serenity's hand, she took off her apron. While rushing toward the kitchen, she exclaimed, "Thanks for coming in. Jonas is overwhelmed with lunch orders. After I help him get caught up, I'll come back and help you."

Laughing, Serenity said, "Go. I got it covered."

Thirty minutes later, Serenity was leaning against the counter staring out the window when Ariana returned. "Woman, you are a miracle worker. I don't know how you took all those orders and had time to relax."

Still staring at the large pickup parked where Scarlett normally did, Serenity murmured, "It's nothing. I've been doing this for eight years. I'm used to it."

She turned back to Ariana. "Have you heard from her?"

Ariana shook her head. "No, but I'm sure she's all right. Physically, anyway. Scarlett puts up a good act, but she's really quite sensitive. Nobody could possibly be harder on her than she would. Give her time, she'll come back. It's only been a day."

Nodding distractedly, Serenity decided there was no way she'd simply wait for her friend to come back. Instead, she decided as soon as she got off, she'd go looking for Scarlett. She could be hurt, dying…

Serenity shook her head. She knew if she continued this line of thinking, she'd leave right now. No. After work would be soon enough.

She looked up when Gage and Marcus pushed through the door. From the looks of them, she'd guess they'd been rolling around in leaves. But that didn't sound quite right for grown men. She walked over with two cups of coffee, as well as two glasses of ice water, and waited for them to sit down.

When they got closer, she stepped back and waved a hand in front of her face. Looking from one to the other she asked, "Would it have hurt to take a shower before you came in?"

Gage answered, "Wouldn't have done any good. As soon as we finish eating, we're going right back to it."

Chuckling, Serenity asked, "And by *it*, you mean what exactly?"

Gage smiled. "Cutting firewood, of course."

Serenity glanced out the window. "Of course."

After she took their order, she walked into the kitchen to question Ariana. "You have furnaces up here, right?"

"Of course, we do. Why?"

Serenity glanced over her shoulder, through the café doors. "Then why are Gage and Marcus so intent on chopping firewood?"

Understanding lit Ariana's face. "It's what they do when something's got them upset. Which translates into something's going on. Since it's both of them, I'll bet it's something big."

Serenity stopped beside the swinging doors. After pushing one open a crack, she looked at the table where Gage and Marcus were having a heated discussion. Just then, Marcus's gaze switched from Gage to her.

Chapter Twenty-Five

Morning wore into late afternoon. The dual stacks of firewood had grown into ridiculous proportions. Marcus looked up from the log he'd just set down and noticed Gage didn't show any sign of slowing. After spending thirty years immobile, his muscles were screaming their protestations. His arms were shaking. And with hands so weak, even holding the axe was a struggle.

Gage threw his own axe across the yard, embedding it in a tree. He turned to glare at the other man, snarling, "How can you not be tired? I feel like my muscles are going to explode."

Marcus laughed. After taking one final swing, he left his axe in the log. He wiped a hand across his forehead. "I wasn't about to give you the satisfaction of quitting first."

Huffing, Gage nodded. "I'll give it to you. Gladly. Early dinner?"

"Who's cooking?"

Gage walked toward his truck. "Who said anything about cooking?"

Keeping pace, Marcus looked at his sweat-soaked shirt and filthy arms and hands. He glanced back at the house again, then asked, "Shouldn't we wash up first?"

Not slowing his steps, Gage replied, "Cleaning up will definitely take too long. And I'm way too hungry. Besides, they have soap at the diner."

Gage steered into the parking lot and a twinge of guilt washed through him. It'd be strange not seeing Scarlett here. He knew he'd been hard on her, but not nearly as hard as she'd been on herself. Instead of offering her comfort, he'd walked away. And that's what bothered him the most.

As if reading his thoughts, Marcus patted his back and said, "Sometimes, being alpha sucks."

Gage jerked his head in a quick nod. They stepped inside then walked over to the only available table. He stared down at the menu that also served as a placemat, allowing his thoughts to wander. He knew that if Scarlett was there, she wouldn't even bother walking over to his table since she always knew what he wanted.

Marcus stared at the surprisingly large selection. "What do you normally get?"

When Gage didn't answer, he went on, "I was thinking about the meatloaf. Is it any good?" Still no answer. Slapping a hand down, he watched the other man jump. He grinned when Gage looked up.

The other man shrugged. "I honestly don't know what to get. Scarlett usually just brings me something."

After Serenity left their coffee, Marcus said, "I'm not chopping one more piece of wood."

Gage laughed. "Would you have rather I told her we were too lazy to get cleaned up?"

"*You* were too lazy. If you remember correctly, I said we should've showered before coming in."

Shrugging, Gage said, "So you weren't as hungry as I am. Which means I obviously worked harder."

Marcus scowled. "Considering I spent the last thirty years standing in one spot, I think I did pretty good. Speaking of thirty years, I have a favor to ask of you."

"Of course. You can ask. But that doesn't mean I'm going to do it."

"I want to go home."

Gage's brows arched over wide eyes. He stared at Marcus a moment. "Sorry, I thought you wanted to—"

"No. My home. I want to go back to Whitebark Stand."

Gage's expression turned from friendly confusion to determined irritation.

Before he could respond, Marcus explained himself. "I don't mean I want to move back there. Well, eventually, I want to. But not yet. I need to see what needs to be done…and to get it ready for my pack."

Gage shook his head. "I don't think it's a good idea. It's been thirty years. What if humans have moved in? Even if they haven't, can you imagine what it'll look like? Major renovations. Not to mention, we don't know how long it'll take to get your pack back together."

"All the more reason. If there's a lot of work to be done, I might as well get started, regardless of how long it'll take to wake everyone. And if humans have taken over, which I doubt, then I'll need to find a new home. That or run them out, which sounds better to me. But the wards were there for hundreds of years. There's no reason to believe something happened to change that in only thirty."

Gage sighed. "We should at least wait until we hear something from Lena and Allister."

Movement from the kitchen caught Marcus's attention. He saw Serenity peeking through the doors. Judging by the intensity of her stare, he realized she'd figured out they were keeping secrets from her. Leaning over the table, Marcus whispered, "Gage. I think she knows we sent Lena and Allister to check on my pack."

Without turning around, Gage pushed away from the table and walked out.

***

After calling her goodbyes, Serenity stepped into the cool evening air. She couldn't believe that by the time she'd walked back into the dining room to give them their order, Gage and Marcus were gone. Now, she'd have to wait until tomorrow to learn whatever secret they'd decided to keep from her.

Serenity unlocked her car then slid into the driver's seat. She closed her eyes and sat quietly for a few minutes to unwind before starting the car. She had no idea that Scarlett's typical day was ten grueling hours long. Waiting tables was hard work. And since it was the only restaurant, there was very little down time. When the few breaks in customers did come, Serenity found herself sitting in a booth staring out the window, thinking about Scarlett.

After the day she'd had, she wasn't sure she even had the energy to go looking for her friend. But she remembered what it was like having no one. Sure, she'd had brothers, she even had a few friends from school…and Lena. But there was nobody who really understood her, let alone cared that much. Certainly not a best friend. That's when she realized how important Scarlett had become to her in such a short time.

That thought filled Serenity with new determination. Not only to find Scarlett but to bring her home. She drove over the curb, past her house, and wove her way through the tall pines. She didn't stop until she couldn't go any further. She stepped out of the car, leaned against the hood, and stared into the shadows. She ran back, yanked the passenger side door open, and grabbed her flashlight.

Giving no thought to her own safety, Serenity began climbing. Waving the light back and forth, she was startled when she heard movement off to the right. She hissed into the darkness, "Scarlett. Where are you? Please, we need to talk. I know you feel bad about what happened, but what you're doing now isn't going to help."

When she got no answer, she continued searching. She didn't stop until she thought she'd collapse from total exhaustion.

Serenity turned around to go back but was shocked to see how far up she'd climbed. She huffed in annoyance and began making her way back toward her car. That's when she realized just how stupid it was to go into the dark woods at night.

And if it weren't for Gage's huge house on the hill, she'd never have been able to find her way home. The steady incline, reversed, now looked steeper than it had in the beginning. Then the worst possible thing that could happen, did.

Her light blinked off, casting her into nearly complete darkness.

All around her, she could hear the animals of the night. More cautious than before, she began picking her way down the hill. Nervousness got the better of her…she then began babbling. She knew it was all nonsense words, but she prayed the noise would keep predators away.

With a nervous laugh, she said, "I really hope there aren't any mountain lions around here. Or I guess there could be wild wolves. But bears, please don't let it be bears. Are bears nocturnal? Maybe it's just little bunnies." She nodded, then began again. "Yes, just bunnies. Or skunks. Oh, no. Please don't spray me, little skunks."

She yelped when something suddenly stepped from behind a tree, blocking her path. Fearing the worst, she debated on whether she should try to outrun whatever animal it might be.

"No. You're not going to run into any bears around here. As for mountain lions, we ran them off long ago. Wild wolves? Of course, there are. And pleading with a skunk to not spray you will only guarantee it happens."

Serenity ran and grabbed Scarlett, hugging her tightly. With tears running down her cheeks, she said, "You nearly scared me to death! Do you know how long I've been looking for you?"

Scarlett stepped back. "Yeah. For about two hours. Are you out of your mind? There's been a pack of wolves trailing you for over an hour. I was having a really hard time chasing them off. But evidently, they freak out when another wolf suddenly becomes human. Why are you out here? Didn't anyone explain things to you?"

Serenity huffed. "Yes. But I decided it was time for you to come home."

Scarlett turned away. "I can't go home."

Serenity nudged her. "My home. I've come to bring you home with me."

"You really like to pick up strays, don't you?"

Serenity walked past her. After a few feet, she looked back. "Well? Stop being so selfish. Do you have any idea how exhausted I am after working your shift? And I still have to get up early tomorrow." She gave her a pointed stare and snorted, hoping Scarlett's wolfish vision worked enough to see how perturbed she was. "And if you don't show up, I'll have to work a double. By myself. You know, I'm amazed at exactly how much work Ariana can find to keep her off the floor."

Scarlett laughed then began making her way down the hill. "Yeah, she really hates waiting tables. She made a big deal out of acting like she was upset when Jonas bought the restaurant twenty years ago. But every time Jonas told her she didn't have to work there, she told him he'd never make it without her. And you know what? She's right. They balance each other out. When one is ready to throw in the towel, the other is there. They—"

Scarlett grabbed Serenity's arm and stopped walking. Her head swiveled to the left. Closing her eyes, she lifted her nose and inhaled deeply. A low animalistic growl rumbled from deep inside.

Serenity stared into the darkness. "What is it?"

Scarlett angled herself in front of Serenity then snarled, "We're not alone."

Serenity searched the shadows, inching closer to her friend. "Could it be Marcus? Or one of your brothers?"

Although Scarlett and she were about the same size, she trusted the wolf to protect her.

Scarlett pushed Serenity further behind her. "No. It's not a wolf. The scent reminds me of you. Human, but not quite."

Serenity paled. Lena called her early that morning to confess to her that her and Allister were on their way to check on the rest of Marcus's pack.

So, she knew it couldn't be her. That just left other members of her family. Could they have found her? What would they do to her new friends? Grabbing Scarlett, she pushed her back then stepped in front of her and screamed, "No."

Looking back at the woman she now considered her best friend, she said, "If it's someone from my family, they can't hurt me. But they can do horrible things to you."

Serenity scanned the shadows, looking for any sign of movement. Raising her voice, she called out, "Who's there? Whoever it is, come out now."

Scarlett added her own threat. "I suggest you do as she says. You're surrounded by monsters that even your wildest imaginings couldn't think up."

A figure stepped from the shadows and into the moonlight. What Scarlett saw caused a shiver to run down her spine. She stepped back and mumbled, "Or not."

Standing in the glow of the midnight moon, a woman hovered inches above the forest floor. Her long dark hair floated around her, with black locks that were somehow moving independently, each as if they were alive. Her onyx eyes gave off an eerie glow, lending an ethereal appearance. Between her splayed fingers, a gyrating blue ball hovered and spun. Streaks of swirling shades of the darkest blues to nearly white occasionally shot out blinding streaks of lightning. The power she possessed radiated from her. Her gaze flickered between Scarlett and Serenity.

Both women knew without a doubt that should she desire it, they would be dead in the blink of an eye.

The woman cocked her head. Her penetrating dark eyes shifted from Serenity to Scarlett. Then, after returning her gaze to Serenity, a moment of recognition passed over her features. And then it was gone. After giving a slight nod, she settled on the ground. In an instant, they watched the spectral figure transform into an ordinary woman.

Stepping forward, she said, “My name is Jasmine Jäger.”

Chapter Twenty-Six

After slipping unnoticed out of the diner, Gage and Marcus headed back to the house. Pulling into the driveway, Gage said, "I guess while I start the food, you can grab that shower. Then you can take over while I get mine. And after that, you can explain why you felt the need to leave the restaurant before we even had a chance to eat."

Gage was still staring into the refrigerator when Ariana walked in. He stepped back, allowing the door to drift shut. He inhaled then followed the alluring scent of whatever was hidden inside the brown paper bag. When she set it down, he reached for the bag.

Ariana batted his hands away. "Just because you're the alpha, don't think I won't knock you into next week. You'll not get a single bite until you get cleaned up. And while you're doing that, you'd better decide how you're going to tell me whatever secret you're keeping from Serenity. That little girl's been through enough without you adding more stress."

Gage walked out of the kitchen, pulling his shirt over his head. Before he started up the stairs, he called back, "You'll have to talk to Marcus. I have no idea, he just…I don't know. Talk to him."

Now, he felt like an idiot. He'd only assumed Marcus wanted to get out of there before Serenity started asking questions about what Lena and Allister were doing. Could that have been his own guilty conscience instead?"

Showered, shaved, and half starved, Marcus could smell the delicious food. Loping down the steps, he headed for the kitchen. Before walking in, he said, "I had no idea you could cook. It smells amazing. You probably shouldn't count on me as far as cooking goes. I have trouble boiling—"

His footsteps stuttered when he walked into the kitchen and his mouth slammed shut.

Ariana looked up from her cup of coffee. "Boiling water? Well, then you have an advantage over Gage."

"Does not." Gage walked in behind Marcus. "I can boil water just as well as the next guy. I only have trouble with anything more complicated than twisting a can opener."

Ariana began with the place settings then grabbed the containers of food she'd brought from the diner. After setting them down, she resumed her seat. "Okay, now it's time to talk. Why were you in such a hurry to leave? And don't try to fool me. I already told Serenity why you were chopping wood."

Confused, Marcus looked from Ariana to Gage. "It's for the coming winter, isn't it?"

Gage stopped mid-bite to stare at Marcus.

Ariana choked on her coffee, spitting it across the table. She jumped up to get a towel. "I was surprised by Serenity's question." She shook her head then sat down to finish her coffee.

"What question?" Then turning to Gage, Marcus asked, "Also, I want to know, if we're not chopping wood for the winter, then why are we?"

Ariana held her hand up. "I can answer both of those. First, she asked if we have modern heat up here. As far as why you were chopping wood…I think the testosterone leaks out in the chopping process."

Marcus said, "But your fireplace?"

Gage winced. "Bon fires? It looks cool stacked next to the cabin?" He shrugged, then said, "I don't know. We've never used it."

Smiling, Marcus said, "So, I guess that means you finally got natural gas up here? Back then, we still relied on wood stoves and fireplaces. Wow. So that means that even if Whitebark Stand is still there, I'm going to have even more major renovations to worry about."

Ariana held up her hand. "Before we go into any of that, tell me why you left so abruptly."

Gage pushed away from the table. He strode to the window and stared across the darkening horizon. "We sent Lena and Allister to check on Marcus's pack."

Marcus interjected, "*We* didn't send them. They offered to go. I wanted to go. By myself. I didn't want to put anybody else in harm's way."

Gage interjected, "Which I immediately nixed. The only thing that would accomplish, in the least, would be him ending up turned into a frozen statue again. At the worst, they could've just outright killed him. I didn't like sending them, but at least Lena is family. As such, I doubt they would hurt her. Besides, if they used their magic on Allister, she can bring him back."

Ariana crossed her arms and scowled at her alpha. "Didn't Lena say someone killed their own daughter? And if they would kill their own daughter, what's going to keep them from doing the same to another relative?"

Gage nodded. "You're right. But Lena can take care of herself. We saw that when she came here. Plus, I made them promise to check in twice a day. If they miss one call-in, we'll go after them."

Marcus growled. "If they were able to overpower my entire pack, how do you suggest we go after them?"

Gage turned to stare out the window that overlooked his community. He tried to imagine what it must have been like to watch helplessly while each member of his pack was taken down by the Dämonejägers. The idea was too horrible to contemplate. Putting himself in Marcus's shoes, he found a new respect for the man. Turning back to face him, he said, "I don't know how you do it."

"Do what?"

"How you can go on every day after what happened. That, and knowing there wasn't a single thing you could have done to prevent it. As for Lena and Allister, they're only supposed to check on the pack. Nothing beyond that. In fact, as soon as I hear from them, I'm telling them to get back here."

Chapter Twenty-Seven

Scarlett leaned closer to Serenity and murmured, "Do you know her?"

Leaning forward, Jasmine whispered, "I can hear you. No. She doesn't know me any more than you do. Just as I don't know either of you. But you…" she nodded toward Serenity. "You resemble the pictures I've seen of my mother." She looked around the shadowy woods. "Do you think we could go somewhere else?" She winked. "I hear there are wild wolves around here."

Frowning, Scarlett said, "No, we're not going anywhere. The only thing we know about you is your name. Which by the way, only reinforces our wariness. Oh, and my own desire to rip your throat out."

"I'm the last person in the world you should be afraid of…wolf. Now, how about telling me who you ladies are. I sense a very powerful magic in her," she nodded toward Serenity. Then she glanced back at Scarlett. "Obviously, you're a wolf. But still, I would like to know who I'm talking to."

Serenity stepped closer. "This is Scarlett. She's the pack alpha's sister and my best friend."

Grinning, Scarlett asked, "I am?"

Serenity returned her smile, nudged Scarlett with her shoulder, then said, "Of course you are.

You're more like a sister I didn't have but always wanted." Then turning back to Jasmine, her smile died. She inhaled deeply. "My name is Serenity Chase. But the name I was born with is Erika Jäger."

Scarlett gasped, and her form shimmered. Jasmine locked her fingers around Scarlett's wrist, which caused her human form to solidify again. Squirming, she struggled against the hold. Finally accepting she wasn't going to break the other woman's grip, she turned to Serenity. She fought back tears. "It all makes sense now. I understand how you were able to sneak onto our lands. And you have the gall…" she sobbed, "to call me your sister."

The air around them became charged with the power radiating from Jasmine. The leaves swirled around their feet, growing in volume until they were spinning mini tornadoes around the three women. Jasmine closed her eyes and took several deep breaths. After the leaves floated back to the ground, she said, "Don't make harsh judgements until you know all the facts. Now, can we please get out of here? I don't know whether you realize this or not, but wolves have a natural hatred for us. I would much rather be somewhere safe if they decide to attack."

Serenity brushed a hand across her eyes. Then turned away from the others and led them down the hill.

***

Scarlett glanced at the clock on the stove. "If this is going to take very long, it'll have to wait until tomorrow." Without looking at Serenity, she said, "It's after midnight and I have to be at work at nine."

After a quick glance at Serenity, she flinched seeing the hurt in her eyes.

Biting back the pain, Serenity said, "Jasmine, you get the couch. I already made up the guest room for you, Scarlett. I just want you to know that you have no reason to fear me. When I came here, I had no idea what kind of people I grew up with. I just thought they were nuts. I have a feeling Jasmine is no more of a threat to you than I am. And I want you to know that I'm *not* a threat, in any way. I meant what I said when I told you how I felt about you. I didn't choose my family. And I hope you can get past that. I say we should all get a good night's sleep. Tomorrow, we need to get a hold of Gage. Not to mention, we need to include him and Marcus in this conversation."

Jasmine walked over to the couch, grabbed a throw off the back, and laid down. "Yes. Tomorrow sounds wonderful. I'm no threat to any of you. That is, as long as you don't threaten me. Just remember one thing. I can, indeed, kill you in less than a blink of an eye."

Chapter Twenty-Eight

Lena turned onto the mountain road. Very soon, they'd be at the house where her grandfather lived and died. The closer she got, the more nervous she became. She knew that her family could sense Allister just as easily as she could. She just hoped they'd mistake him for one of the many spelled wolves on their property.

She grabbed her visor then spun it toward her window. Were anyone to notice, they'd simply assume she was blocking the glare of the late afternoon sun. Instead, she was hiding her face from any Jägers who may be out driving. Then setting her elbow on the door, she allowed her hand to sail nervously on the wind.

A moment later, she twisted the visor around, closed the window, and pulled over to the side of the road. The moment the car stopped, she shoved the door open, slid down the embankment, and collapsed.

Allister ran after her, leaving his door open. He knelt. "What's wrong?"

His own nerves were on end. He kept glancing at the road while waiting for her answer.

Lena cradled her head, resting her elbows on her knees. Finally, looking at her traveling companion, she said, “You can feel it, too.”

Allister wanted to pretend he didn’t know what she was talking about. He wanted to pretend he didn’t feel the evil that permeated the air around him. But he also knew no amount of denial would make it so. Giving a quick nod, he dropped to the ground beside her. “Do you think they know we’re here?”

Groaning, Lena admonished herself. “How could I be so stupid. What was I thinking? I should have stopped sooner. I could’ve masked our presence. It may not have completely hidden us, but it would’ve made us less noticeable.”

She stood and began making her way back to the car. “We need to go back.”

Allister grabbed her shoulder and spun her around. “We’ve come this far—we need to finish it. I can’t imagine what Marcus is going through, not knowing the fate of his pack. I only know how I would feel. We need to keep going.”

She glared at him. “And how do you think Gage will feel if you become one of them? All it takes is a few words and you’re ensnared. It’s a fate worse than death. At best you would be trapped in your mind. At worst, they can make it so you could feel everything. If they wanted to, they could torture you, and there’s nothing you could do to stop them.”

The idea of something so horrifying was almost enough for him to agree with her. To leave and never look back. Almost. But not quite. He opened his mouth to argue.

Lena stopped him.

"We can argue in the car. As long as we're standing here, it gives them that much more of an advantage. If we're going, we need to keep moving. It's hard to hit a moving target."

Smiling, Allister asked, "Really? That's all we have to do?"

Lena snorted. "No. Of course not. You don't have to be standing still to hear a phrase. I was just being facetious. I just don't want to be standing here when they come looking for us. They've probably mistaken me for Serenity. If that's the case, we're both in trouble. They may cast a spell on you, but they'll outright *kill* me."

Lena drove a few miles further then turned onto a narrow dirt road. She pulled off the road and into the beginnings of a forest. She parked behind several trees and got out. Standing by the truck, she waited for Allister.

He stopped beside her. "I thought you wanted to keep moving."

She shook her head and pointed through the trees. "We're here. Make sure the ringer is off on your phone. The last thing we want after coming all this way is to be found because someone decided to call at the wrong time. I'm not sure where they're keeping the pups, but I know they have several large barns. We can check those. On the way, we should come across some of the wolves. I can lay a hand on them and begin the waking process. But that's all I'm going to do. We're not prepared to take an entire pack out of here. The best I can promise…if we don't get caught, is to maybe bring a few pups with us."

They made their way closer to the large house. A few minutes later, they came across a huge white wolf. Lena looked from the wolf to Allister, then whispered, "Any idea who this is?"

Shaking his head, he said, "All this happened long before I was born. But we can take pictures to show Marcus."

After Allister took her picture, Lena laid a hand on the wolf's shoulder. She closed her eyes, mouthed a few words, then walked away. After repeating the same process with each wolf, she hurried toward a break in the trees.

Allister noticed after passing the first few wolves, she was getting more anxious to move on. He glanced back. "What's happening?"

He watched her stare into the darkness behind them. "Every minute I stay in here, they become more aware. If they happen to wake before we're ready, it'll alert the Jäger's, then we're going to be in serious trouble. As it is, we're going to have to find another way back. As soon as we check on the pups, we need to get as far from these woods as we can. As fast as possible."

They'd found a dozen wolves in the fifteen minutes it took to get to the house. A few had a pup lying behind them. Allister nudged Lena and asked, "Why are these pups here while the others are supposedly in the barn?"

She shrugged. "Beats me. Maybe they thought it would create a more impressive scene for anybody who happened upon them…a mother defending her baby. They're an arrogant bunch if nothing else."

They paused and looked toward the house. All the lights were off. Either nobody was home, or they'd already gone to bed. Allister tapped Lena's shoulder then pointed past the house. Behind it, a large barn sat with the back end extending into the woods.

They made their way closer then paused outside the barn. After ensuring nobody had come out to investigate, they stepped inside. The moment they crossed the threshold, Lena's phone began ringing.

Lena slapped a hand over her hip pocket then pulled her phone out. Without bothering to answer, she silenced it as quickly as she could. She gave Allister a sheepish smile. "Sorry."

The barn was too dark to make out much, but not so dark that it concealed how many pups were crammed into the small space.

Alister flicked on his flashlight then cursed. There had to be at least fifty pups varying in ages.

Lena gasped. "How many can you carry?"

The floorboards above them creaked and a lone voice called out, "I can help."

***

Gage had just put the coffee on when the doorbell rang. Everybody in his pack knew to come through the kitchen in the morning, so he figured it had to be Serenity. When he opened the door, he was shocked to see Scarlett standing there.

She pushed past him, murmuring, "She made me."

He saw Serenity looking over her shoulder toward someone standing a few feet away. Whoever it was, he heard her ask, "Are you ready?"

A dark woman stepped in front of Serenity. Barely contained power radiated from her. His wolf took notice. He wasn't afraid of much, but this woman terrified him.

Stepping into the foyer, Scarlett said, "Yeah. She has that effect on everybody."

Gage spun toward his sister. "So, she's safe?"

Scarlett walked toward the kitchen. "Nope. All I said was she had that effect on everybody."

Gage scowled and stood his ground, blocking the door. "You're not invited in."

Snorting a laugh, Jasmine pushed her way past him. "That only works on vampires."

Twisting around he said, "Wait. Vampires are real?"

"Of course not. Why would you think they're real?" Serenity asked, following the other woman.

Gage stood with an empty cup in one hand and the door gripped in the other. Finally slamming the door, he commented, "But she said…"

Following the women, he stopped in the doorway. A moment later, two wolves knocked him over. The darkest wolf stopped in front of Serenity. The other, in front of Gage.

Gage kicked his brother away and snarled, "I don't need my brother protecting me."

Noah's wolf morphed, leaving a large man writhing on the floor. Noah glared at his brother and growled, "I wasn't trying to protect you. I was giving you a chance to get away."

Gage kicked him again and shouted, "That's even worse. What kind of an alpha would leave their pack vulnerable?"

Jasmine took a sip of Gage's freshly brewed coffee then spit it into the sink. "What's this supposed to be?" She grabbed the pot then walked over to the sink.

Gage lunged toward her, shouting, "No…wait…I haven't…"

Jasmine poured the pot down the drain then started scooping fresh grounds into the filter.

Gage threw his hands up. "My house. My coffee. But does that matter? No. Of course not." He glared at the others. "Hey, why don't you guys all just make yourselves at home. Especially you, random stranger."

Unphased, Jasmine waved a finger toward Gage and smiled. "Why, thank you, alpha wolf."

Scarlett jabbed an elbow in his ribs and whispered, "This is where you say thank you for not killing me, powerful magic stranger."

Jasmine chuckled. "Even though I could kill all of you, at once, with just a single thought, I would never. Is there somewhere more comfortable to talk? It's getting a little crowded. You also might want to call in your officers. I don't want to repeat myself. I also don't want what I have to say passed around second hand. That often results in things getting left out or end up being completely wrong. Which leads to misunderstandings. Misunderstandings which could get someone killed."

Thirty minutes later, they were sitting in the large meeting hall while breakfast was served. Jonas and Ariana had been called when Jasmine requested that he call in the pack's officers. Jonas was sitting beside Luke, holding Celeste. Serenity, Scarlett, and Ariana were setting up the breakfast buffet.

Jasmine sat in the middle, watching everything around her. Smiling, she'd never felt as comfortable in a group of people as she did then. She just hoped they'd welcome her when she finished telling them everything.

After the meal was finally finished, cups were filled, and conversation picked up.

Jasmine decided it was time to tell these strangers who she was, as well as what they could expect going forward. She also suspected Serenity didn't fully understand herself, or how much power she wielded. Otherwise, she never would've had any fear when they met.

She stood and walked to the head of the table and asked. "Can I have everyone's attention?" She waited until the talking stopped and everyone turned to face her.

Smiling, she began. "For those of you who don't know who I am, my name is Jasmine Jäger. Now, I know I'm not the first Jäger you've met. However, I also know I don't fit the typical profile of the Jäger clan. For centuries, they've married only within the original Dämonejäger descendants. Except for two. The first being Sabrina. I believe you know who I'm talking about?" She waited until everyone nodded.

"Good, then I don't have to go over that. The second to mate outside her clan was Gabriel Jäger…my mother." She paused, waiting for that information to settle. She wanted to give them plenty of time to understand, especially Serenity.

Serenity wasn't sure how to feel. Of course, she'd known about Lena. After all, they'd grown up together. She also knew she had other cousins but wasn't sure where they stood as far as the family secrets went. But this. This was over the top surprising. Unable to hold back any longer, she said, "I thought Gabriel was killed not long after she turned sixteen."

Jasmine picked up her coffee. She stared into the cup. "I don't suppose you have any coffee cake to go with this?" Blank stares were her only answers. Nodding, she said, "Sorry. I have a terrible sweet tooth."

Frowning, she turned her attention back to Serenity. "Yes. My mother was murdered by her father after she turned sixteen. I'm not completely certain of the story. But from my understanding, she suspected something was up when her father insisted on her coming home for her birthday. However, they refused to allow any of her friends or family to come. All girls dream about their sixteenth birthday. Gabriel's mother was even more excited about it than she was. So, of course, my mother made sure she wasn't home for her birthday. She'd met a boy at summer camp and fallen hopelessly in love. When he found out what she suspected, he insisted on bringing her home with him. Well, one thing led to another…and here I am. Of course, her father eventually caught up with her. She'd gone into town to pick up a few things for her newborn baby girl and he was waiting for her. Nobody saw her again. My father, unable to live without her, walked into the woods and never returned. I was raised by his family. Thank goodness Grandfather Jäger didn't know about me, or my father's people. I'm from Montana. More specifically, the Sycamore Strand Pack."

Chapter Twenty-Nine

Lena felt power radiating from this girl and knew she had to be connected to the Jäger's. But how? Then she remembered her father talking about how upset her Uncle Paul and Aunt Sofia were because all attempts at having another child failed. Could it be that her uncle had cheated? Anxious to know, she asked, "Who are you?"

The young girl climbed down from the loft then walked toward them.

She stopped when Allister snarled, "That's close enough. I don't know who you are. Considering where we are right now, not to mention what we're about to do and suddenly you show up out of nowhere. If Lena doesn't know you, I'm not about to trust you. So, whatever you have to say can be said from where you're standing."

She took a few steps back then leaned against the ladder. "I guess I don't blame you for not trusting me. My name's Anna Wilson. I came here looking for my father. But of course, he's not here. But I did manage to find several rather twisted relatives. I was standing on the porch, poised to knock, when I overheard one side of a conversation.

Let's just say I didn't wait around to see what the person on the other end was saying. If anyone has a reason to be scared, it's me."

Lena opened her mouth to say something when Allister stopped her.

"I think this is a conversation we can have later. May I suggest we get out of here as soon as possible. Personally, I don't want to be here if someone looks outside and notices our flashlights."

Lena glanced toward the door. "Right. Let's get as many of these babies out of here as we can. And as fast as we can. I know we're not going to be able to take them all…"

Anna walked into the dark space beneath the loft. She emerged a moment later with a large wheelbarrow. She knocked her head back and said, "There's more."

Allister and Lena ran toward their waiting vehicle. Both wheelbarrows were overflowing with pups stacked in complete disorder. When Allister thought to complain, Lena reminded him that the pups were frozen in exactly the same position they were thirty years ago. They felt nothing. At least for now. The longer they were handled by her, the faster that would change. Both had pups over their shoulders as well as tucked inside their shirts. Between the three of them, they'd managed to clear out the barn.

After setting the last pup inside the SUV, Lena said, "I just hope they don't find out we took them until we've had a chance to come back for the others."

Allister climbed into the driver's seat. "And I hope that girl wasn't messing with us. If she doesn't meet up with us in Whiting, then we'll know."

Lena had barely sat down when Allister slammed his foot down on the accelerator. She belted herself in as they spun out of the forest and onto the highway. While watching the passing trees, she asked, "Do you remember where you need to turn the lights off?"

Frowning, he asked, "Why do I need to do that?"

Lena kept her gaze on the dark woods. "Trust me, the last thing we want is for my uncle to make a connection between the missing pups and the random car driving past their house. There's not much traffic up here, at least not on a weeknight."

Finally coming off the mountain pass, they pulled into the agreed parking lot.

When Allister opened the door to get out, Lena grabbed his arm and hissed, "Where do you think you're going?"

His head swiveled from her to the diner. "I'm hungry."

Lena stared at the many blond-headed patrons and shook her head. "No. As soon as Anna gets here, we need to leave." She nodded toward the happy diners. "If I'm not mistaken, every person in there is somehow connected to the Dämonejägers."

Allister slid behind the wheel, shut the door, and kept his gaze on the people inside. Then he started the car and backed out. He left the lights off and drove to the corner furthest from the building.

Fifteen minutes later, they were about to give up when a compact SUV pulled into the parking lot. After stopping, the window was opened, and a blonde head peeked out.

"That's her," Lena said, "flash your lights."

After pulling alongside them, she asked, "Okay, what now?"

The door to the diner opened and two families stepped out.

Lena cursed. "What's he doing here?" She glanced between Allister and Anna. "We need to leave. Now. And not through the exit."

Allister looked toward the restaurant. "Why?"

"Those people…that's my dad over there talking. And the man he's talking to is Serenity's dad. And trust me, my dad will know my car since he bought it."

Allister pulled onto the main highway. He glanced at Lena. "So, we're just going to bring her back with us? I mean we don't know anything about her. For all we know, she could be on the phone with the Jäger's right now."

Lena continued to stare out the window at the headlights in the mirror. "She has two dozen pups in her car. She also helped carry them out of that barn. Now let me ask you this. Did you want to just leave her and the pups in our dust? Because…I don't think that's such a good idea. But if you want, we can stop somewhere, shove all those other pups—"

"—Fine. I get your point. But do you understand where I'm coming from?"

"Allister, I'm sorry. Of course, I understand. The people we come from are best described as monsters. Trust me, if anyone knows that it's me. I grew up with those people. Your life, and the lives of every member of your pack is about to change forever. I know that mixing with the hunters is a hard pill to swallow, but it's going to happen. I'm sure you've noticed what's going on between Serenity and Marcus."

Allister laughed. "And you and Gage."

"No. There's nothing going on between us. I'm not looking. And if I was, it wouldn't be with someone like him. The first argument we had would end up with one of us dead. Nobody… absolutely nobody will ever treat me that way again."

The car swerved. Allister turned his gaze toward her. Then, after regaining control, he snarled, "What do you mean, again?"

Lena blushed. "That's…just never mind."

Chapter Thirty

Marcus looked at Gage, whose face mirrored his own feelings. Rage battled with confusion. Looking at the stranger, he said, "You expect us to believe your father was a shifter?"

She shrugged. "Believe what you want. My father was to be the next alpha. After my mother vanished, he mourned for a month before leaving. I was raised by my uncle, who was forced to step into his brother's shoes."

Gage spoke up. "You expect us to believe that you're half wolf? You threatened to kill us. In my house. Why shouldn't I kill you myself?"

Scarlett scooted away from the table. She shook her head while watching Jasmine and backed toward the door. Then looking from Gage to Jasmine, she said, "Just remember, I had nothing to do with this." She glanced back at Serenity. "You coming?"

Serenity glared at her friend. "Don't be so dramatic, Scarlett, sit down. Gage, you really don't want to challenge Jasmine." She pointed to herself, then Scarlett. "We've seen what she can do. Well, not exactly. But still."

Jasmin walked back to the table and sat down. After taking a sip of her coffee, she mumbled, "Are you sure you don't have anything to go with this coffee? At least a…"

Ariana left the room, returning a few minutes later with a large cookie jar.

Jasmine's eyes got big. "Bless you, woman." After taking the lid off, she gasped, exclaiming, "Chocolate chip to boot." She dipped one of the cookies in her coffee and bit off half. "Now this…this is what I'm talking about!"

When she noticed nobody shared her glee, she sighed. She dusted her hands off, then grumbled, "Okay. Chill. I've had enough coffee and gotten my sugar fix. I'm more than ready to be reasonable. Just so you know…"

She waved a hand and everything that was on the table hovered above it for a moment before coming back down. "And…"

She backed away from the table. Her body shimmered for a few seconds. Then, standing in her place was a wolf as light as she was dark. Instead of her black eyes, the wolf's eyes were an icy blue. Where Jasmine was a dark mocha, her fur was as white as snow.

A moment later, Jasmine, in her human form, was standing there again. She returned to the table. "Now, I'm not sure if every child born will be magic and have the ability to shift. I don't broadcast this information since people aren't always receptive to my mixed genes. After listening in on the conversation between my two uncles, I especially don't want them to find out I'm half wolf."

After taking a deep breath, she continued, "So I'm trusting you with a secret that could get me killed. After my mother fled, she realized what could happen. My uncle gave me the letter she wrote just in case anything ever happened to her. As it turns out, she was right in doing it. I'll sum up what she said for you. Because of the journals handed down through generations, she learned she was magic. The men of the Jäger clan also have magic. However, every time they use their magic for evil, it's diminished. This carries into each generation. So, basically, at birth, you don't get a clean slate. It's kind of one of those sins of the father things. Because the preceding generations used their magic for ill will, by the time it got to this generation, it was nearly nonexistent. And now they're limited on which spells they can cast. I'm able to use my magic with just a thought. However, *they* must recite incantations. That's the reason the shifters who refused to change were killed. They aren't able to force them to shift."

Serenity asked, "What about the women? Do the same rules apply to them?

Jasmine winked, pointed to her, and said, "Bingo. Lucky for us, the women from years gone by were smarter than their husbands. Still, a few in the past have used their magic to aid the men. Imagine what could have been. Did you know, in the beginning there was no sickness in our villages?

What a shame to have thrown away something so magnificent."

Serenity interjected, "I would imagine it was a surprise to them when that ability was lost. Someone, somewhere had to have been the first to discover the consequences of doing evil."

Jasmine thought about it a minute. "That's true. There are other Jäger clans out there. I don't know what they're capable of. Maybe someday, we'll find them."

Marcus leaned in. "So, about your threat to kill all of us at once?"

Smirking, Jasmine said, "I said I could. That wasn't a lie. That's also the reason I said I wouldn't do it. However, if it comes down to me or you…it will be you who loses."

Serenity asked, "Hey, what about this conversation between your uncles?"

Jasmine resumed her seat. "Oh, yeah. I went there before I came here. I wanted to see firsthand if what my father's family said was true. Let me just say, I agree."

***

Gage hadn't been asleep long when something woke him up. A sound. Creaking floorboards. Someone was in his house. Someone who didn't belong there. Instantly alert, he rushed to the door. He pulled it open a few inches and peeked out. Someone was standing in the hall outside his bedroom. He jerked the door open then leapt toward the intruder. Fist drawn back, he jerked the man around. "What are you—"

Marcus shushed him. "Someone's downstairs."

Before they could start down the steps, they heard a loud commotion coming from the living room. They ran down the stairs and Gage flicked the light switch. Rolling around in the foyer, Allister and Noah—caught by surprise—stopped fighting.

Rolling away, Noah snarled, "Why were you sneaking around?"

Rubbing his jaw, Allister growled, "Because we didn't want to wake anyone up?"

Gage chuckled and walked toward his brothers. He reached a hand to Allister, then Noah. Grinning, he said, "Really? You thought—"

Lena stepped inside. "It was my idea."

Allister smirked. "I told you that wouldn't work. I just wish I'd thought to have you come through the door first."

The screen door opened. A woman Gage didn't know stuck her head in. "Is it safe yet?"

Gage snarled, "Why would you bring a stranger here? And judging by her scent, she's another Jäger."

Lena scowled at Gage and pulled the young girl inside. "We can talk about that in the morning—"

—"We'll talk about it now."

Lena glared at Gage. "And just exactly what will talking about it tonight accomplish? When everything could easily be resolved tomorrow? I mean, other than depriving us of sleep after a long drive. Besides, we have more important things to do right now." Thumbing toward the door, Lena said, "Help us get them out of the cars."

Chapter Thirty-One

Marcus was sitting in his usual place at the island drinking coffee when everybody began stumbling into the kitchen. Instead of speaking, he continued staring into his cup. After hours of tossing and turning, he'd finally given up and came downstairs. He'd already finished a pot of coffee and had started on a second.

Gage sat beside him. "Couldn't sleep?"

Marcus looked from his coffee toward the patio. "All I could think about were the ones who didn't make it. How…"

He stared at his coffee another moment. Swallowing a lump, he turned toward Gage. With tears in his eyes, he asked, "How am I going to tell their parents?"

Gage slumped into a stool. He knew this was one of the most difficult alpha responsibilities. Most people only saw the perks. Unless you had to live it, you couldn't understand. He was deep in thought when a cup of coffee was slid in front of him.

Lena sat beside him. "And it's watered down, just the way you like it."

She looked at Marcus. "You won't have to do it alone."

The back door opened and Scarlett, Jasmine, and Serenity walked in and began preparing breakfast. Lena got up and called out, "Anna can you come help me set the table?"

Anna squealed, grinning. "Yay! Family stuff."

Lena laughed. "I'm glad such a simple thing makes you happy. Did your mother's people sit around the table, too?"

While adding napkins and utensils beside each plate, Anna casually said, "I don't know anything about my mother's people."

Shocked, Lena stopped and looked at the young girl. "What do you mean? How could you—"

Taking the plates from Lena, Anna continued setting the table. Without looking up, she said, "I grew up in foster care. Well. Mostly."

Lena's eyes rounded. Shocked by what her new cousin said, she murmured, "What—"

Gage laid a hand on her shoulder. "In due time. Let's eat. Then we can all get to know each other. I'm sure you've noticed she's not the only new person here. After breakfast, we'll move into my office and everyone can introduce themselves."

Thirty minutes later, they were seated in a circle similar to the one they were in when Serenity revealed her secrets. It was also when she'd learned the truth of who—and what—she really was. They were things beyond Gage's comprehension. He couldn't imagine growing up in a family like hers.

Jasmine spoke first. "I already know most of you, so to the newcomers, I'll introduce myself. My name is Jasmine Jäger. What that means to you," she stared at Lena, then added, "I'm your cousin. I'm the daughter and only child of Gabriel. I was raised by an uncle after they killed my mother. Unable to go on without his mate, my father died shortly after they took her. So, yeah, in case you haven't figured it out yet, I'm half wolf. And please, don't ask for me to show you my wolf. It doesn't actually hurt, but it's not pleasant either." She glared at first Marcus, then Gage. "If I'd known I would have to repeat myself, I would've waited."

After hearing the low growl coming from Gage, Lena laid a hand on his arm. When he looked at her, she gave him a knowing smile. Then turning to Jasmine, she said, "We're all very sorry to have cost you thirty wasted seconds of your life." Then facing Anna, she said, "Anna, the only thing we," she waved a hand between her and Allister, "really know about you is your name. So, if you wouldn't mind…?"

Anna squirmed. "There's really not much to tell. My name is Anna Wilson. All I know is that my mother left a few hours after I was born. I had to break into the office to learn who my parents were and discovered that mother died a few years after I was born. Drugs," she shrugged. "When I found out who my father was, and that he was still living, I was really excited to meet him. Until I overheard his brother on the phone. That's when I realized sometimes… not knowing is better."

Lena leaned forward. "So you don't know who you are. I mean not really. The Jäger's—your father's people—possess some very powerful magic. And before you give me the teenage eyeroll, let me tell you that magic is very real. We can talk about this later if you want. I'm sure the others have no desire to go over that conversation again."

Smiling, Gage agreed, "Yes, please. After we finish here, we're going to have to address what to do with the pups. So, Allister, if you wouldn't mind recounting what happened…"

Lena and Allister took the next fifteen minutes to explain what happened on their trip to Serenity's family home. Allister finished by telling them about their narrow escape at the diner.

Gage leaned forward. Staring from Allister to Lena, he asked, "Wait. Did you say her father bought the car for her?"

Lena's gaze swept the room, noticing everybody else's confusion mirrored her own. Finally, looking back at Gage, she said, "Well, yeah. I'm only nineteen. How else could I have afforded such a nice vehicle?"

Gage paled; his mouth hung open while he stared at Lena. Visions of the Dämonejägers ascending on his community flashed through his mind.

He was even more shocked when Scarlett grabbed Serenity's arm and exclaimed, "Your car."

Gage's gaze swept from Lena to Serenity. Overwhelming dread filled him before asking, "What about your car?"

It was Serenity's turn to pale. "Um. It's not really my car... I kind of just took it."

Tapping her foot, feeling nervous, Anna said, "Well, *now* that phone call makes sense."

Attention switched from Lena and Serenity to Anna.

Gage leaned forward and demanded, "Tell me everything that was said."

Anna plucked at the threads in a frayed split in her jeans. She was quiet for a moment, then closed her eyes for a second. "It went something like…*No. I haven't seen her. How long has she been missing?* There was a pause before he went on. *Really? I hadn't thought of doing that. Can you come over and show me how?* And then the last thing he said was…*Of course, I'll come with you. You know we'll have to take care of her and Erika.* That's when I decided it was time to get out of there. I didn't know what *take care* of meant, but I had a pretty good idea that it wouldn't be something good."

When Serenity gasped, Lena gaped at her and asked, "What? Do we know somebody named Erika?"

Marcus answered, "After leaving her abusive family, Serenity changed her name. It used to be Erika."

Allister bounded out of his seat. On his way out the door, he yelled, "We need to move fast. Lena and Serenity, you follow me. The rest of you stay here and watch the pups." When Gage and Marcus snarled, he said, "Okay. Everybody else, stay here and watch the pups."

Scarlett argued, "I'm not leaving—"

Jabbing a finger in her chest, Gage demanded, "You will do as you're told. You're lucky to even be allowed in this house."

Running out of the house, Allister called back, "Lena and Serenity, get your cars and follow me. We need to get them as far from here as we can."

Serenity watched Marcus follow her out to the car. For a long time, he fidgeted in his seat, obviously unable to get comfortable. Finally, he reached for her hand, kissed it, then said, "I have no idea why everybody's so freaked out."

Serenity's face flushed after Marcus kissed her hand. It was a reminder of their one and only kiss and how much she wanted to do it again. If she hadn't invited so many people to stay with her, maybe things could go to the next level.

She glanced at Marcus and wondered if Gage could be persuaded to let Scarlett go home…and take Jasmine with her. Then she remembered how upset he'd been before they left. All hope vanished.

Marcus began kissing his way up her arm. Reaching a hand across the console, he turned her face toward him. In a husky voice, he repeated his question, "Why is everyone so freaked out?"

Serenity found herself focusing on his lips. It wasn't until she heard the horn from Allister's car that she remembered what she was doing. Twisting her gaze away, she sputtered, "What?"

Marcus laughed then repeated his question once more. "Why did Gage and Allister freak out over your family buying you and Lena cars? I can kind of understand Gage being upset, since Lena's his mate."

Waggling her finger at him, Serenity said, "We'll address your stone-aged thinking later. For now…" She shook her head. "I'm such an idiot. I should have thought of it." She glanced at Marcus. "When I left home, I tossed my phone out the window since they can trace it. I never even thought about them tracking the car. My family believes the rest of the world is as evil as they are. So, I'm sure they've enabled GPS tracking on all their vehicles. Because of that, I pretty much told them where to find us."

An hour and a half later, they pulled into a suburb on the outskirts of Portland. Serenity followed Allister into a grocery store parking lot. She watched as he pulled into a space at the end of one lane. Then stepping out of his car, he waited for her.

She opened her window. "Now what?"

He leaned in. "Go find you a parking spot. Get as close to the store as you can. Then shut the car off and wait for me."

After she parked, Allister said, "Close your windows and get out." He opened the back door. "Hit the lock then toss the keys in."

Serenity shook her head. "Won't do any good. You can't lock your keys in the car."

Grinning, Allister said, "After I finish with it you can."

Fifteen minutes later, the five of them were piling into Allister's small car.

Allister watched Gage fold his large form into the tiny seat.

Gage asked, "Why didn't you bring one of the SUV's?"

"You're the one who insisted on coming, so don't complain."

Gage snarled, "When we get home—"

Lena threw both feet into the back of Gage's seat. She looked at Allister and said, "Good thinking, Allister. Thanks for saving our hides, Allister."

He chuckled when Gage crossed his arms, said nothing, and stared out the front window.

Marcus spoke up, "Yes. Thank you. I had no idea technology had advanced so far. Are we safe now?"

Allister glanced at Marcus in the rearview mirror. "I honestly don't know. Serenity's been with us for quite a while. But hopefully, we were able to move the cars before they found them. If they haven't started searching yet, it should be good. The GPS will only show their last location, which is far enough they shouldn't be able to find us."

***

The phone on the table beside Luka's chair vibrated. A happy tune announced an incoming call. He flipped it over then frowned at his brother's smiling face. What could he possibly want? It'd been years since they'd spoken, and he would be more than happy to never talk to the man again. Instead, he swiped a finger across the phone and growled, "What do you want?"

His brother's frantic voice came over the line. "Have you seen or heard from Lena?"

"No. I haven't seen her."

He thought about his own missing daughter, then asked, "How long has she been missing?"

A loud sigh came over the line before his brother said, "It's not really been that long. But when I pinged her phone, it came up close to you. I thought maybe she'd come to visit Erika."

Luka was surprised to learn his niece was in the neighborhood but hadn't bothered to stop by. "Really?" He paused, then went on, "I hadn't thought of doing that." His mind drifted to his daughter's phone. "Can you tell me how to do that?"

Anton laughed. "If Lena hasn't been to your house, I don't know where she is. Will you help me look? Then after we find her, I can show you how to track a phone. There're all kinds of ways to find missing children."

"Of course, I'll come with you. You know we'll have to take care of her and Erika."

The line was quiet for a moment before Anton responded. "It'd better not mean what I think it means when you say, *take care of.* I love my daughter, and I would never do anything to hurt her."

"No. Of course I would never do anything to hurt the girls. I just meant bring them home."

After a pause, Anton asked, "Bring them home?"

Luka answered, "Erika snuck out of the house about a week ago. We tried calling her, but she never answered."

"Have you traced her car?"

Instead of answering, Luka asked, "When can you be here?"

Without hesitation, Anton said, "I can leave right now."

"Meet me at the diner at the bottom of the hill." Without waiting for a response, he dropped his phone in a pocket. Then walking toward the kitchen, he called to his wife, "Sabine, get ready. We're meeting Anton in three hours at the diner. Call Paul and tell him to meet us there. Anton's going to help us find Erika."

Sabine came out of the kitchen drying her hands. "And then what? That ungrateful child has done nothing but rake us over the coals, over and over."

Sneering, he told her, "The first thing I'm going to find out is what she did with Dad's money. Then we're going to take a little walk out to the woods."

"You're more patient than I am. I don't know if I could wait that long. Stupid curse, anyway. We should've gotten rid of her a long time ago."

Chapter Thirty-Two

Serenity stood under the starlit sky staring at the big house on the hill. She couldn't help thinking about the wolves she'd left behind. If only she could've brought more of them with her. The helpless babies in the barn who were tossed haphazardly into corners. And the many, many wolves positioned around the property. With each suffering their own living nightmares. Then, of course, there were the ones who didn't make it, like Henry.

But there was one above all that weighed heavily on her mind. The first wolf she'd met, the one who'd visited her dreams. Then another thought came.

What if her family decided to kill the remaining wolves after they'd discovered the missing pups? She prayed they hadn't yet discovered them gone. Gazing at the stars above, she murmured, "Chance, I'm so, so, sorry. I promise I'll come for you. Please don't give up."

She closed her eyes and leaned into Marcus. She'd felt his presence long before she'd felt his touch. His warm hands caressed her bare arms, sending shivers down her spine. She turned to face him. When she nodded, he took her hand and led her back into the house. After remembering the women sleeping inside, she realized she really didn't care. She wanted him. And she wanted him now.

He led her through the kitchen and into living room. The curtains were still open, allowing the moonlight to spill into the room.

Her gaze landed on the empty couch. She felt a feather light kiss on her neck, then heard Marcus's whispered words, "I sent them away. It's just the two of us."

***

Serenity watched Marcus sleep. He'd told her last night they were now mated for eternity. Not even death could separate them. She could feel him deep in her soul, and now understood what happened to Henry.

If Marcus were taken from her, she knew she'd never survive it. The mating had linked not only their lives, but their souls as well. She remembered their first meeting. Although she'd been a child at the time, she realized even then that she'd felt their connection.

Memories returned from the shadowy realm of dreams. In them, she'd lost count of how many times she'd watched her father give a sinister laugh and shoot Marcus. In slow motion, she'd watch the bullet explode from the gun and into its target. Sometimes, it was his head, others, his chest. And she was helpless to do more than watch him die.

It was a recurring dream. Each time it sent her flying from bed, only to find nothing had changed.

A moment of dread overcame her. Could it have been an omen? Panic swept through her. No. She couldn't lose him. Not now. Not ever.

Marcus was instantly awake. Something was wrong. His mate. Was she in danger? Had he somehow slept through a break-in? His eyes snapped open. A low growl rumbled up. Lying still, he listened to every sound. He inhaled deeply. The only scent that came to him was his mate's. He sat up, propping himself on an elbow, then leaned over her. After wiping a tear from her cheek, he asked, "Why are you crying, my love?"

She closed her eyes and tried to turn away. When Marcus's arms came around her, she stopped. She peered into his glowing obsidian eyes. "It's silly."

He kissed her nose. "Nothing you say could ever make me think that."

Serenity struggled with mixed emotions. She wanted to make love again, but she also needed to tell him her fears. Finally, she asked, "What if something happened to you? Marcus, I couldn't take it."

Her scent was driving him insane. Smiling, Marcus scooted closer. "My love. I'm a very powerful wolf. Nothing is going to happen to either of us."

She looked down, swallowing the sob that threatened. "But before…when my family came…"

"Knowing what I do now, that is something that won't be repeated. Ever."

Serenity decided to give voice to her thoughts and fears. While tracing a finger down his chest, she said, “I remember running out to check on you after a storm. When I woke up, I saw the limbs that littered the front yard. All I could think about was you. What if something like that happened again?”

She sighed. “I remember when I was ten, running out there with an umbrella and a blanket. I wanted to save you from the cold winter rain. It took me forever to get that umbrella propped up enough so that it wouldn’t fall. Then I covered you with a blanket. When I got home from school, the umbrella was upside down and the blanket was lying half inside the umbrella pond, with the other half in the mud. Let me tell you…my mother’s reaction when she saw—”

Marcus snarled, “Do not speak of your family. What they did to you…it’s taking everything I have to not go after them.”

She locked her arms around his neck and pulled him closer. “Promise me you never will. Whatever you think you could do to them is nothing compared to what they could do to you. Thirty years. Marcus, if you… How could I go on if—”

“My love. To wipe away those tears, to erase that fear, I will give you my vow that I will never.”

With tears rolling down her cheeks, she smiled then whispered, “Make love to me.”

***

Gage was sitting in the kitchen enjoying his morning coffee when he heard a conversation coming from the stairs. When he recognized his sister's voice in the mix, he set his coffee down and waited.

Scarlett stepped into the kitchen. She stumbled a little when she noticed Gage's angry glare directed at her. She decided to play it off. She smiled and said, "Good morning, brother. You're up bright and early." She winced, wishing she could take the words back. Since there wasn't a single day when he hadn't been awake before her, she knew she'd messed up.

Gage arched a brow, crossed his arms, then waited.

Sighing, Scarlett threw her hands up. "Busted."

Gage wanted to be angry. Instead, he only felt joy. Not only was his sister home, but she was back to her old self. He couldn't believe what Serenity had accomplished in only three days. He'd not expected to see her again until winter set in. Yet here she was. Then a thought struck. Had the implications of the seriousness of her offense really sunk in? Or had her normally flippant attitude caused her to downplay what could've happened?

Scarlett watched Gage's shifting expressions. She'd always prided herself on her ability to speak her mind. She didn't believe in playing games. Anyone who knew her, knew where they stood. Because she was quick to tell them. Even though telling him how she felt would leave her vulnerable, she couldn't *not* tell him.

She strode across the kitchen and poured herself a cup of coffee. After sitting a few feet away, she looked her brother in the eye. "I know I don't deserve to be here. I…"

She swallowed a sob, pushed the cup away, then stood. She walked toward the back door but couldn't hold back the sob that worked its way up.

Gage was across the room in an instant. He caught Scarlett just as she collapsed. He carried her into the living room then sat with her on the couch. Gage held her while she wept, then began rocking, and kissed her forehead. He remembered the first time he'd done this. It was just a few hours after learning their parents had died. He'd given her promises of how everything would be all right.

Instead of comforting her, she'd screamed, "It'll never be all right. Nothing will ever be right again." After that, Scarlett kept her heart locked up tight.

A few minutes after they sat down, she scooted off his lap. In a teary laugh, she said, "I'm a little big for that."

He shook his head and put an arm around her shoulder. "Baby girl, you'll never be too big for that."

She leaned her head on his shoulder. "Gage, I can't get the images out of my head, of what could've…"

He leapt off the couch then reached for her. "I have just the thing to cheer you up. Is Jasmine here, too?"

Scarlett allowed herself to be led away, answering, "Yeah. Marcus kicked us out last night."

Gage walked to the bottom of the stairs, then shouted, "Anna, Lena, Jasmine! It's time to wake up."

He led his sister toward his office and walked over to the bank of windows. Opening the slider, he whispered, "Wanna wake up some pups?"

Fifteen minutes later, they were standing on the deck, surrounded by the spelled wolf puppies. The pups, each different, were somewhere between quite young and half grown. However, each had one thing in common—a shared state of terror. He figured that must have been the reasoning behind dumping them in the barn. After all, a bunch of cowed pups wouldn't impress anybody.

Lena and Jasmine were standing by the door watching them. Jasmine couldn't hide the shock and horror brought on by seeing what her people had done to the incredibly young.

Lena shook her head. "I don't think this is such a good idea."

The moment of joviality broken, Gage's grin died. "Why not? What if they're awake enough to know what's going on, and yet unable to tell us what they're feeling?"

Lena sighed then walked to one end of the deck. She looked at her cousins. "You go to different sides and follow my lead. We can try, but I'm sure it would work better…and faster… if Serenity were here."

Gage and Scarlett moved to the edge of the deck. "I don't want to disturb them right now. They're newly mated, and I'm sure they have much better things to do."

He smiled at his sister and nodded. "Begin."

Lena raised her hands, closed her eyes, and started chanting. Following her lead, Jasmine and Anna began. The air around them stilled for a moment before the wind picked up. Gusts blew across the deck. Papers and dead, brown leaves began swirling around the still figures of the wolf pups caught in magic's embrace.

A roar from below stopped them from going any further. Gage, Scarlett, Anna, Lena, and Jasmine ran to the railing. All of them stared down at the wolf charging toward them, then saw another figure not far behind. When the wolf disappeared under the deck, they backed away. As the wolf rounded the last curve, he leapt toward the pups, shifting as he did. After stopping in the middle of the pups, Marcus snarled.

Serenity was right behind him. Panting, with her hands clasped over her heart, breathless, she said, "What…what do you think you're doing? Better yet, what's the matter with you?"

Gage scowled. "We were just going to wake them up."

Throwing her head back, Serenity bellowed, "Just? Just? We were *just* sound asleep when the wave of magic washed over us. Do you have any idea how much magic it takes to awaken so many pups at once?"

She staggered back, realizing that even she didn't know. But she knew it had to be a lot.

Marcus snarled, "If you'd succeeded, what were your plans after that? How were you going to care for fifty wailing children? While you're at it, what are you going to tell them about their parents?"

The sliding glass door was thrown open. Allister, pale and looking both furious and terrified, stepped onto the patio. Glaring at the group, he shouted, "This is just great. After everything we did to keep the Jäger's away, you go and do this."

He waved a hand around the deck. "You might as well have sent them a map with a big red X marking our location."

***

Humming while she worked, Sabine reached for another egg. Before she could add it to the first, a powerful wave of magic washed over her. Gasping, she dropped the egg and stumbled back. The hot skillet was forgotten. Her gaze swung toward the back door.

In the upstairs bathroom, Luka had just lathered his hair when the wave hit him. Frowning, his jaw set, he twisted the knobs and reached for a towel.

He rushed toward his bedroom, grabbed a pair of pants, and began dressing. He was just buttoning his shirt when Sabine appeared in the doorway, turning her wide gaze toward him.

Luka nodded. "That wasn't from just one person. I think we've found the girls. I'll call Paul. But you can call Anton. I'm still mad over the last time we spoke. He's gone soft. But this…this is going to need to be taken care of. You know what those girls can do."

Sabine reached for her phone then turned to leave. She paused in the doorway. "What about the boys?"

Luka shoved a foot into his boot. "They'll have to stay. We can't take the chance that any of them might get sentimental over their sister."

Sabine thought back to all those years ago when her children were still small. A slight twinge of guilt pervaded her thoughts when she remembered Erika's joyful face on Christmas mornings. After presents were handed out, she'd ignored her daughter while watching the boys open their gifts. One year, she hadn't even noticed that Erika left. Dieter, however, was quick to point it out. He'd wanted to know why she hated his sister so much. Angry that he'd question her, she'd told him that if he was so concerned, he could give her his presents. After that, he'd kept his opinion to himself. Now, she wasn't sure if his feelings had changed over the years, but she wasn't willing to take a chance. She turned back to the stairs. "Of course. I'll grab my purse."

Chapter Thirty-Three

After hours of carrying pups from Gage's deck to the forest, they were finally finished. Serenity set the last pup in position, nodded, then waved a hand toward her house. She stepped into the kitchen and waved an exhausted arm toward Gage. "Sorry, I don't have a fancy bar to make drinks. But there's beer in the fridge and I can put on a pot of coffee if anybody wants some."

Fifteen minutes later, everybody had wandered out to the porch. Some sat on the swing, others on the railing, while the rest either leaned against the house or sat on the stoop. Everybody was tired. The dire situation had demanded they act quickly. For Marcus and Serenity, they were just now enjoying their first cup of coffee for the day. She was about to suggest a donut run when Gage spoke up.

"Do you think that'll work?"

Shrugging, Serenity answered, "I have no idea. All I know is the wave of magic from Lena, Jasmine, and Anna woke me out of a sound sleep. I would imagine anybody sensitive to magic would've felt it from miles away. How far…?" Again, she shrugged.

At the trilling, melodic sound of Lena's phone, everybody stopped and turned toward her. She pulled it out of her pocket and stared at her brother's smiling face. She glanced at the group, mumbling, "Sorry."

Aside from Serenity, David was the only person in her family she trusted. At least until she'd met her two new cousins. As always, every call she got from her brother was a delight. She walked out to the yard, then tapped the screen. "Hey, David. What's up?"

David's frantic voice came over the line. "I don't know what happened but Dad just got a call from Aunt Sabine. He said they found you. I didn't know you were missing."

Lena laughed. "I'm not. I just missed my usual call in."

She paused then said, "Wait. What do you mean, they found me? That can only mean they felt the magic that far away. Great—"

David interrupted, "Listen, we're on the way out the door to meet them. But I thought I would let you know that you're about to get a visit from..." His voice cut off for a moment before he continued, "from everybody. Hey, sis, I wanted to warn you that Dad already narrowed down the general area of where you're staying. I don't know what's up with Uncle Luka. When Dad called him, he said Erika was missing as well—"

—"I'm not missing."

"Whatever's going on, it's got to be big. I don't think I've ever seen Dad this upset."

With a fading smile, she glanced back at the group, who were now watching her with interest.

She turned her attention back to the phone. "Thanks for the heads up. How much time do we have?"

David answered, "Not much, maybe four hours."

"Thanks, bro." Ending the call, she shoved her phone into a hip pocket then raced toward the porch.

Marcus met her halfway. "What is it?"

She looked from him to the others. "That was my brother. He said that wave of magic was felt as far away as Washington. He also said they knew exactly what it was. They'd already had a pretty good idea of where to find me." She glanced at Serenity. "And you, as well. But now they have it narrowed down to this section of the mountain. When Aunt Sabine called my dad, she said they were already in the car. So, after they meet, it won't take them long to get here. We might have four hours. Might."

Gage paled. "I did this."

Scarlett laid her head on his shoulder. "It's not your fault. You were just trying to help the babies."

He kissed her head. "Thank you. But you and I both know that's not why I did it."

She laughed, slapped his arm, then said, "Couldn't you have just let me have that one? After all, you don't want everybody thinking you're going soft, do you?"

Lena rolled her eyes. "You didn't do this. Not alone, anyway. Now, regardless of whose fault it is, we need to figure out what we're going to do. I have an idea, but you're not going to like it. The first thing we need to do is take down those wards. When the Dämonejägers get here, it'll be a beacon directing them to the center of town."

Gage argued, "That's why they were put up in the first place, to keep them out."

"And that's exactly why they won't work." Lena turned toward Marcus. "Before the attack, were your wards up?"

Marcus was fighting to stay calm. But he wasn't sure it was a fight he could win. If anyone knew what the Dämonejägers were capable of, it was him. Swallowing a lump, he answered, "We did, and it didn't even slow them down."

Lena waved an arm toward Marcus. "See. The wards are magic. They can feel magic. Because they *are* magic. So, we need to take the wards down."

Gage leaned against the porch railing. "And if we could do that…what then?"

Lena frowned. "What do you mean, if?"

Gage shrugged. "It's never been tried. I can get someone on it, but then what?"

"Simple. Anna and I will drive down the mountain and find a secluded spot to set up camp."

Marcus cocked his head. "And that helps us how, exactly?"

"They know I travel and like being on my own. The second I turned eighteen, I left…"

Serenity snorted a laugh. "Like a year ago."

Glaring at her cousin, she said, "Anyway…I just happened upon someone else with powerful magic. After a huge match off, we settled into spending a few days camping and getting to know each other." She laughed. "Imagine Uncle Paul's shock when he learns he has a daughter. Better yet, imagine Aunt Sophia's surprise."

Serenity said, "I wish I could be there. Hey, can you video it?"

"I think that can be arranged."

She added, "There's more. Nobody. And I mean nobody, can shift until I give the all clear…or until I hear from my brother. That means that the pups need to be taken somewhere else. One screw up—that's all it would take."

Jasmine said, "I'm sure they can go to my pack. It's not very far. Only about half a day's drive. But they'll be safe there. It wouldn't hurt to get to know another pack, anyway. And as for the wards, I can take them down, then put them back when it's safe."

Gage shook his head. "I don't like it. My parents were visiting another pack when they had their accident. As were Marcus's parents."

Allister interjected, "It was pack business, an annual meeting of the alphas. And everybody knew about it. But this is different. Nobody but us will know what's going on. I think it's our best chance. In fact, I think the elderly should go as well. Some of them also have trouble with shifting back and forth. I'll get the school bus. With that and a few SUV's, we should be able to get everybody out. But we need to move quickly."

***

Lena and Anna drove to an isolated area about ten miles away.

Lena pulled off the road. "This should do it."

She parked far enough away from the highway to be hidden from any car that may pass. She got out and asked, "Can you help me with my gear?" She opened the trunk then began pulling everything out that they'd need to convince her family.

Anna stopped by the opened trunk then peered toward the road. "What's the purpose of coming here if we're just going to hide from them."

"We're not hiding from them—we're hiding from everybody else. The last thing we need is for some badge to chase us out. We couldn't hide from our family if we wanted to. As soon as they turn onto this highway, we'll literally be a magic beacon."

Anna put on the pack, grabbed another bag, then followed Lena into the woods. After dropping their gear in a small clearing, she asked, "What if they try to make me go back with them?"

Lena dropped the tent and began setting it up, talking while she worked. "They're not going to try anything. Together, our magic is much more powerful than theirs. Even combined, they couldn't take us."

Anna began gathering firewood and rocks for the pit. "I thought you said that if we used our magic to do harm, we would lose it."

"Given a choice of losing our magic, or losing our lives, which would you prefer?"

"Good point. What are we going to do now?"

Lena crawled inside the tent and began making up their beds. Without looking back, she said, "We need to make our camp look like we've been here for a few days."

Anna looked around. "Um…Lena. We don't have any food."

Lena popped her head out and tossed Anna her keys. "Sorry, it's still in the car. Red cooler in the backseat."

Ten minutes later, Anna set the ice chest down. After a quick glance inside, she sighed then yelled, "You know the ice is almost completely melted. Also, there's not much food in here."

"Go back and grab some of the empty cans out of the back seat."

Anna let the lid fall then stared at Lena.

After tossing a few more pieces of wood into the fire, Lena began gathering small twigs and branches. She returned to the fire, then noticed her cousin was still standing in the same place. Exasperated, she said, "We need to make it look like we've been here for a while. For that, we need trash."

Anna climbed into the car muttering, "Gross."

She found an empty bag and tossed a few cans in, then got another one and began filling it with trash from the back seat. Satisfied she had enough, she headed to the campsite. When she stepped into the clearing, she was surprised to see the flames shooting into the branches of the trees overhead. Whatever Lena had done, worked. The camp looked like they'd been there for a week. All that was missing were the empty cans and food wrappers.

Lena grabbed the bag and dropped a few empty cans beside one of the chairs then tied it to a low hanging branch. She walked over to the cooler, grabbed a cola, and sat by the fire. She waved toward the empty seat. "Pull up a chair, take the load off. We've got time. I don't know how long it'll take them to get here, but we might as well enjoy ourselves while we wait. Maybe even compare magic. Have you mastered levitation yet?"

Beyond nervous, Anna stared at her newfound cousin. "You can't be serious? I didn't even know magic existed before meeting you guys."

Lena leaned forward and allowed her magic to roll from her in waves. The air around them rippled with power. Next, Lena's hair lifted and writhed around her head. The flames flickered, rose, then fell. They dipped so low the pit was left with nothing but glowing embers. Once again, the fire came to life, shooting flames into the heavens even higher than before. Lena rose from her chair then hovered ten feet above the camp. She raised her arms above her head, closed her eyes, and drifted back to her chair.

A few seconds later, Anna found herself flying. Deeper into the forest she sailed. When she looked down, she noticed a doe and her fawn drinking from a small creek. A moment later, she was hovering above the forest. From there, she could see everything.

In the distance, she saw the school bus full of children followed by several cars and SUV's. She looked the other way. Far below the mountains there was a caravan of trucks filled with men carrying shotguns. She also knew the moment they felt her gaze. And then, in a blink of an eye, she was back in her seat.

The flames had died down to something more typical of a campfire. Beside her, Lena was sipping a beer. In her other hand was a stick with a charred hot dog. When she looked at the flames, she realized she, too, was holding a hotdog on a stick. Mouth gaping, she stared at her cousin.

Without looking up, Lena said, "The camp must be filled with our magic so they won't look any further."

Anna looked from her hotdog to her cousin. She was about to ask how she could be in two places at once when Lena reached into a bag beside her chair. After pulling out a bun, she slid her hotdog off the stick, and asked, "So what did you see?"

Anna was unable to do more than stare at her cousin.

Lena sighed then said, "Yes. You never left your chair. It was a simple spell that allowed you to leave your body while it stayed here."

She nodded toward the fire. "Just how burnt do you like your hot dog?"

Lena looked at the black thing on the end of her stick, curled her lip, and tossed stick and all into the fire. "How can you eat that crap?"

Lena shrugged. "I guess you're going to go hungry. That's the only thing I brought…aside from chips and a few granola bars."

Anna found the bag hanging from a branch. She looked inside. "Seriously, this is all you have? Let's hope we don't have to wait too long."

Lena gave Anna an exasperated sigh. "You don't eat granola, either?"

Anna returned empty handed to her chair. "Peanut allergy."

Lena tossed her the keys again, saying, "There's other kinds in the trunk."

A moment later, Anna returned with two unopened boxes and a smile. She sat down and ripped a box open. Then moaning around her first bite, she said, "I love, love, love blueberry."

"Happy to be of service. Now. Again. What did you see?"

After stuffing the last bite into her mouth, Anna held up a finger. Then, washing it down with her cola, she said, "They're not quite to the road leading in, yet."

She leaned closer. "They knew I was there. How did they know I was watching them?"

"I told you. They can feel magic. Just like I could feel your magic when we met."

She studied Anna, then asked, "What did *you* feel when we met?"

Anna was quiet for a moment, staring into the flames. "I didn't know what it was. I knew someone was coming. I just…then when you went into the barn." She shook her head. "I…I don't even know how to explain it."

Twirling her stick, Lena said, "That's what magic feels like. Now that you know, you'll recognize it right away. When they come, you'll feel their magic. But it won't be the same. It'll feel…wrong. It's like something that leaves a bad taste in your mouth. But when they feel our magic…I'm not sure what it feels like to them."

"My brother said it's like a hunger. That's why he left. He told me that growing up, he would sometimes wake up and find Keith, our other brother, standing by his bed. Let me tell you. If there was ever anyone born evil, it was Keith. He started using his magic against other people early on. From the first day of school, he was a bully. Things…" she shuddered, "things started happening to the other kids. After starting a fire…magically, of course…one of the boys in Keith's first grade class walked into it. By the time they got him to the hospital, he was dead. Another boy just vanished. I don't know where he got those spells, but it's..." She leaned closer to Anna. "Did you know that's the only way they can use their magic?"

She sat back then continued, "Anyway. It only got worse. I guess David finally asked what his deal was. Now this part is really creepy. Keith grabbed David's shirt, then burying his head against his throat, he said, *you smell delicious*. That night, as soon as everyone was asleep, he left. After some research, he found out that if you kill someone, you take their magic."

She shook her head. "Can you believe it? I don't know if my parents would've gone that far, but Keith? Yeah. In a heartbeat."

So shocked by what Lena said, Anna couldn't do more than stare at her in disbelief. Finally, she whispered, "Why did I ever go looking for my family?"

Lena winked, then answered, "To meet me, of course. Now I figure we have about an hour before they get here. We need to practice. We need to make sure you've got levitation mastered. I can get one of us out of here, but not both. We can kill them with our magic. But if we can get away without doing it, that's what we should do."

Chapter Thirty-Four

Gage snarled, "It's all I can do not to shift. If ever there was a time that I wanted… needed, to run, this is it."

Marcus laughed. "Maybe you should've gone with the pups and elders since you're having trouble controlling yourself."

Gage glared at Marcus, snarling, "My pack is in danger…sorry. I know there's nothing anyone can do about it. And I'm sorry for taking it out on you." Then he added, "However, going for a run would help relieve some of the tension."

An hour later, nothing had changed aside from Gage's continued pacing. He'd questioned Marcus's ability to stay calm at least half a dozen times.

It wasn't that Marcus was calm. Inside, he was a wreck. It wasn't that he didn't want to burn off some excess energy. Instead, he was frozen where he stood, paralyzed by the fear of history repeating itself.

Marcus walked over to the railing and stared across the horizon. From where he stood, he could see every house. But more importantly, he could see the entrance to Willow Run.

Visions of the streets of Whitebark Stand filled with truckloads of the Dämonejägers returned. From his deck, he couldn't see everything that was happening at the time. But he'd seen enough. Now, he knew more. Including the deaths of several members of his pack.

Chance's message replayed in his mind. *"It's old man Jäger, himself."*

When he felt a hand on his shoulder, he whipped around, ready to attack.

Gage backed away and held his hands up. "Hey. It's okay. I just heard you growling. I wanted to stop you before you did something we'd all be sorry for."

Rolling his shoulders, Marcus relaxed. He glanced once more toward the road. "Sorry. I was just…" Marcus ran a hand through his hair, then asked, "Want to chop some wood?"

Two hours later and sweat-soaked from the exertion, the tension melted into something more manageable. Gage pulled out his phone. "I can't believe we haven't heard anything."

He watched Marcus bring the axe down again, leaving it embedded in a log. After wiping sweat from his brow, Marcus said, "You do know it could be days before they get back, or even call? We're going to have to get our minds off what may or may not happen, or we'll go nuts."

Gage arched a brow. "We?"

Marcus laughed. "Did you really think none of this was bothering me?"

Gage mumbled, "I was beginning to."

Marcus grabbed a bottle of water. After drinking half of it, he dumped the rest over his head.

He shook out his wet hair, scowled and said, "It brings everything…"

He left the words hanging. "Maybe if we keep our minds busy with something else, it'll help. Just go about business as usual. What do you normally do during the day?"

Gage walked away while pulling his shirt over his head. "Let's get a shower then we can go check on the rest of the pack. If we're feeling this way, I'm sure others are as well."

An hour later, Marcus and Gage were standing in front of a house. The door opened before they got there. A young woman stood in the doorway, her eyes wide in terror.

She gasped and flung the door open wider before throwing herself into Gage's arms. Between sobs, she said, "Gage, what are we going to do? What if they come and take me from my babies?"

Gage stared into the darkened interior. "Where's Cooper?"

Diana stepped back, wiping her eyes. "I'm sorry. It's just that…well, since you're the alpha…"

He stepped off from the porch, then backed up a few feet. "Maybe you should go to work? Try to go about your day as usual." He nervously looked around. "So, where did you say Cooper was? Might I suggest a shower?"

Diana laughed. "He went to work. By the time he gets home, your scent will have worn off. But I'll take a shower just to make sure. As for me going to work…"

He'd forgotten she was a teacher. "Sorry."

Then an idea struck. "Diana, how about you go check on the other mothers? I'm sure you can imagine how upset they must be. And who better to do it than their kid's teachers?"

Marcus stepped closer. "I have an idea. How about a picnic?"

When Diana looked from Gage to Marcus, she lowered her head then cowered back.

Gage suddenly realized very few pack members knew anything about Marcus. Upon meeting him, they would know him for the alpha he was, just as he had when *they'd* met. The members of his pack would feel confused or threatened by another alpha. He needed to explain if they were going to keep everyone from panicking. "Diana, this is Marcus. He's visiting from the Whitebark Stand Pack—"

She gasped and stepped further away. She waved her hand around behind her, searching for the doorknob.

Gage swore under his breath. Then he grabbed her wrist before she could run away.

Eyes wide in panic, she stared up at him.

He soothed, "I'm sorry. I guess if anyone would know about Whitebark, you would. Have you met Celeste yet?"

Her free hand fluttered nervously behind her while her gaze pinged between them. Relaxing slightly, she smiled. "She's adorable. I met her when she was at the park with Luke."

Gage nodded. “Celeste and Marcus recently came here with the human.”

Her gaze widened and she tried to pull away again.

Gage tightened his grip, being careful not to bruise. “Now, please just listen to me before you freak out. Can you do that?”

Diana nodded, then looked from him to Marcus and back. Understanding crossed her features. “She’s from Whitebark, too, isn’t she? I mean Celeste.” Her smile fell. With her gaze centered on him, she asked, “Gage what’s happening? Why did the children have to leave? And why did they take our seniors, as well?”

Gage looked away. “I have a feeling this is going to take a while. Can we come in?”

She, nodded, stepped back, and opened the door wider. Then, after giving Marcus a cautious glance, she asked, “Coffee or something stronger?”

Marcus gave her a small smile. “How about coffee with something a little stronger added?”

Thirty minutes later, Marcus and Gage returned to the car with a promise from Diana. She was going to visit the other mothers. First to make sure they were all right but then to plan a picnic for later that afternoon.

While driving toward the main road, Gage said, “I like to check on the local businesses a few times a week. And I haven’t done that since Serenity got here.” He pulled into the diner’s parking lot. “How about some lunch first?”

After stepping through the door, the first thing they noticed was how quickly conversations ceased. Next, was how packed it was. When they were unable to find an empty table, they waited by the door.

Then two chairs were pushed toward them from a table in the center. Looking at the three men, Gage nodded and sat down. "I'd like to introduce Marcus. He's the alpha from another pack and came to talk about doing an exchange."

The youngest of the three, Brian, grinned. "Welcome, Marcus. You have no idea how glad we are to see you. It's been a long time since another pack invited us in."

Gage felt his temper rise when Brian then turned a glare toward him.

Marcus laid a hand on Gage's arm and cleared his throat. "I can understand your alpha's reluctance. Tell me, boys, how are your parents?" He knew what happened to Gage's parents would be common knowledge for every pack member. If ever there was a reason for hesitancy, that certainly qualified.

The three men bowed their heads and didn't say anything else.

Nodding, Marcus continued, "A lot of packs lost their alphas in questionable circumstances. My parents included. Now, I'm sure you don't want to start something you can't finish, so let's just leave that be. What do you say? Maybe a fresh start?"

One of the other men shoved his hand out, then said, "My name's Ryan. My brother sometimes speaks before he thinks. It wouldn't be the first time his mouth got him into trouble." Grinning, he elbowed his brother. "Nor would it be the first time he got in trouble with Gage."

More serious, he said, "He's just giving voice to what some of us are feeling. There are a lot of single men and women here. However, not many that aren't related in some way. As for me…I wouldn't mind meeting a few women, but I don't want to move away. As the oldest, I need to keep my roots planted where they belong. If you know what I mean."

Marcus nodded. "I know exactly what you mean."

The third man looked from Gage to Marcus, then stuck his hand out. "My name's Wayne. I agree, we need to start fresh. How about with the truth?"

Gage hung his head. A moment later, he stood. "Can I have everyone's attention? Diana and some of the other mothers are putting together a picnic at the park around four. I want all of you there. Call your friends and family. I know there are a lot of questions. I'll answer them the best I can, at that time. In the meantime, I'm hungry."

An hour later, they were walking out of the restaurant when Jonas caught up to them. "A picnic, huh? That's not much time to get things together."

Gage leaned against the building. "I told Diana not to go overboard. Just sandwiches and chips will be fine."

Jonas stood still, silently watching the other men a moment. Then narrowing his eyes, he asked, "Are you sure that telling them what's going on is such a good idea?"

Gage winced. "I know it's risky. But, leaving them in the dark is worse. Imagination is a powerful thing. Who knows what they'll come up with if we don't tell them what's really happening? Besides, it's a good way to prepare them in case Lena's plan falls through."

Nervous, Jonas shuffled from foot to foot. "*If* it does fall through. And *if* the Dämonejägers come here...and *if* we do fool them into believing we're not wolves…how do you explain the absence of children? Or grandparents for that matter?"

Gage smiled. "Easy. Field trip. Since the parents are at work, the grandparents volunteered to be chaperones."

He glanced from Gage to Marcus. "Let's just hope their plan works. I don't like the idea of trying to fool them. I already lost two brothers. I don't want to lose my kids, as well."

Narrowing his gaze on Marcus, he asked, "Do you have any idea what happens when they freeze a pregnant woman?"

Gage pushed himself away from the building. "Who's pregnant?"

Jonas crossed his arms. “The girls thought it would be cool to do it together. They told us last night. Emilia and Bethany are both due at the end of May. They’re talking about inducing, so they can have their babies together.” He shook his head, then smiled. “Hey. I’m going to be a grandpa.”

Gage laughed and slapped him on the back. “Congratulations, old man.”

Marcus frowned. “We don’t know what’ll happen. Let’s just pray they don’t come here. Gage, I think it’s time to talk about bringing in the rest of my pack. If they discover the pups are missing, then what will they do to the others?”

Chapter Thirty-Five

They heard the rumble of the approaching trucks before they saw them. Lena looked at Anna. "Don't let them see you sweat. And whatever you do, try to keep your distance." She took out her phone, then walked over to a nearby tree and set it in a place she'd previously chiseled out.

"Why are you doing that?"

Lena grinned. "I promised David and Serenity that I'd video it. Can you imagine finding out like this that your husband was cheating on you? Let me tell you, it couldn't have happened to a nicer couple. In case you missed it, that was sarcasm."

Anna glared at Lena. "That's just great, cuz. Why don't you just throw me under the bus?"

Lena grabbed her arm before she could walk away. "What he did isn't on you. That was just wrong. But if he hadn't done it, you wouldn't be here. And I, for one, am glad you are. You really stepped up when it was time to rescue those babies. And his wife? She's a terrible person. She lost her magic before she was eighteen. So even if they'd had any more children, they would've been born with little to no magic." Then she asked, "Do you know anything about your mother?"

Anna looked down. "Yeah. She had me then died a drug addict. I guess she was a distant relative of yours who was here as an exchange student."

Lena's face paled. She felt like she was going to be sick. She ducked her head to meet Anna's gaze. "Please tell me it was a college exchange."

She shook her head. "She was fifteen when I was born…*just* turned fifteen." While fighting back tears, she continued, "That's all I really know. I'm sure you can imagine how surprised I was when I saw his picture. I was expecting someone much younger." Then, wiping the tears that wouldn't be denied, she said, "Yeah. You're right. He deserves whatever happens."

Lena grabbed her hand then backed away from their camp. A second later, she felt someone coming up from behind and dragged her cousin closer to the fire.

Two men stepped through the trees, both middle aged.

One man, greying, with more than just a little extra around the waist, was the first to speak. "Lena, nice to see you again. You should've stopped by for dinner."

The thinner, balding man, licked his lips and asked, "Who's your friend?" He absently rubbed his hands down his thighs then took a few steps closer.

Anna felt like she was going to be sick. Lena was right about how their magic would make her feel. But worse was the way her own father was looking at her. Heart racing, she realized how stupid the plan to meet her family was.

She heard Lena ask, "Where's Aunt Sofia? I can't imagine she'd let you have all the fun without her."

A woman stepped from the woods behind them, saying, "You're right, Lena. They haven't gone on a hunt without me, yet."

When Anna turned toward the woman, she was surprised at how beautiful she was. She stood just over five feet and had all the curves guaranteed to satisfy any man. Her hair hung past her waist in long brown waves. However, the stench of evil radiating from her nullified everything that could've made her attractive.

Sofia directed a glare on the man who'd asked about Anna, then snarled, "If you know what's good for you, you'll put that tongue back in your mouth."

Lena laughed. "Yeah, especially since she's your daughter."

Paul staggered back a few steps. His gaze shot from Anna to Sofia. Finally landing on Lena, he took a few steps closer and he growled, "Your daddy should have taught you better, little girl."

Not the least bit intimidated, Lena taunted, "Little girl? Is that what you called her mother when you raped her?"

Paul paled then twisted back to face his brother. His gaze swept from one person to the next until finally stopping on Sofia. He stuttered,

"N…now…y…you…j…just w…w…wait a minute. I never—"

Grinding her teeth, an enraged Lena yelled, "She was fifteen when she had Anna. That would have made her…"

Lena swung her gaze toward her new cousin and waited.

Looking at the ground, Anna whispered, "She was fourteen when she got pregnant."

Luka's head twisted toward his younger brother. Never taking his gaze away, he said, "Now, you girls enjoy your camping trip."

He glanced once more at Lena, then added, "You come on by before you go home. We'd like to see you."

Then, knocking his head toward the road, he snarled, "Let's go. We got some family business to take care of."

A minute later, Lena and Anna were left alone. For the first time since arriving, the silent forest around them gave Lena the chills. She ran over to the fire. After kicking the logs away, she dumped the cooler of half melted ice on the hot embers. Without looking up, she said, "Pack up."

Anna watched while Lena frantically gathered everything around them. Then she looked from Lena to the path that led away. "What…"

Without stopping, Lena shrieked, "Move. We need to get out of here. Now."

Ten minutes later, they were driving down the mountain. Then Lena pulled into a bar just off the highway and shut the car off. Loud country music drifted from inside. Every now and then, the door opened, spilling someone out.

Anna watched Lena walk all the way to the door before the woman realized she was alone. Stalking back to the car, she knelt beside Anna's open door. "What are you doing?"

Arms crossed; Anna glared at Lena. Tilting her head, she said, "That's what I'd like to know?"

"I really, really need a drink. Something a lot stronger than beer."

Anna scoffed, "And what am I supposed to do while you have your *something stronger than beer*?"

"Well, you could come in and have one with me."

Anna threw her head back and laughed. "I'm seventeen. And while we're having this little discussion, do you mind telling me where we're going? Oh, and why we're not going back to Willow Run?"

Getting in the car, Lena squealed out of the parking lot. After driving for an hour in silence, she got off the interstate and turned around. Thirty minutes into their drive, they passed a line of pickups driving in the opposite direction. Lena breathed a sigh of relief then sped up.

After they began their climb into the mountains, Anna said. "Please, Lena. Tell me what's going on."

"We'll talk about it when we get back to Willow Run. Serenity's going to want to know what happened. And I'll need that much time to wrap my brain around it…Oh…My phone. I left it in that tree."

An hour later they were back at the camp they'd just left. While leaving the motor running, Lena cautioned, "Don't get out. I'll be right back."

Anna watched her run toward the tree on the other side of the clearing. After Lena picked up her phone, Anna watched in horror as her cousin collapsed. Without thinking about it, Anna leapt out and ran to her. Then dropping to the ground beside her, she put an arm around Lena's shoulders and waited.

After a few minutes and a lot of tears, Lena stood then silently strode back to the car. While driving out of the forest, she said, "We'll be there in fifteen. Please don't ask me to explain anything until I'm ready." Lena shook her head. "I don't know how I'll ever be ready for something like this."

Their drive home was in silence. The only sound was that of the wind coming through the opened windows and the hum of tires rolling over the blacktop. The darkened houses and empty streets only added to the somber mood inside the car. A few minutes later, they pulled into Gage's driveway. Neither spoke as they listened to the ticking engine while it cooled. For five long minutes they sat in silence. Anna watched while Lena, unmoving, continued to stare straight ahead.

Gage stood in the living room watching the front door. He'd heard the car pull up. He knew they should've been at the door by now. When he was unable to wait any longer, he walked down the long winding path toward the driveway. Instead of coming in, they were sitting in the car. Stepping closer, he stopped to stare inside, wondering what was going on.

When Anna noticed the movement in front of the car, she looked from Lena to the dark figure. While looking at him, nerves got the better of her. The whole scenario took a humorous turn. The longer she watched, the funnier it seemed. A grin formed as she imagined him waiting for them to release the hood so he could check the oil.

She was brought back to reality when the glowing silver eyes turned toward her. While maintaining eye contact, she knocked her head toward her cousin, who still hadn't moved. Then opening her own door, she climbed out. After closing the door with a quiet snick, she left them alone.

Gage stared at this woman. A woman who'd come to Willow Run such a short time ago. Her only intention was finding and saving her cousin. But Lena had changed his life in ways he wasn't sure he would ever understand. There was one thing he knew for sure, though. He wanted to learn everything there was about her. And he knew he wanted to keep her in his life… Forever. Now, he just had to figure out how to get her to agree to it.

He walked around the car to the closed door. Peering inside, he hesitated a moment. Then opening the door, he knelt beside her and took her hand. "Lena. What is it? Tell me what has you so upset. Please."

Watery blue eyes turned toward him. Trails of tears coursed down sooty cheeks. When her gaze finally focused on him, she crumbled into his arms. Burying her face in his neck, she sobbed.

Gage lifted her out of the seat and climbed the long winding stairs to the deck, all the while, whispering soothing words into her silky blonde hair. Then walking across the wooden planks, he settled onto a chaise lounge with her still in his arms. He brushed her hair away and turned her face toward him. While holding her chin, he kissed the side of her mouth then whispered, "Tell me. Whatever it is. Please."

Jerking her chin away, she wiped her tears, leaving behind long dark smudges.

Gage smiled and decided that was very much a part of this strong woman he could very easily fall in love with. Then he was stunned by the realization that he'd already fallen hopelessly in love with her. He leaned back. "Tell me what happened." When Lena tried to scoot off his lap, he tightened his grip, holding her in place.

Forgetting everything that had happened up to this point, Lena focused a glare on Gage. When she realized that he wasn't going to release her, she crossed her arms and stared at the house.

Then Gage noticed her attention was focused beyond the windows. Everybody had stopped whatever they were doing and were now watching them. Growling his displeasure, he set Lena on the chair and stalked toward his office. He jerked the door open, ready to lay into the curious group. Instead, Lena ducked under his arm and walked over to pull Serenity into her arms.

Lena's fingers curled into Serenity's thin blouse, gripping it tightly. Her shoulders shook with the force of her sobs while she kept repeating, "I didn't mean to. I didn't mean to. I didn't mean to." Pulling away, she stared into Serenity's eyes and begged, "Please believe me."

Serenity patted her back. "Whatever it is, I'm sure it'll be okay."

Turning away, Lena ran to Anna. "I'm so sorry." She shook her head, then whispered, "So, so, sorry. I didn't mean to tell them. Not all of them. It's—"

A look of stunned surprise passed over her face. Looking down, she grabbed her vibrating pocket. Her wide-eyed gaze swept through the crowd. A moment of sheer panic came over her. Yanking her phone out, she stared at David's smiling face. She blinked down at his name, knowing he wouldn't be smiling now. After sinking into a nearby chair, she squeaked, "David?"

***

Luka shoved Paul toward the trucks. He jerked open the passenger door then pushed him inside.

Before he could close the door, the handle was jerked out of Paul's hand by Jon, a distant cousin. The large man pushed Paul over, climbing in to sit beside him.

Luka drove away. The silence dragged on for several miles. Then, he glanced at Jon and said, "Call Anton."

Paul stammered, "Luka…you got to believe me. I…I…never knew. I mean…she looked older." He pleaded, "How was I to know?"

Looking past Paul, Luka asked, "Jon, how old do you think that girl is?"

Jon swept his gaze from the passing scenery to Luka. "Best guess? Sixteen, seventeen at the most."

Luka nodded and gripped the steering wheel tighter. Narrowing his gaze, he looked at the other man again. "Tell me again, how old is your daughter?"

Jon glared at Paul. "Fourteen, Luka. She *just* turned fourteen."

***

After taking a moment to find his composure, Gage looked from Lena to Anna. "I think it's time for someone to tell us what happened."

He squeezed Lena's shoulder, then asked, "Anna, do you want to start until Lena can calm down a bit?"

Anna looked around the room. "I have no idea what upset her. We were sitting around the campfire practicing magic. Then suddenly, we were surrounded by people. She told them about my mom and they left. After we drove around for a few hours, she took us back to the place we were camping because she forgot her phone. And that's when she started crying. Before that she was just kind of freaking out…Like a lot."

Gage walked over to the bar and poured Lena a shot of brandy.

Lena tipped the glass and downed the entire shot. Then, pushing the glass across the bar, she said, "More." She turned her stool to face the others, making it a point not to look at Serenity. "After I told Uncle Paul that Anna was his daughter, he made some kind of remark about my upbringing. But it was the last thing he said that got to me. He referred to me as *little girl*. I guess it upset me enough that I said a few things I shouldn't have."

Gasping, Serenity took a few steps closer. She ducked her head, forcing Lena to look at her. "What did you do, Lena?"

Lena winced at her accusatory tone. "I'm sorry. I wasn't thinking. I was just upset. Really, really, upset."

Serenity turned to face Anna and asked, "How old was your mother when she got pregnant?"

She looked down, suddenly finding something on the floor very interesting. "Fourteen."

Throwing her hands up, Serenity paced toward the dark windows that overlooked Willow Run. She found herself half laughing and half crying. Then turning back to the group, she explained. “The Dämonejägers take care of their own. Someone who commits a minor offence might be laid up for a few days…or weeks, depending on how bad it was. They have a tendency sometimes to go a bit overboard. But for the big stuff? Like raping a child?” She shook her head, gazed up at the ceiling, and took a few deep breaths. Then biting her lip, she turned her tear-filled gaze back to the others. While sucking back a sob, she continued, “They just vanish.”

Stepping forward, Marcus gripped her arms. “What do you mean, they just vanish?”

Unable to speak for a moment, Serenity gave up fighting the tears. On a sob, she said, “It’s going to fall on my father’s shoulders to deliver justice.”

Unable to go on, she turned her head away. Wiping the tears, she sniffled then looked back. “My father will have to kill his little brother.”

Chapter Thirty-Six

Luka pulled into his driveway and waited until everybody got out. Then he walked over to the white pickup driven by Sabine and pulled the passenger door open. When he reached inside, Sophia batted his hands away.

She scooted out, growling, "Just don't. I don't need for you to coddle me. I'm so mad right now…I could just spit."

Sabine walked up to her, chuckled, and said, "You know—"

Sophia waggled a finger in her sister-in-law's face. "Just keep your trap shut." She looked at Luka. "Should I call the boys to come help me get him home?"

He gave her a pitying look, shook his head and said, "I'm sorry, Soph."

Sophia stumbled back. She looked from Luka to Sabine then swept her gaze over the half dozen big men waiting by their trucks. That's when she noticed nobody would look at her. She shook her head, then collapsed, sobbing, "No. No, Luka…He…"

Sabine helped her up and led her toward the house, leaving the men to their business.

Jon walked over to Luka. "Anton said he'd be here. He's not happy, but he agrees. Something like this needs to be dealt with."

Luka looked away and fought the swirling emotions raging through him. It was his brother. He knew what he had to do. But that didn't make it any easier.

Finally, after he regained his composure, he said, "We need to send a message to everyone that something like this will never be tolerated." He shook his head, mumbling, "I just wish…"

Then turned and walked toward the forest.

***

After leaving the meeting, Marcus and Serenity strolled back to her house. While holding her hand, he said, "I think it's really important for me to go check on my pack. I also believe we need to seriously think about waking them up."

"I agree. After learning what happened with Lena and Anna, I don't want to take any chances. I think the time has come for us to do something. It's time to bring them home. I couldn't live with the guilt if anything happened to Chance. Not to mention all the others. But especially Chance. I can't explain what it is, but there's something about him that speaks to my heart. Maybe it's because from my earliest childhood memories, it was him who called me to save all of you."

Marcus knew he shouldn't be jealous over Serenity's feelings toward his beta. It was because of Chance's calling to her that they were brought together in the first place. He looked down at Serenity then wondered if he had anything to fear once Chance was awakened. Could she be in love with Chance? He decided the best thing to do was ask her how she felt. He also knew humans didn't feel the mating bond as strongly as shifters. But if she told him Chance was her mate he'd step down. It would break his heart, but the most important thing for him was her happiness. Suppressing a growl, he asked, "Is Chance your mate?"

Serenity laughed. "Why would you think that?"

Marcus sighed. "You did say there was something about him that spoke to your heart. When you say something like that, I think it's only natural for me to think you love him."

Serenity suddenly stopped walking to center her gaze on him.

His heart melted. He knew he could gaze into those beautiful, blue eyes for an eternity. Stepping closer, he leaned into her. More than anything, he needed to taste her lips. That is, until what she was saying sank in.

"Of course, I love him. But—"

Marcus felt like he'd been sucker punched. He jerked his hand away and staggered back. He needed to get away. Away from here. And away from Serenity. Now. Turning toward the forest, he ran. This time, there was no suppressing the anger he felt building inside. Hadn't he just told himself that if she loved Chance, he would step down? He knew, no matter how much he cared for his friend, if Chance was there, he would tear his throat out. Such was the pull of a mate. Unable to live without the one who completed his soul, he knew there was only one thing to do. When a wolf lost his mate, a piece of them died inside. The emptiness lingered and increased every day until nothing was left. He'd never fully understood the enormity of it, until now.

Serenity was left standing alone under the moonlight. Twisting around, she stared at Marcus's departing figure. She'd waited for him her entire life and she wasn't about to lose him now. She ran to catch up then reached for him. Interlocking their fingers, she gave a swift jerk. While gazing into his glowing black eyes, she immediately understood what he was feeling. More than anything, Marcus was afraid. Afraid of losing her to a man he loved like a brother.

She stood on her toes, kissed the corner of his mouth, then whispered, "I also love my cousin. And of course, Celeste. And chocolate, brownies, donuts, oh and…"

She laughed. "Marcus, of course Chance is close to my heart. But you...Marcus, *you* own my heart."

Marcus stared into Serenity's big blue eyes and wondered at what an incredible gift she was. Kissing her deeply, he lifted her into his arms then turned toward the house. He carried her into the bedroom and laid her on the bed. Then, kneeling beside her, he said, "You are my mate. I love you more than anything. I have loved you since that first day, the day you awakened me. And I will continue to love you until the end of time."

***

Lena stood on the deck, staring into the night sky. The same stars that now twinkled above her were also hanging over a forest two-hundred miles away. But she knew the men standing in the woods couldn't see them through the thick canopy of trees. Still, she knew they were there. And stars were the last thing on their minds.

While staring into the night sky, she wondered. Would her uncle's death be swift? If she knew her family at all, she also knew the answer. And it wasn't a pleasant thought.

Gage stood in his dark office watching Lena. He tried to imagine what she was going through. However, no matter how much he tried, he just couldn't get past the whole killing your family thing. It was true. What he'd done was horrendous. There was no doubt. But he also wondered what had gone wrong in this man's life to have created such a monster in the first place. Whatever the reason, he knew there was no going back from something like this. He also knew the only thing he could do was offer comfort to this beautiful woman. A woman who was suffering so much over something she'd had nothing to do with. Even though she blamed herself, he knew the fault fell solely on the man. Now, if only he could convince her of that.

He walked outside then stopped beside her and gazed at the clear night sky. Putting his elbows on the banister, with one foot on the bottom rail, he waited for her to speak.

Lena could feel him watching her before he came out. And when he did, her body stiffened. What must he think? Of her. Of her family. Did he think of her as much of a monster as her uncle? Or was he shocked at the violence one man could bring against his own brother? A single tear trickled down her cheek. Lena had been sure there weren't any more tears left since she'd already cried for hours. She felt sick. And not just from crying.

Lena murmured, "I don't understand. How…how can…"

Unable to continue, she shook her head and stayed quiet.

"How can a man do such a thing…to a child? How can a man kill someone he loves?" He turned to Lena and pulled her into his arms. He could feel her shoulders shaking and heard the quiet sobs. He was the alpha. The leader of a large pack of wolves. Almost nothing frightened him. He'd always prided himself on his ability to protect those he cared about. But this?

He'd never felt so helpless. If he could take her pain, he would. But he also knew that the only thing he could do, he was already doing. Kissing the top of her head, he said, "You do know that none of this is your fault. Right?"

He felt her pulling away. She walked to the other side of the deck. Spinning around, she crossed her arms, nodded, and said, "It is my fault. I didn't have to say anything. I could have kept my mouth shut. I should never have mentioned the age of Anna's mother. I should—"

In three long strides, Gage had Lena in his arms again. "No. None of it. Not one single thing. It wasn't your fault that man raped a little girl. Neither is anything else your family did. They made their own choices. You stood up for someone who wasn't around to defend themselves. You stood up for Anna. She's also just a child. And don't forget, she may not be his only victim. Not to mention those he has yet to hurt."

"You're right of course. But they can't take the law into their own hands. They should've left it for the police. Let them take care of him."

Tilting his head, Marcus thought about everything he'd learned since the first day Serenity showed up. "Let me ask you how that would work? You're no more human than I am. Do you really think there's a prison that could hold a man with the kind of power he has?"

Lena was quiet a moment. "I hadn't thought of it that way. I…"

She sighed then murmured, "I guess you're right." Staring up at him, she said, "But there's something I need to know."

Smiling, Gage kissed her forehead and said, "Anything."

Lena was afraid of what his answer would be, but she had to know. After taking a deep breath, she asked, "Do you…"

She tried to pull her face away. But Gage wasn't about to release her.

She sighed, then asked, "Do you hate me now?"

Of all the things Lena could have said, he'd never expected that. Leaning closer, he whispered, "I could never hate you. As a matter of fact, I may well be very much in love with you."

***

Jasmine was sitting at the bar where she and Allister had been enjoying a few beers.

Allister asked, "So…what do you think of your family, now?"

Smiling, Jasmine shrugged and said, "Nobody's family is perfect. Besides…."

She looked through the window at the couple who should've already found someplace more private. Then turning to Allister, she asked, "Are they going to…?"

Chuckling, he said, "I'm sure they are."

While trying not to look outside, she started fiddling with the label on her beer bottle. She tried to focus her attention on the single corner she'd managed to pry up. She frowned then asked, "Do you think maybe…we should go somewhere else?"

Alister walked around the bar then pulled the empty bottle out of her hands. When she looked up, he winked and said, "Only if we value our lives."

He knocked his head toward the hallway and asked, "How about a midnight snack."

"It's not midnight."

He pulled his phone out then corrected, "Well, how about a ten pm snack? I think there's blueberry pie in the fridge and ice cream in the freezer."

Pulling the door shut behind her, she said, "Throw in some coffee and you're on."

Chapter Thirty-Seven

Propped on an elbow, Serenity laid on her side watching Marcus sleep. The swaying trees cast dancing shadows across his face with occasional speckles of early morning sun. Long strands of black hair were curled around his neck while the rest fanned across the pillow. She scooted closer, admiring his long eyelashes. She loved watching him sleep almost as much as she loved gazing into his smokey grey eyes. The dark shadow of a beard on his normally clean-shaven face was a testament of everything that'd happened in a very short time. It was hard to believe she'd been here for just over a week. For her, it felt like a lifetime.

Marcus's body stiffened before his nostrils flared. With his eyes closed, his lips curled into a small grin before he asked, "How long have you been watching me sleep?"

Serenity's breath caught when he opened his eyes. "You're so beautiful."

Marcus laughed. "Beautiful, huh?"

He took in her delicate features. From her bright blue eyes, upturned nose, and bow shaped lips to the golden curls that hung in rings around her head. Then lifting his hand, he watched a blonde lock curl around one of his fingers.

Marcus pushed her back. with his elbows on the bed, he looked at her slightly parted lips and got closer. Under heavy lidded eyes, he whispered, "My mate. You are the one who is beautiful."

When Marcus kissed her, Serenity was lost to everything but him. She was shocked a moment later when he leapt off the bed.

Struck speechless, she watched him walk out of the room. She heard the shower come on a moment later. Throwing the covers off, she mumbled, "You're not getting away that easy, buddy."

When Serenity stepped into the kitchen thirty minutes later, Marcus was sitting at the table sipping a cup of coffee. And in front of him was a box of stale donuts. Grabbing a mug, she poured herself a cup and sat down. Then looking from his sugar-coated lips to the box, she asked, "How can you eat those?" To prove her point, she grabbed one glazed donut and knocked it against the table.

Marcus pulled the last donut from her hands. He walked over to the counter, calling over his shoulder, "Easy. Just put them in this magnificent box for a few seconds and they're as good as new." After pulling the now soft pastry from the microwave, he frowned, then added, "But I don't suggest doing it for more than a few seconds."

"So what was the big hurry this morning? I thought we were going to—"

Stuffing the last of his donut in his mouth, he bopped her on the nose with a sticky finger. Grinning, he said, "And we did. However, I'm always up to it if you want to go again. As for why I was in such a hurry…we need to talk to Gage and start planning our next move."

The discussion from last night came back, bringing with it a harsh reality. She knew she'd have to go back there. Back to the home she'd run away from. To the family she now knew wasn't above killing the ones they were supposed to protect. In her mind, she pictured a mound of dirt in the middle of the forest. Along with that, her own rotting corpse. Buried and forgotten.

Serenity's hand went lax, spilling her coffee down the front of her shirt. The second the hot brew met her skin, she sprang out of her seat.

Marcus was there in an instant with a cold towel, dabbing at the mess.

Frowning, he asked, "Are you okay? I thought this was what you wanted."

He looked away, shook his head, and added, "You do realize that every minute we delay puts my pack in danger."

She pulled the towel from him then tossed it toward the sink. And missed. Next, she pulled her shirt over her head. She walked over, dropped it in the sink, and added the towel from the floor. Then she began filling the sink with cold water. She looked down and frowned at her favorite white lacy bra. A moment later, bare from the waist up, she walked out of the kitchen.

After stepping into the living room, she let out a startled yelp. Luke was standing on her porch with his hand poised to knock. His gaze went from her to an enraged Marcus. Averting his eyes, he backed away from the house, mumbling his apologies.

Before Marcus could take more than two steps, Serenity blocked his path. Gripping his arms, she bobbed her head back and forth. While blocking his view, she said, "It's not his fault. I shouldn't have been walking around half naked."

Marcus glared over her head, snarling, "I saw the way he was looking at you. I need to—"

Standing on her toes, she weaved back and forth until he finally looked at her. She cupped his face. "You don't need to do anything. I forgot he asked me to pick up Celeste from daycare this afternoon. He was probably coming over to make sure I didn't forget."

Marcus spun toward the kitchen. Then Serenity heard the back door slam. And she had a feeling it would be hours before he was cooled off enough to talk.

***

Awed, Gage rolled over and kissed Lena. He smiled, thinking about the night before. A mate. He had a mate. How did he get so lucky? She was everything he'd ever wanted in a mate, and more. Including her spunk. No. Especially her spunk.

She didn't put up with anything. She was exactly what an alpha needed. She'd never let him intimidate her. She was her own woman. And she wasn't afraid to put anyone in their place, including him. But more importantly, she always put others first. She cared. Plus, she was fiercely loyal. Those she cared about knew exactly how she felt. And he knew she would do everything in her power to protect the ones she considered family. And his pack had now become a part of the family she held so dear.

Sleepy blue eyes opened to stare up at him. Smiling, Lena murmured, "Good morning."

"I have an idea."

Wiggling beneath him, she said, "I see that."

Before he could say anything more, his phone rang. He groaned. "Ah, the privilege of being the alpha." Picking up his phone, he snarled, "This had better be important."

Luke's frantic shout was loud enough Gage didn't need the phone to hear it.

"Gage. I messed up, man."

Gage growled and leapt off the bed. An instant later, he was standing on the deck staring down at his beta's house. He could hear Luke pacing while he struggled to put into words what had him so upset. This was his beta. His second in command. Aside from Gage, Luke was the most powerful wolf in the pack. His pack… "What happened?"

"It's Marcus. I think—"

Enraged, Gage threw his phone. His body shimmered a second before a dark grey wolf ran toward the stairs.

Dressed in coffee free clothes, Serenity was standing at the stove frying eggs when her phone rang. She pulled it out of her back pocket and stared at the smiling faces of Luke and Celeste.

It was easy now to see the family resemblance. She couldn't imagine growing up thinking your entire family was dead. But his joy of finding his sister alive…It was something she'd seen every day since they were reunited.

At first, she'd selfishly wanted to keep Celeste. Unlike Luke, she'd grown up with the little pup. And even though all she'd done was sit beside her, she was still very much a part of Serenity's life. When she was a young girl, she used to take her toys down to the forest and pretend they were playing together. She'd even dressed Celeste in some of the grownup princess gowns that she'd stolen from the attic.

But now she realized that Celeste belonged with her family. And Serenity never regretted putting them back together.

After the ringing stopped, she realized she'd gotten caught up in the daydreams of the only part of a happy childhood she could remember. A few seconds later, her phone dinged. Pressing a button, she heard Luke's voice.

"Serenity…I don't know what to say. I'm really, really, sorry. I hope you can find it in your heart to forgive me. I just keep messing up when it comes to you. I honestly don't mean to. Well, at first—"

His message cut off.

Laughing at Luke's nervous rambling, she called him back.

He answered before the first ring ended. "Serenity?"

She walked over to the door and stared across the street. In the window, she could see Luke watching her. Sighing, she said, "I'm making breakfast—"

The line went dead. And Luke was gone from the window. Hurt by the call cut short, she fought against impending tears. She'd finally found a home here. And people who cared about her. She might even venture to say some of them loved her. Now, because of one tiny incident, it was over. She knew Luke was Gage's second. His beta. Would they ask her to leave? She returned to the stove and stared down at the three plates of bacon and eggs. She picked up one then turned toward the table.

When she saw someone standing in the kitchen, she yelped in surprise, nearly dropping her breakfast.

Luke reached for the plate then looked behind her and asked, "Is one of those for me?"

Serenity scowled and grabbed her plate then sat and facing the back door.

When Luke noticed where she was looking, he froze. Sweat poured down his back. He slowly turned his head, expecting to see Marcus standing there. After finding the door empty, he nervously laughed. He strode over to the table. "He's going to kill me. Isn't he?"

Serenity's head twisted toward her neighbor then back to the yard. After a minute, she mumbled, "I honestly don't know."

Turning back to Luke, she screamed when she saw an enraged Gage standing there. His silver eyes glowed. His curled fingers ended in sharp, deadly claws. Serenity's heart nearly pounded out of her chest. She knew if he wanted her dead, there wasn't a single thing she could do to stop it.

Then she felt a moment of déjà vu when the back door exploded inward. Marcus's dark wolf landed in the kitchen. His obsidian eyes were glowing a midnight black. His lips, pulled back, revealed deadly canines. Crouching, poised for attack, he leapt toward Gage.

Serenity screamed.

Chapter Thirty-Eight

Serenity was confused. What she saw, she knew couldn't be. Yet there it was. She stood from the table and walked closer. Luke's fork was frozen, poised in front of his mouth. A string of yellow egg yolk hung suspended from his fork. She waved a hand in front of his face. He didn't blink, much less move.

Looking past Luke, she noticed Gage's wild-eyed expression. His hair was frozen in place. A few long, black strands were blocking his silver eyes, while still others hung in the air around his face.

Shaking her head, she turned to face the man…the wolf, who'd claimed her as a mate. Mouth gaping, she stepped closer. Amazed at what she saw, she whispered, "How…"

Behind him, shards of her ruined door hung in the air, while others were scattered across the back yard. His wolf though…his wolf hovered several feet above the floor.

"I knew something was up when I saw Gage fly out of the bedroom."

Spinning around, she saw her cousin walking into the room. After slapping a hand across the back of Gage's head, Lena strolled over and stared at Marcus.

Serenity's gaze pinged between the three men…she shook her head then looked at her cousin. Deep in thought, Serenity picked up her cup and brought it to her lips. Then, pulling it away, she frowned at the dark brew. She then turned the full cup upside down. While shaking it, she said, "Lena?"

Lena laughed, walked over and took the cup from Serenity. After waving a hand over the top, she gave it back.

Serenity gaped at the steaming cup for a moment before setting it down. Then waved her arm, encompassing everything in the room. She crossed her arms and asked, "Want to explain?"

Lena bent over, giggled, then pulled the bite of egg off Luke's fork. Then she moved the fork toward his chin. "Now, *that* is going to be hilarious."

Lena walked over to the counter and waved a hand over one of the plates. After taking Marcus's breakfast to the table, she waved her fork around "This…"

With a piece of bacon in her hand, she stabbed her fork toward the plate. After taking a bite of the crispy bacon, she smiled at her cousin and said, "Exactly the way I like it. Thanks."

"Yeah, you're welcome to eat Marcus's breakfast if you want."

Lena set her fork down. "Trust me, he's not hungry. If he is, some little bunny, somewhere—"

Serenity held a hand up. "Nope. Don't even go there. Now." She waved her hand between the three men. "What, pray tell…is this?"

Lena kept eating. With a mouthful of bacon and eggs, she said, "This is me preventing our mates from killing each other."

"You…" Serenity looked from Gage to Marcus. "You did…" She shut her mouth, opened it, snapped it shut again. "You can do something like this?" She stared at her own hands as if they'd suddenly turned into serpents. Gawking at her cousin, she squeaked, "Can I do this?"

Lena laughed and said, "In time, I'm sure. You're just now starting to understand your magic. I've been using it for a long time." She shook her head. "Man, I still can't believe they kept that from you all those years."

Resuming her seat, Serenity stared down at her plate. She waved a hand over her breakfast. When nothing happened, she tried again. Finally, she turned a glare on her cousin.

After Lena flicked a hand toward Serenity's plate, the smell of fried bacon and eggs filled the kitchen.

When Lena began eating again, she said, "But you really shouldn't."

Serenity paused with a forkful of eggs halfway to her mouth. "What do you mean?"

Lena set her fork down to explain. "Every time you use your magic for harm, you lose a little."

Serenity looked from Gage to Marcus. "I don't think this was for harm. You were protecting…well, you were protecting all of us. Not to mention my newly renovated house."

It doesn't matter. Magic doesn't differentiate. You can do anything with yourself. You can soar above the trees. You can…" Looking around, she said, "Oh…curl your own hair, or straighten it if that's your choice. You can even heal certain illnesses and minor injuries. But this…" She sighed. "This is messing with another person." Shrugging, she added, "Or wolf. If your magic interferes with another, nature doesn't like it. Regardless of why you did it."

Lena pushed her empty plate away. "Now help me separate these two alphas."

Marcus suddenly found himself standing, waist deep in the river. He shifted from wolf to man. Then he stared down at the muddy, sopping wet jeans he'd put on not even an hour ago. At least he thought it was an hour ago.

He stepped onto the bank and wiggled his toes inside mud filled sneakers. Then after looking around, he realized he had no idea where he was. A second ago, he'd been standing in the kitchen ready to attack a male who'd threatened his mate. Now he was in a forest, standing beside a river, completely alone.

Alone. Panic raced through him. His mate. Where was Serenity?

A sound coming from across the river had him spinning around. Gage was standing on the opposite bank staring at him. While cupping his mouth, Gage yelled, “Do you have any idea what happened?”

Marcus frowned at his clothes and muddy shoes. He shrugged, then stepped back into the water. He was able to wade in about ten feet before he was forced to swim. After reaching the other side, he clasped Gage’s outstretched hand. He pulled his shirt off, wrang out as much water as he could, then threw it over his shoulder. After looking around, he said, “Better yet. Do you know where we are?”

Gage nodded toward the path leading away from the river. He walked over to his friend. “My house is about a mile and a half from here.” He looked at Marcus. “Any idea how we got here?”

Marcus shook his head. “I’ll just be glad to get out of these wet shoes.”

Laughing, Gage said, “I know right? Is there anything worse than walking in wet shoes?”

They continued down the path for a few minutes before Marcus said, “The last thing I remember was the scent of fear radiating from my mate.”

Gage nodded. “I remember Luke saying something about…”

He cocked his head then squinted at Marcus. After a moment, he continued, "You know…I have no idea what he was going to say. I was still in bed when he called. All I heard was, I messed up." He gave Marcus a sidelong glance. "Then he said your name."

Stopping, Marcus suddenly remembered what happened. Rage blinded him for another moment. He snarled, prepared to run back to his mate. Before taking a single step, Gage blocked his way.

With his nails digging into Marcus's shoulders, Gage said, "Wait. I'm willing to bet my mate had something to do with what happened to us."

Relaxing, Marcus grinned. "Your mate, huh?"

Gage thought about the night before and waking to Lena in his arms. Resuming his trek, he grinned and said, "Yes. I knew she was my mate the moment I saw her. But as they say, she doesn't suffer a fool. That fool being me, of course. After Luke called, I left her in bed alone. She had to know something was going on. So…again, what happened."

Marcus gave an exasperated sigh. "Looking back on it now, I'm sure it was an accident. After Serenity spilled coffee on her shirt, she tossed everything into the sink. I mean *everything.*"

Understanding dawned on Gage. "He saw her."

Marcus nodded. "I was out of my mind. I guess I overreacted a bit."

"No. I don't think you overreacted. I would've done the same. I think that's why Luke said he messed up. It's in our nature to protect our bond, as well as our mates."

When his house came into view, he asked, "You're okay now, right?"

"Yes. Your beta has nothing to fear from me."

In the distance, the Jäger women could be seen sitting on the deck watching them.

Marcus looked at Gage. "We need to talk. Serenity and I were getting ready to come over when everything happened."

***

Luke laughed, then looking at Scarlett, he said, "Imagine my surprise when I shoved the empty fork into my cheek." When Serenity and Lena laughed, Luke smiled. With a twinkle in his eyes, he continued, "But that wasn't all. When I saw my plate, I nearly vomited. I think they must've taken every single piece of leftover food and condiment out of the fridge and dumped it on my plate. Not only did it look nasty…" He cringed, then said, "But the smell…"

Serenity chuckled. "That's what you get for not telling me you called Gage."

"Yeah… about that—"

Luke's chair was suddenly jerked backward. Surprised, Luke's arms flailed around, which sent his drink sailing across the deck. His wide-eyed terror was followed by a very unmanly scream. His arms and legs flailed around before he realized he wasn't falling.

Marcus stepped from behind him and held out a hand.

Luke looked from the proffered hand to the man who'd wanted to kill him not even an hour earlier. He stood, grabbed his hand, then said, "Thank you for not killing me."

"It was a mistake." Marcus glanced at Lena. "Now that I've calmed down, I can see that."

Serenity spoke up. "Since we're all here, there's something we need to talk about. And for what I have planned, I might need the help of all my cousins. My *female* cousins, that is."

When she looked around, Serenity knew most of the people would be against her. But she also knew she could at least count on Lena. Maybe even Allister. After all, they'd put themselves at risk only a few days ago. All they were supposed to do was check on the wolves. Instead, they'd brought all the pups from the barn back with them.

She sucked in a deep breath. "Marcus believes it's time to bring his pack home. And I agree. If my family discovers the pups are missing, who knows how they'll react. I don't even know if they have—"

Lena spoke up, "I would've heard if they had. My dad has no idea that David is acting against him. My dad and my uncles may have their differences, but they're still blood. For something like this…something this big…" She looked down and mumbled, "I mean, Uncle Paul."

After taking a deep breath, she continued, "It would be an all hands on deck thing. The wolves, I mean. Not only would they call in my dad and my brothers, but they'd also call in every relative on the west coast. That would give us at least a few days' notice. Plus, they'd have to move them. There's no way they could fire off that many guns on my grandfather's property…" She looked at Serenity and amended, "Uncle Luca's property, without drawing attention to themselves."

Serenity stared at her cousin for a moment. "Where do you think they would take them?"

Lena was quiet for a moment, then said, "Best guess? Home. *Their* home, that is."

Serenity stood and paced across the deck. While standing by the railing, she swept her gaze through Willow Run and beyond.

A thought came to her. She spun around. "Why did your pack pick here...this location?"

Shrugging, Gage said, "Easy answer. Because of the isolation. We're far enough in and high enough up to avoid contact with the outside world. Not to mention, we're nowhere near any place humans might go for recreation."

Silent a moment, Serenity nodded. "And how do you keep your wards up?"

This time, it was Marcus who answered. "We don't have to do anything. We never even knew how they got there in the first place."

Jasmine stepped onto the patio. Glaring at the others, she said, "It would've been great if you'd invited me."

Serenity winced. "Sorry. I just saw—"

Waving her hand, Jasmine interrupted, "You either forgot I was here, or you just don't trust me yet. Which I can understand you're not trusting me. But to forget? I was sure I'd made more of an impression than that."

Anna stepped outside behind Jasmine and said, "I think they were just so caught up in what was happening, they didn't think past who was and wasn't here." She looked at her cousins. "Am I right?"

Ashamed, Lena stared down at the red boards beneath her chair and nodded.

Serenity gave a heavy sigh. "Guilty."

Luke interrupted, "In their defense, it's been a pretty crazy morning."

He went on to explain everything from the moment he'd seen Serenity standing in her living room to when Gage and Marcus joined them.

Jasmine smiled. "Good job, cousin. And congrats on the mating, both of you. Now, about the wards. You're all very lucky my mother thought of everything."

She turned to Lena. "I'm guessing you haven't read all the journals?"

Scoffing, Lena said, "Have you seen how many there are? That must be at least thirty generations. With each adding at least twenty journals…"

Jasmine corrected her, "Twenty-four, to be exact. And there are just over five-hundred journals. All of which constituted most of my early curriculum, along with mastering my magic. I had to read…and study each one. I was tested regularly by members of my pack. Each family was given different journals to learn. You know how they say it takes a village to raise a child? They weren't kidding."

Jasmine sat in Serenity's vacated seat. "Now the wards. They were put there after our ancestors came to this country. And your family, Gage, were drawn here because of the wards that were already in place."

Leaning forward, Luke's gaze swept through the four cousins. "And why would anyone from the Jäger clan help us?"

Smirking, Jasmine said, "Because they were mated to the alphas."

Chapter Thirty-Nine

Marcus could barely contain his excitement. When everybody agreed that he should return to Whitebark Stand, he nearly cried. Home. He was finally going home. When they'd told him they wouldn't be making the trip until the next morning, he'd tried to argue. But after learning how far they'd have to drive, he relented.

To say sleep had evaded him was putting it mildly. The night before had been spent tossing and turning in anticipation of what was to come.

But it was here. He was going home today. Even if it wasn't to stay. Still, it was more than he'd dared to hope. However, along with the joy the prospect brought was the looming apprehension. He had no idea what thirty years of sitting empty had done to the houses.

Two large SUVs pulled up in front of Serenity's house. Gage got out of one, Luke the other. Marcus stepped off the porch and met Gage halfway. He looked from Gage to the darkened windows behind him. "Who's going?"

He nodded toward the house. "No offense, but how about if we wait for Serenity before we begin talking about details?"

Behind him, he heard the front door open. Serenity stepped out, juggling a bucket and several bags. After setting them on the porch, she went back inside.

Luke ran past them, yelling over his shoulder, "You gonna help or just stand there?"

Bags and boxes filled with cleaning supplies, plus mops and brooms, were sitting by the trucks. They were nearly ready to go. Serenity stood beside the car. "Just one more thing."

She turned toward the house and waited.

The screen door opened one last time. Luke walked out carrying a large cooler with a picnic basket on top. Grinning, he strode toward his vehicle.

Serenity shrugged and followed Luke.

Luke slammed the hatch then walked over with a sandwich in one hand and a can of cola in the other.

Serenity scowled and said, "Those are for lunch."

"I'm hungry. Besides, we can always stop before we get there for more food."

He winked and added, "At least I didn't touch the chicken."

Gage stared at his beta then glanced at Serenity. He nodded toward the hatch, murmuring, "Chicken?"

After stuffing the last half of the sandwich in his mouth, Luke replied, "And potato salad."

Jabbing an elbow into Luke's side, Serenity said, "Yes. I brought food. It's a long drive there and back. And with all the work we have to do, I figured everybody would get hungry."

When Gage noticed Marcus was as perplexed as him, he asked, "What are you talking about? We're just going to check on everything."

Serenity walked past them to the front of Luke's car and opened the passenger door. "As long as we're there, we might as well start getting it ready. A little cleaning won't hurt."

Another SUV pulled up to the curb. A door opened and Ariana stuck her head out. She looked around for a moment until she found Serenity. Smiling, she said, "I got seven volunteers."

From inside, someone mumbled, "We didn't volunteer. You *told* us we were doing it."

Grinning, Ariana winked and said, "Same thing."

Then, frowning at Gage and Marcus, she asked, "Are you ready to get the show on the road, or are you going to stand there all day with your heads up your—"

Gage laughed when an arm appeared and yanked Ariana back inside. He was glad he wasn't riding with them. He knew Jonas wouldn't get off lightly for doing that. He looked at his own SUV then thought about Lena.

Smiling, he couldn't be happier knowing how similar to Jonas and Ariana his life would be after finding Lena. He'd always admired Ariana. He remembered asking Jonas if he ever regretted mating such a fiery woman. Jonas had winked, smiled, then waggled his brow saying, "Not even a little." To say that made him uncomfortable was putting it mildly. He'd always considered them family and imagining how her passion played out behind closed doors wasn't something he wanted to picture.

Marcus watched Serenity get into the front seat of the car driven by Luke. He frowned then strode over to the large vehicle and yanked the back door open. He reached inside and pulled Anna out. Then, after opening the front door, he grabbed Serenity. While glaring at Luke, he replaced Serenity with Anna. Then shoved Serenity into the back seat and climbed in after her.

The first thirty minutes of the drive was spent in uncomfortable silence. Arms crossed, body rigid, Serenity fumed. Turning a scathing glare on Marcus, she said, "You know that we're just friends."

Luke's eyes met hers before returning to the road. Without looking back, he said, "It's okay. I totally understand. Give him time. It's a wolf thing."

Snorting, Anna corrected, "It's a man thing."

It was exactly what they needed to break the tension. For the next two hours, they talked about friends and family.

At noon, the caravan pulled off the highway. Everybody got out to stretch their legs and have lunch.

Gage came over to where Serenity and Marcus were standing. He leaned against the car and looked over Serenity's shoulder. Heads bowed, they both were intent on the video they were watching. He waited a moment longer for it to end. Then looking from Serenity to the phone, he waited for her to explain why they were watching countdown videos from New Year's Eve, several years ago.

After cramming her phone in a pocket, she explained, "A lot has changed in the last thirty years. I thought I would show Marcus a few videos."

Laughing, Marcus commented, "And I see cars still don't fly. But the things you can do on just a phone. Amazing. Then she told me you can actually see the person you're talking to." He looked between them. "She also said not very many people have house phones anymore."

Lena joined them. "Although we can do video calls, most people choose not to."

Marcus's jaw hung open. "Why? That's such an incredible thing."

Serenity scrunched up her nose. "Well, for one thing, you can imagine that most people aren't going to want others to see them in all their grunginess."

Gage laughed. "Not to mention, most people don't have time for something like that. Life has been made easier through technological advances. But instead of using that time to enrich their lives, people tend to fill the extra time with other things."

Marcus shook his head and sighed. "Which is exactly why I've always chosen to stick with a simpler life. Time goes by much too fast to take anything for granted."

After his statement, everybody got quiet.

Gage cleared his throat, then asked, "Ready?"

After a few nods, everybody made their way back to the cars. Gage stopped beside Luke's. "Did Scarlett stay behind to run the restaurant?"

Luke answered, "No. They decided to close down for the day." Laughing at the echoed gasps, he said, "I know, right? No, Scarlett stayed behind to watch the pups."

Gage bowed his head. With a stiff nod, he returned to his car.

After being on the road for fifteen minutes and enduring another long, uncomfortable silence, Serenity asked, "How long is Gage going to feel bad about what happened?"

Marcus squeezed her hand. "Until he doesn't. I don't have any siblings, so I can't really understand what he's going through as a brother. But I do know as an alpha. It's just going to take time."

Anna turned in her seat. "You feel bad about what your father has to do. Even if you don't agree with everything he's done, or what kind of person he is. He's still your dad." She shrugged. "Family is family."

Serenity's eyes burned with the tears she was fighting. Unable to hold them back, she turned her head toward the window. While watching the blurring hills beside them, she nodded.

Luke glanced in the rearview mirror. When he'd first met Serenity, he'd wanted to rip her throat out. Now, she'd become more like a little sister to him. Because of that, he hated seeing her sad, especially over something she had nothing to do with. Instead of pointing that out, he changed the subject. Glancing over his shoulder, he asked, "So, Marcus. What's the first thing you want to do?"

The rest of the trip was spent talking about cleaning and renovations.

They agreed that modernizing the houses would be the most difficult challenge. Nobody in Whitebark Stand Pack would know how to help with the upgrades. And then once the upgrades were completed, they'd need to be taught how to use modern technology.

Anna and Serenity involuntarily shuddered when they turned off the highway onto the narrow road leading into the small community.

Marcus noticed Serenity's discomfort. "What is it?"

"First of all, nobody's here. Now that I know what it feels like, I'd know immediately if anybody from my family was here. But best of all, the wards are still strong. It kind of feels like…" Shrugging, she looked at Anna.

Anna said, "Like something's got a hold of your skin and they're pulling it back. Not in a painful way, but like…"

Serenity nodded and said, “Yes, that’s it. Gravity. It’s like a super strong pull. Kind of like at the fair when you get on a ride that spins you around really fast.”

“Exactly.” Anna continued, “Like trying to lift your arms away from your sides. You can, but it’s really difficult and a little uncomfortable.”

Everybody felt it. Driving through the streets was like visiting a ghost town. Most of the houses looked exactly the same. In some, the doors were still standing open, some windows, as well. A few yards had bicycles laying in the front yard.

Upon closer inspection, Marcus noticed a few roofs had caved in. On one porch, a post was busted in half, causing part of the roof to collapse.

He felt Serenity’s hand on his arm. When he looked at her, he saw his own defeat reflected on her face. Lifting her hand, he kissed her knuckles. “It can all be fixed.”

Then, looking out the window again, he pointed to a house rising above all the others. Releasing his belt, he scooted up, then said, “That’s my house.”

Luke whistled. “And I thought Gage’s house was opulent. What is it, like four stories?”

“No, just three.”

Luke laughed. “Just three, huh? Basement?”

Turning his gaze from the house to Luke, he said, “Yes, it runs the full length of the cabin.” After he returned his attention to his house, the only home he’d ever known, the full impact hit at once.

"Stop the car." When Luke glanced back and kept driving, he shouted, "Stop the car." He felt a little guilty for yelling at him. "I need to walk the rest of the way."

After they stopped, Serenity reached for her door. But Marcus put his hand on her arm and shook his head. "I need to do this myself. I need to let everything…" His voice trailed off. Without looking back, he turned and walked away.

Luke waited a few seconds then continued driving to Marcus's house. While watching the lonely alpha in his mirror, he said, "Remember, to him this was just a few weeks ago. Can you even imagine? He lost everything. His pack, his house…everything."

They were still unloading when Marcus arrived. Everybody stopped when they saw him. He said nothing, just walked over to the winding stairs that led to his deck. Nobody moved until he leaned over the railing and yelled, "It's safe. Come on up."

When they got to the deck, Marcus was standing in front of a large desk. His finger hovered above a button on a small beige box. Shaking his head, he sighed and walked away.

Jonas wandered over to the desk. Then looking from the box to Marcus, he asked, "Do you mind? I'd really like to…" Unable to continue, he stared out the window.

Without hesitation, Marcus walked back and punched the button. Everybody was shocked when they heard the frantic voice.

"Marcus, pick up! Marcus! Man, where are you? A caravan of pickups and box trucks just rolled in. Marc, I think it's them. Riding shotgun in the lead truck…it's old man Jäger, himself."

Once the message was over, Jonas walked out of the room with his mate right behind him. Their low voices filtered through the door. When they heard the soft sobbing coming from the hallway, everybody returned to the deck.

Marcus was grateful for the distraction when Gage asked, "How is it you still have power?"

Marcus pointed to the roof, then said, "I've always considered it my duty to take care of the environment. We were nearly self-sufficient. Solar power, wells, septic, plus we used wood to heat our homes. But I had a guy tap into the phone lines to keep us off the grid. I'm not sure if it still works." He gave a sad smile, then added, "I guess it doesn't matter. There's nobody here to call anyway."

Serenity waited until Gage walked away before questioning Marcus about the voice she'd heard. She stepped closer. "That was Chance, wasn't it?"

Marcus looked inside then nodded. "He was my beta. And my best friend. But he was also Jonas's brother." Wiping a hand down his face, he cleared his throat. "We need to get them back."

Serenity curled into his arms. "First we need to make sure they have a place to live."

Leaning in, Marcus kissed her. "We can start with my house. It'll be a bit cramped, but there's room enough for everybody here."

It was past midnight when they finally got home. Serenity walked behind an exhausted Marcus. While gripping his shoulders, she directed him down the hall and into the bedroom. As soon as they walked in, he moaned and fell onto the bed. She grabbed his legs, pulled his shoes off, and began undressing him. Afterward, she pushed, pulled, and tugged him the rest of the way into bed. Although she was just as tired, she knew there was no way she'd be able to fall asleep. After locking up, she took a long shower and got ready for bed.

After climbing in beside him, she tossed and turned for thirty minutes before giving up. She walked toward the kitchen then noticed Luke standing in the window across the street. She grabbed some mugs then made two cups of hot cocoa. After walking out to the porch, she waved them toward him then sat on the swing.

A minute later, Luke stepped onto the porch. "You do know if Marcus sees us, I'm as good as dead."

"No you're not. I'll protect you."

Luke laughed, sat down, and inhaled the rich aroma. He took a sip. "What? No marshmallows?"

Crinkling her nose, Serenity said, "Gross."

Luke chuckled. "Agreed."

Chapter Forty

Serenity awakened to snuggles and kisses from Marcus. With her eyes still closed, she mumbled, “Don’t think you’re getting off that easy.”

He continued kissing her and asked, “Whatever are you talking about, my love?”

Opening one eye, she focused a glare on him. Then, rolling away, she murmured, “Like you don’t know.”

Kissing the back of her head, he said, “You’re my mate, and I love you. What was I supposed to do?”

“I love you, too. But in the future, how about if you don’t explode through the door and nearly kill Luke?”

She tried to get up, but Marcus grabbed her. Then pulling her back, he said, “You love me?”

Serenity threw the blankets off then rolled to the floor and snorted, “Of course I do.”

She stood with her hands on her hips and glared at him.

“It’s difficult to concentrate while you’re standing there in all your naked glory.”

Serenity threw her hands up and bellowed, You’re impossible!” She stomped across the room and put on her terry cloth robe. Then turning back to face her mate, she crossed her arms and waited.

Marcus sat up. "Please don't fight with me. I'm sorry. How should I have reacted when I found you two snuggled up together on the porch?"

He waved a finger toward her, saying, "And…with your head on his shoulder, arm in arm, no less. I know how males think. After seeing you…I know he wants you."

Waving her hands around, Serenity growled and left the room.

When Marcus walked out a few minutes later, he found her standing in the kitchen, watching coffee drip into the pot. Leaning over, she squinted at the extremely slow rising line.

"You know, it's not going to brew faster with you watching it."

"I happen to know for a fact that Luke doesn't want me. He's more like a brother."

Marcus paced across the room a few times. "And just how do you know this? Because, let me tell you, no man sees another woman as a sister. They're all—"

Striding across the room, she poked a sharp nail into his bare chest. Then punctuating each word with another poke, she growled, "No. Don't try to make the friendship between Luke and I dirty. Do you even know why I know he's not interested in me?"

Marcus grabbed her finger then frowned at a few drops of blood from the crescent holes in his chest. Backing away, he dropped into a chair, crossed his arms, and shook his head.

Smirking at Marcus she said, “He’s crushing on Jasmine.”

Resting his elbows on the table, Marcus leaned forward. Then, reaching for the big white box on the table, he cursed and tossed the now empty box into the trash. Then, he started getting ingredients out for breakfast. After setting an onion and pepper on the counter, he reached for the knife. “And how do you know this?”

Serenity pulled out three large potatoes and began peeling them. “Well, first, I’m not blind. Second…” She shrugged, then mumbled, “He asked if I thought he had a chance.”

“Do you want to see if he’s hungry?”

***

While sitting at the breakfast bar with a cup of coffee hovering a hair’s breadth from his lips, Gage’s eyes flicked between his three early morning guests. Without taking a sip, he set his cup down and asked, “Does anybody want to tell me how my beta got a black eye?”

Grinning, Luke waved it off. “It was just a misunderstanding. So, are we going to plan this trip or not?”

“Um…No. Not right now. Maybe we could wait until…Oh, I don’t know… maybe, nine? Ten or eleven would be great. Coffee would also be good. Breakfast. Even better. Oh, I know. Sure, let’s do this. Why don’t you call and get Ariana out of bed for this early morning meeting?”

Holding his hands up, Luke said, "Eleven sounds fine to me."

Marcus chuckled and muttered, "It's my fault. I was so excited about seeing my own beta…and my own pack, that I couldn't sleep."

Sighing, Gage set his cup down again. "I get it. Really. I totally understand—"

Marcus shoved his stool back then slammed his cup down hard enough for it to shatter. Ignoring it, he glared at the other alpha. "No. Gage. I don't think you do understand."

He shouted, "Thirty years. That's how long I stood in that forest. For a while, I had no idea what was happening. I was stuck inside my own head. I relived the same day over and over. It was the day the Dämonejägers drove into our community and changed our lives forever."

Lowering his voice, he continued, "And then, about twenty years ago, Serenity came into my life. Day by day, I slowly started to wake. After that came the real agony. For most of those twenty years, I was completely coherent, yet unable to move. That," he bellowed, "is what every member of my pack is feeling right this minute. I could feel the wind, the rain, and the snow. The scorching summer sun, while it relentlessly beat down on me day after day. Yet I was unable to move into the shade. In the winter, my fur froze to my skin. At times, I was buried chin deep in the snow." Jabbing a finger at Gage, he yelled, "Understand that!"

Tossing a final glare at the other male, Marcus walked out.

Serenity felt like all the air had been sucked out of the room. Her hands shook so hard, the coffee sloshed out, spilling all over the counter. Then she felt the sting of tears seconds before a sob escaped. Looking from Luke to Gage, she cried, "I did that. I wasn't helping them. I was hurting them. I just…I just wanted to give them comfort." Gasping, she whispered, "The pups."

Gage abruptly stood, knocking his stool over. Then, looking at Luke, he said, "You make the calls, I'll wake everybody upstairs. I want those pups out of the forest and up here. Now."

Serenity stopped him. "Wait. That's not what I meant. Well, of course I want them brought in. But they've been sheltered since the beginning. No. I mean there are still pups out there. In the forest."

Marcus was still running through the forest thirty minutes later when movement from below caught his attention. The woods behind Serenity's house were filled with people. When he moved closer, he noticed they were carrying the rescued pups. Fear battled with reason. Instinct took over. Although he knew they were safe, his past refused to allow the thoughts to stick. The dark wolf ran toward the nearest person and lunged for their throat. He was determined to kill whoever thought to harm the most vulnerable.

A thickly muscled arm knocked him away. While rolling across the ground, he shifted back to his human form. Sitting up, he stared at a very angry Jonas.

"Boy! Do not start with me! It's bad enough I had to listen to…"

He paused then looked around and whispered, "Do you see Ariana?"

Laughing, Marcus said, "Do you have any idea how much you remind me of Henry?" Looking at the sudden sadness on Jonas's face, he wished he could take the words back. "I'm sorry. I wish…"

After taking a deep breath, Jonas said, "No. None of this is your fault. Not one single thing. Do you hear me? Nobody could have known what was going to happen that day. And you telling me that I remind you of my brother…"

Jonas cleared his throat, then looked away for a moment. After wiping a sleeve across his eyes, he shook his head. "It's a compliment. I always looked up to him. Having Luke, and now Celeste, has enriched my life beyond measure. Even if I couldn't save Beth, I raised their son the best I knew how. Then when Ariana came into my life, she loved him like her own. I couldn't be prouder of that boy. So, you see, my life has already been filled with so many, many blessings."

Offering his hand, Jonas added, "And pretty soon, we'll have Chance back. How about that, huh?"

When Marcus walked into the basement with two pups, he couldn't help laughing. It looked like a giant toy box had exploded. From one wall to the next, everything from plastic army men to life size dolls covered the floor. Someone had papered the walls and set tables of paints and crayons along the parameter. The scene was completed by the aroma of baking cookies.

Marcus set the pups down then went looking for Gage. He found him sitting in a corner on the floor assembling cribs. He walked over and picked up the directions. He looked from the pile of nuts and bolts to Gage. "I think you missed a few."

Shrugging, Gage said, "Directions. Who needs them? Right?"

Marcus knelt beside him. "Well, how about the toddlers you're planning to put in there?"

Gage looked from the screw he was turning to the growing pile of discarded pieces. "Oh…I guess that's true."

While running a finger down the directions, Marcus began searching for where Gage had gone wrong. Then grabbing a ratchet, he said, "Look about earlier—"

"—Give me that…" Looking at Marcus, he yanked the ratchet out of his hand. "Do you see the 3/8th inch socket?"

Hours later, they'd finally finished the last crib. After stretching out his cramped legs, Marcus said, "Let's go upstairs."

He followed Gage toward the hall that led to the stairs and didn't stop until they reached Gage's office.

Gage walked to the bar and grabbed two beers. After handing one to Marcus, he stepped onto the deck. Then propping a foot between the balusters, elbows on the rail, he scanned the horizon. "You're right. I don't understand. Well, at the time I didn't. But I do now."

Turning around, he narrowed his eyes and continued, "I sent a few members of my pack out to get two large trucks. They should be back any time now. I figured if we leave within the next few hours, we should get there sometime after midnight. With enough of us, it shouldn't take long to find your pack and load them onto the trucks."

Marcus staggered back; he couldn't speak. For a moment, he was back at Whitebark Stand. Far below him he saw the Dämonejägers carrying wolves, tossing them with little care into the backs of their trucks. But more than that were the shots he'd heard ringing through the valley. He now knew exactly what that meant.

"Thank you. But what about *them*? They could do the same thing to us they did all those years ago."

"I don't like it. In fact, I was totally against it, until…"

Scowling, Marcus growled, "No."

Serenity's voice came from the doorway. "We have to. We're the only ones who can protect you. Alone, one of us may be very powerful. But, together, nobody can stop us."

***

Lena drove the lead car with Serenity riding shotgun and Anna and Jasmine in the back seat. Trailing not far behind were two large SUVs, along with two huge moving vans. After four long hours, they were nearly to Serenity's childhood home. Before starting up the mountain, she pulled into a parking lot then waited until the others stopped.

Calling everybody over, Serenity said, "Hopefully, we'll catch them off guard. If not, you need to be ready. None of them are strong enough to cast a spell without chanting the incantations. So, if you hear anyone speaking, you need to shift into your wolf."

A man standing in the back called out, "If we do that, then we're going to end up like the same wolves we're here to rescue."

Lena glared at the man,, then shifted her gaze to the others. Raising her voice, she called out, "We can override their spell. But we can't save a dead man. If they can't spell you, they'll just shoot you. It's as simple as that. So, unless you'd rather die…" Letting her words hang, she went back to the car.

Marcus turned to address the group. "She's right. They won't hesitate to kill you. These are the same men who came into my community, walked into our homes, and…"

Unable to go on, Marcus shook his head, whipped around, and stalked back to the SUV parked behind Lena.

Gage stepped in front of the others then waited until Marcus was in the car. He lowered his voice, then said, "They killed the most vulnerable."

The man who'd spoken earlier mumbled, "The babies." Snarling, he said, "I just wish we could kill them all."

Gage nodded "I do too. But they're more powerful than we are. The only thing we can do is try to save as many as we can."

A little after one in the morning, Serenity directed Lena to the same narrow lane she'd used to get Marcus and Celeste. Before the men exited the trucks, the women separated. Fanning out, each stood ready, with Serenity closest to the house.

As the night unfolded, one after another, each wolf was carried into the waiting trucks. Serenity had spent her childhood in this forest and knew exactly where each one was. After only an hour, everything began falling apart.

The dark night became as light as day. Spotlights and headlights from the trucks that surrounded them came on.

Caught unaware, the men froze mid step.

The voices of those who'd hunted the wolves filled the forest, beginning low, then growing in volume.

In seconds, wolves replaced men. They'd already been told of the futility of attacking. A spell could freeze them mid-lunge just as easily as a bullet could penetrate a human chest.

A moment later, a gunshot echoed through the forest, quickly followed by another. A single voice rose above the others. “Go! Now, while they’re distracted.”

Chaos ensued.

Lena, Serenity, Anna, and Jasmine lifted their hands. Their bodies, rising above the forest, became ethereal. Magic flowed from them into the wolves who’d been kept in stasis for so long. The men from Gage’s pack shifted once again, then, carrying a wolf, each rushed toward the trucks.

Marcus ran back to where the women were still hovering above the ground and shouted, “Everybody out!” He had no idea who’d come to their rescue. And even though he wanted to, he knew he couldn’t wait around to find out.

Doors slammed, engines roared, and the clearing emptied.

Luka stepped into the light. While looking at his daughter, he said, “Welcome home Erika. We’ve been looking for you.”

Serenity watched the trucks drive away. While floating back to the ground, she looked from them to the man who’d always terrified her. She realized then, she didn’t feel even a glimmer of the love she’d once had for him.

Eyes narrowed, Luka said, “I understand you recently came into a large sum of money.”

Serenity cocked her head and glared up at him.

Arching a brow, he asked, “Nothing to say for yourself?”

When she continued to stare, he bellowed, "Where is it?"

Smirking, she said, "Let's just say the local wolf preserve has a large plaque hanging in honor of their most generous benefactor…Oscar Jäger."

"Why, you little ungrateful—"

Serenity bellowed, "Ungrateful? Please tell me, what I have ever had to be grateful for? Years of torment and abuse? Should I be thanking you for that, Father? You know…because you and Mother were such shining examples of what a parent should be? No, I don't think so. If ever there were people who shouldn't have had children, it was you."

"I don't have to…" He pulled his fist back. Then sneering at his daughter, Luka swung.

Serenity flinched, knowing how powerful her father was. She knew she may well be experiencing the last moments of her life.

Chapter Forty-One

Gage slammed a fist against the truck's hood. They'd parked in the same parking lot they'd stopped at before going into the mountains. For thirty torturous minutes they'd waited. Pacing the length of the caravan, he bellowed, "Where are they? They should've been here by now."

He walked to the back of one truck then watched a few of the newly awakened members of Marcus's pack. He'd been surprised after learning half of them woke by themselves. After what he'd learned, he had a feeling they were the ones Serenity spent the most time with.

Mates were reunited. Joyful parents were clinging to their children. But it was the sight of his good friend, Jonas, that really got to him.

He and Chance clung to each other and wept. They cried for the years gone by, and they cried for those they'd lost. For Chance, only a moment ago, he'd been standing with Henry. And now, he had to deal with the loss of his brother.

Marcus stopped beside Gage. "You know, the flow of time…when you're…"

He sighed then looked away. Clearing his throat, he continued, "It feels like an eternity. Yet at the same time, it feels like the blink of an eye. Chance will have to mourn, not just for Henry, but for Beth, as well. But right now, for most of them…" he waved an arm toward the group, "it's all about finding loved ones. But sooner than we're ready, they'll begin noticing who isn't here. Then when we get back…"

Gage shook his head thinking about how many mothers and fathers had lost their precious babies. His thoughts turned to his mate, Lena. The thought of a loss like that was too much to bear. In his mind, he pictured their own child then having it ripped from their arms.

He was shocked back to reality when Marcus slapped him on the back. "I'm going to go see my beta."

Looking back toward the SUV, Gage saw Luke. Although overjoyed at finding his uncle, there was still the lingering painful reminder of who wasn't there. On the seat wrapped in a blanket were the remains of his father. They'd be returned to Willow Run where they'd be taken to the same forest his mate had wandered into all those years ago.

Gage walked back to the car and stopped in front of his beta. After glancing at the truck, he said, "You should go meet your uncle."

Luke looked away. "Why? I really don't know him." He nodded toward the truck. "They're all strangers to me. I've lived for thirty years without them; I don't need them now."

Gripping his arm, Gage said, "You didn't know Celeste either. And now look." He glanced back at the truck. "Go. Welcome your family."

Luke hesitated. "I'm not going back with them. I belong here."

Smiling, Gage said, "I sure hope not. Who could replace you? Hot-headed Noah, or irresponsible Alister? It's not a commitment, Luke. It's just welcoming them back."

While leaning against his car, Gage watched Luke hop onto the back of the truck then turned his attention to the dark highway leading into the mountains.

What had happened to Lena and her cousins? Why weren't they here yet? Someone, he suspected was Lena's brother, had opened fire on the Dämonejägers. It was the chance they'd needed to get away. He'd suspected her brother was on their side to begin with. But could he trust the man to turn against his own family for strangers? He knew he'd just have to believe it, if not for the sake of the pack, then for Lena, at least.

In the distance, he could see headlights through the dense trees. Coming to attention, he bellowed, "Somebody's coming!"

Instead of hiding, everyone ran to stand around him. If there was going to be trouble, they would face it together.

As the SUV neared, his hope soared. The large vehicle slowed. A yellow turn signal briefly flashed before the truck turned into the parking lot. Then pulling alongside him, the SUV stopped. The doors opened, spilling out four frantic females.

Running to the back of her car, Lena yelled, "Help me. It's my brother. He and my dad came after they learned what happened with Uncle Paul."

When Gage opened the hatch, he saw a large man curled into the tiny space. Although unconscious, he continued to moan. Blood stained the beige blanket wrapped around his body. From what Gage could tell from a quick examination, it looked like just one gunshot. Depending on how bad it was, he may or may not make it back to Willow Run. Although they didn't have a hospital, they had a very good doctor.

Chance pushed his way through the crowd. "How far do we have to go?"

Serenity stepped up to the huge man and whispered, "Chance?"

Smiling down at the tiny human, he said, "In a few, baby doll. Right now, we need to get him fixed up."

Serenity nodded, wiped a tear, and said, "About two hundred miles."

Chance shook his head. "He'll never make it."

Lena's sobs broke Gage's heart.

Chance glanced at the woman who'd helped to free them. "Let's get him to Whitebark Stand." He pointed to Lena. "You ride in the back and get busy waking everyone else.

Jasmine said, “We’ll come as well. With the four of us working together, it won’t take long. How far are we going?”

Gage glanced around for a moment, then took out his phone. After a few seconds, he said, “We’re looking at a good hour’s drive. It may not be close, but it’s not as far as Willow Run.”

Luke helped the women into the back of the truck then he got into the SUV they’d been driving. The caravan pulled out of the parking lot then turned left onto the next highway.

Gage sat in the backseat to watch their passenger. Before leaving, Chance had wrapped his wound to slow the bleeding.

Blue eyes, which reminded him very much of Lena, cracked open. With one hand gripping the side that had been shot, he thrust the other toward Gage. “David.”

Taking his hand, Gage introduced himself. “I’m Gage, alpha of the pack that was hauling the wolves out. Let’s just hope it won’t cost you your life.”

Breath heaving, he asked, “Lena…?”

Laying a hand on his arm, he said, “Everybody’s safe. Save your strength. We still have at least another thirty miles before we can get you patched up.”

David’s eyes drifted shut before opening again. Grunting in pain, he said, “They were planning to kill all of them.”

Nodding, Gage said, "We figured that's what they had planned. That's why everybody shifted—"

"No. The girls…my sister…they were…"

***

The four Jäger women separated. Each woman stood on one side of the truck with a man on each side securing them. Magic poured from their outstretched hands. Five minutes into the drive, the women began to rise. Fifteen minutes later, their heads were touching the ceiling. Thirty minutes after they'd begun the climb to Whitebark Stand, the inside of the trailer began glowing. Pulsing waves of colors in hues ranging from the purest white to midnight blue swirled around the still forms below.

Then, as if from a great distance, Serenity heard a faint voice calling to her. A moment later, she felt a tug.

With one hard yank, Chance pulled Serenity into his arms. One by one, the women fell. Beneath them, arms reached up to catch each one. The spell broken; Serenity found herself standing on the floor of the huge truck. Weaving side to side, she smiled her thanks to Marcus and Chance.

In the center, wolves were coming to life. Those who'd been captured in mid leap crashed to the floor. Young pups whimpered and snuggled up to their mothers. As reality began to set in, the pack turned their attention to the outsiders. Snarling wolves inched closer to the women who'd risked everything to save them.

Above it all, a loud shout came from the man standing beside Serenity. In a booming voice, Marcus bellowed, "You will stop. Or you will die."

The animals who'd been prepared to attack shimmered a moment before tight rings of men surrounded the females and children.

Chance and Marcus stood shoulder to shoulder in front of Serenity.

On the other side of the truck, they heard Anna's shouted threats. "Don't make me change you back." Followed immediately by… "Hey! I'm only seventeen."

At once, every head turned. Leaving Serenity alone, Marcus and Chance pushed through the crowd. As the group parted, Serenity saw a very large man leaning over her young cousin. One arm rested on the wall, while he ran a hand down her long blonde hair. She relaxed when she heard him say, "So am I, darlin'."

Tension relieved, the group dispersed and began talking amongst themselves.

Exhausted, Serenity nearly collapsed. With an arm around her waist, Marcus lowered her to the floor and pulled her onto his lap. He kissed the top of her head. "Sleep, my love. I'll wake you when we get there."

***

The world around her was moving but not in the way she'd expect from riding in the back of a truck. The roar of the highway was replaced by the sounds of a forest. Snuggling deeper into the arms that held her, Serenity murmured, "I guess this means were here."

Suddenly alert, she wiggled until he put her down. "Where's David?"

Marcus smiled. "If you mean the injured male, he's with our doctors."

"Doctors?"

Marcus took her hand and pulled her toward his house. "Yes, every pack has at least one doctor. We have two. I don't know anything else yet. So, who is this David to you?"

Grinning, she said, "David's my cousin. The one and only man in my family I don't hate. He's Lena's brother."

Marcus's eyes rounded beneath arched brows. "Well, then I'm sure he'll be all right."

"And how can you be so sure?"

Marcus winked and said, "Under threat of an alpha, I'm sure they'll do everything they can to ensure the well-being of his mate's brother."

Serenity watched as the rescued families began making their way toward the houses below. "I thought they were going to be staying with you?"

Not bothering to look back, he shrugged, then said, "It's their choice. I can't blame any of them for wanting to get their lives back together as fast as possible. The only one who knows how long it's been is Chance. After he saw his brother, there was no denying it. They've been told to get some rest and come on up to the house tomorrow for a meeting to discuss what's happened."

Serenity, watching Luke in a deep discussion with his uncle, asked, "Are we staying here? I mean, forever?"

Marcus replied, "I could only wish. We'll talk more about it tomorrow. I know that no matter what we decide, we can't stay here until it becomes more livable. The years haven't been kind to our homes. Gage may have been right when he said it might be easier to live somewhere else."

Chapter Forty-Two

Someone was in the room with them. He could feel them watching them sleep. After a slight inhale, he knew it was a shifter. A male. There was only one reason he could think of for someone to sneak into their room. Someone meant them harm. His mate. A protective rage crept over him. Whoever it was would rue the day they'd thought to challenge their alpha.

Beside him, Serenity stirred. One side of the blankets lifted. A moment later, the bed dipped ever so slightly. His rage grew when he heard her kissing this strange male.

In a sleepy murmur, Serenity asked, "What's the matter, honey?"

"I miss my sister," came the tearful reply of a very young boy.

Shame overwhelmed him. Only a few seconds ago, he'd been ready to attack. He didn't need to see her to know that Serenity instinctively knew it was a child who'd come into their bedroom. He wasn't sure if it was her magic or her maternal instincts, but she'd immediately opened both her heart and her arms to comfort this little boy. Her softly spoken words of comfort continued.

"I know you do, sweety. What's your sister's name?"

"Her name's Melissa, but we call her Missy," the boy answered.

"Sweetheart…how old is Missy?"

"Same age as me. We're twins."

Unable to endure another heartbreaking moment, Marcus sat up. While leaning over his mate, he said, "Good morning, little wolf. Do your parents know where you are?"

Big dark eyes stared up at Marcus. While slowly shaking his head, little hands fisted the blanket and pulled it closer to his wobbly chin.

Attempting to put the boy at ease, he smiled, then said, "It's okay. You don't have to be afraid."

"But you're—"

"I'm the alpha, this is true. Do you know what my job is?" When the boy shook his head, Marcus continued, "My job is to protect every member of my pack. That includes you *and* your sister. I would die for you. Never, never be afraid of your alpha." He bopped the boy's nose. "Respect him, yes. But never be afraid. Now, how about you go find your parents while Serenity and I get dressed?"

The boy rolled out of bed and left the room just as quietly as he'd come in.

Marcus sat on the side of the bed and began dressing. Without looking back, he asked, "How did you know?"

"Know what?"

Pulling a shirt over his head, he said, "That it was a child who'd come into our room and not someone who wished to do us harm."

Laughing, she said, "Here's a thought…I opened my eyes and looked at him."

Marcus paused with one shoe in his hand, then asked, "You mean you didn't instinctively know it was a child?"

Serenity sat beside him. "Of course not. How would I know that?"

Shrugging, Marcus finished putting on his shoes then stood to leave.

Serenity laughed. "You think that just because I'm a woman I automatically knew? I might have some magic, but I'm not psychic."

He leaned over and kissed her. "Get dressed. We need to have that meeting and get back to Willow Run. I don't know how many parents lost their babies when the Dämonejägers came but we'll wait until we get there to find out. Having found some may be a small consolation, but at least it's something."

Stunned speechless, Serenity stared at him. He was nearly to the door before she found her voice. She stood and shouted, "Small consolation? Really? You're going to tell a grieving parent that…hey, at least your neighbor's child is okay. Because I'm going to tell you…that would not make me feel better!"

Marcus froze with his hand hovering above the doorknob then spun around. In a few long strides he was standing in front of her. Gripping her arms, he snarled, “And what would you have me do? There is no easy way to tell a parent their child was murdered simply because of what they were. That men walked into their homes and shot—”

A gasp sounded from behind them.

Pushing past him, Serenity ran to the door. There, holding the hand of their morning’s visitor, stood a young woman with eyes as dark as coals. Obviously, his mother. Serenity pulled the woman into her arms and held her while she sobbed.

The woman stepped back and stared into Serenity’s eyes for a moment. She glanced down at the boy, who was also now crying.

Kneeling in front of him, Serenity asked, “Hey. How would you like to be Marcus’s number one helper today?”

Marcus stopped beside her. “I don’t know…it’s a pretty big job. I’m not sure you could handle it.”

The boy’s dark eyes rounded. Stepping closer to Marcus, he exclaimed, “I’m five and a half years old. I’m big. I’m even bigger than Missy, and we’re the same age.”

Kneeling in front of the boy, Marcus asked, “What’s your name, boy?”

Grinning, he said, “Jason, sir.”

“I don’t know…I’ll tell you what, Jason. How about you show me how strong you are?” He held out his hand and waited.

Jason stared at the proffered hand, then with fierce determination, he grabbed it and squeezed. His face turned red while his little arm shook.

Marcus collapsed in front of the boy, crying out in feigned anguish. Lying on the floor, he looked up at Jason's smiling face. "Wow, you're pretty strong. Maybe you *can* help me." Rolling to his knees, he held out a hand, then waited for Jason to help him up. While holding the boy's hand, he walked toward the stairs, mumbling, "How about I make you my beta for the day?"

Serenity's gaze followed the pair until they were out of sight. Then turning her attention to the bereaved mother, she said, "I need to get ready. But I can listen while I dress. My name's Serenity Chase."

The young mother followed her into the room. "Marsha Hancock."

Dropping her robe, Serenity began dressing. With her back to the other woman, she said, "Jason told me about Missy."

Marsha cleared her throat. "Yes, his twin." She choked back a sob. "She's not…"

After pulling a shirt over her head, Serenity turned around. "Not all the children are here. Lena, my cousin and Alister…he's the brother of the alpha…it…it doesn't matter. Anyway, they went and picked them up and took them back to Willow Run."

The woman smiled. "I know where that is. I'm actually from there. I met Stan one summer when he and a bunch of other boys came looking for mates. Are we all going there? I can't wait to see my parents—"

Serenity interrupted, "There's a lot to talk about. Marcus wants to leave as soon as possible. I promise we'll tell you everything soon."

It was well into the afternoon when they finally left. If luck was on their side, they'd be home in time for dinner. Gage drove with Lena sitting beside him, with Marcus and Serenity in back.

Marcus looked at Serenity. "Do you want to tell me what happened? You've been quiet since you came downstairs. I also noticed you avoided talking to everybody."

Serenity took a moment to gather her thoughts. Finally, she said, "So you guys send bachelors to other packs looking for mates?"

Gage looked at Serenity in his rearview mirror, then answered, "Of course we do. After a while, almost everybody is related in one way or another."

Serenity crossed her arms and waited.

The car swerved, then Gage murmured, "Oh no."

"Oh, yes," Serenity said.

After a moment of silence, Gage asked, "Who…"

Looking out the window, Serenity fought back tears. She wiped a hand across her face, then said, "I don't know how…Not only are we going to have to tell them about their babies, but somehow, we need to tell them how many years have passed." She looked at Marcus, grabbed his hand, then said, "It was my family that did this to them. They're going to hate me."

Marcus grabbed her hand, kissed it, then said, "You saved them. What your family did isn't your fault. Whatever comes, we'll face it together."

***

Seven hours and six rest stops later, they pulled into Willow Run. Gage drove straight to his house then waited for everyone to unload. While standing in front of the garage, he yelled, "Can I have your attention please?"

After everyone quieted, Marcus walked up to address his pack.

Standing beside him, Serenity squeezed his hand and whispered, "Together."

The incline of Gage's driveway allowed them to see everyone. There was a mixture of joy and apprehension interspersed. He knew that soon, sorrow and anger would also join in. He knew these people. Some were young couples who'd only just welcomed their first baby into the world. Others had just gotten home from visiting parents or grandparents. Gage had told him about some of their parents. There were some who'd mourned their children even thirty years later. Most, but not all, still lived.

Jason came to stand between them. Then looking up at Marcus, he said, "Don't be scared, I got your back, sir."

Right now, the only thing on Marcus's mind was the hope that somewhere in the large group of pups behind them was a little girl named Missy. Nodding, Marcus cleared the lump that had formed in his throat and began. "I would first like to ask all of you to wait until I've finished before you do or ask anything. What I'm about to tell you will shock and horrify you. I know because I felt it, too. For me, the attack felt like yesterday. But…"

His gaze swept the crowd before he continued, "It's been thirty years."

Loud gasps and grumblings sifted through the crowd. Some denied the truth, others were angry, and there were some who wept.

Jonas and Chance came to stand beside them. Chance still looked like the same young man he had the day the Dämonejägers rode in. Jonas, however, although younger than Chance, now resembled their father more.

Jonas raised his hands. "You all know me, but you may not recognize me. I'm Jonas, Chance's youngest brother."

The group grew louder.

Then Chance yelled, "Marcus is still our alpha and I'm still your beta. Now, unless you want us to bring that point home, you will quiet."

Nodding his thanks, Marcus squeezed Chance's shoulder. After the noise died down, he continued, "The Keneally Pack has been kind enough to welcome us while we get ready to live in a world we no longer understand. Gage, their alpha, has opened his home to some of our youngest members. Over fifty pups were recently rescued from the barn belonging to the ones responsible for what happened. Standing beside me is my mate, Serenity."

He scanned the crowd. "Lena, Jasmine, and Anna, if you would, please join me."

After they did, he continued, "These four women are responsible for waking every single wolf. In an act of selflessness, Lena and Gage's brother brought the pups back here. Then after the women awakened the pups, we came for you. So, regardless of what you might think, or hear…Remember, it is these women you owe your lives to. As well as the lives of every pup in that house. However, not every pup made it."

He let the news sink in. After taking a deep breath, he said, "They only captured the pups that had shifted."

Almost a full minute passed before understanding dawned. A woman in front cried out and collapsed. Throughout the group, he heard the heartbreaking wails of grieving parents.

Gage's voice rose above the noise. "If you're missing a child, please come with me."

Marcus kissed Serenity, then said, "I feel like it's my place to be there for the parents whose babies aren't there. Will you be all right?"

Nodding, Serenity said, "You're right, you do need to be there. Gage is a stranger to them, as am I.

They need you right now. I’ll stay here. I’ve got my cousins and friends to watch out for me.”

Chapter Forty-Three

Serenity noticed a young couple walking straight toward her, one of which was Marsha. The man knelt and held out his hands and Jason ran and leapt into his father's arms.

Stepping closer, she introduced herself. "My name's Serenity. I met your wife…I mean mate, earlier."

Giving her a sad smile, Stan said, "It's okay. I know humans don't always understand our ways. I'm one of the pack's doctors, so I spent plenty of time in the human world." His nostrils flared. Then his head tilted to the side while he squinted at her.

Serenity knew then that he realized she wasn't human.

Instead of saying anything, he said, "Honey, why don't you go in and see if you can find the girls." He waited until she was gone before he turned back to Serenity. Looking at Jason, he said, "Why don't you go update Chance on what's happened so far?"

The moment Stan released Jason's hand, he ran.

Laughing, Stan murmured, "The idea of him being Marcus's beta…genius." Then turning back to Serenity, he said, "You saved us. For that, you'll forever have my undying gratitude. Being the mate of my alpha also ensures your position in the pack." While looking from her to the three women who'd helped her, he said, "But I would strongly recommend telling the others before they figure it out for themselves."

Serenity looked at those they'd rescued the night before. With what Stan had just said, she saw them in a different light. Before now, she'd only seen them as men and women. But they weren't just men and women. They were predators. Every one of them could easily rip her throat out. Without thinking, she took a step back.

From behind her, thick arms came around, pulling her against a wide chest. She glanced over her shoulder and stared up at Chance. Her Chance. An enraged Chance. Could she have been wrong to trust him so fully?

Chance scanned the crowd for threats. The sweet scent of fear radiated in waves from Serenity. Other than Stan, everyone else's attention was elsewhere. If there was anyone amongst the pack that could be trusted with humans, it was Stan. Although Serenity wasn't human. Not really. She was more. Turning his glare on the other man, he asked, "Do we have a problem?"

While holding his hands up, Stan took a few steps back. "Not from me. I would defend her with my life. I merely suggested she might want to tell the other members of our pack who she really is before they figure it out for themselves."

Chance nodded his understanding. He released her then moved to her side. Without looking at her, he whispered, "Never fear me, little one. For you…you are family. Always."

Serenity curled her hands around his arm then leaned her head against his shoulder. How could she have ever doubted him? He was right. He was like a favorite uncle. On her worst nights, it was him she'd sought out. On the nights when her father took his wrath out on her, she'd always gone to the forest. Not even fear of retribution could keep them apart.

When Stan moved to stand on her other side, she knew that if any were to look, his emerald eyes would be glowing like beacons in the night, proclaiming him the predator he was.

A few minutes later, she felt a presence behind her. Glancing over her shoulder, she saw Jonas, Luke, and David standing shoulder to shoulder. Then she noticed Lena, Anna and Jasmine had taken up positions not far from where she was standing. She knew that if anything happened, their magic would encompass the entire group.

Gage and Marcus led the group through the house, down the stairs, to a closed door. Behind, the sounds of happy children filtered through. Marcus opened the door, smiled, then said, "Ladies…"

Marcus followed the last woman in. His heart swelled with joy at watching mother after mother reunited with their children. These were his pack. He'd known each of them. Some he'd grown up with. Other's he'd met later, or when they were brought in as mates. He'd watched each of these children while they grew from tiny babies into mischievous toddlers. He may not have known each one intimately, but he'd oohed and awed over every one of them after they were born.

Standing in the center of the room, looking lost, was Marsha. He remembered the devastated look on her face when she'd overheard him talking to Serenity. Knowing Jason had survived, he'd just assumed his twin would.

He walked over and said, "She's not here?"

While frantically scanning the room, she said, "No, they're not."

Angling his head to get her attention, Marcus asked, "They? What do you mean? How many children do you have?"

Marsha stopped searching long enough to answer her alpha. "Three, Jason and Missy are twins. But we had another daughter, Heather." Blushing, she added, "She was a surprise. She's not quite a year younger than the other two."

Marcus was at a loss for what to say. Or what to do. The members of his pack were all dark. Dark brown to black hair, with eyes just as dark, with only a few exceptions. Here and there a baby would be born with red hair. But because they were so few, he'd known the parents of each child. So, if he were to ask what they looked like, it would be dark hair and eyes. Which wouldn't help in searching for them.

Finally, he decided the best thing to do was narrow the search. Raising his voice, he yelled, "If you've found your child, please make your way to the door at the far end of the room where you'll be reunited with your mate."

Several long minutes passed until the last family walked through the door. In the center of the room stood a few lone women. These he knew had to be mothers of the babies who didn't make it.

When he looked across the room, he noticed Scarlett sitting with about a dozen young children. Feeling hopeful, he asked, "Do you want to check…" He pointed to the small group.

His heart broke for them. He'd only considered how the parents would be impacted. Never once had he considered the adults who'd lost their lives that day. Each man or woman who'd died could have had a mate or child. The mate would most certainly die, if not right away, then over time. Such was the way of the wolves.

They were mated and bonded for life, however long that may be. When one died, so too did the other. Explaining the loss to a parent was one thing. But how do you tell a child that their mommy and daddy wouldn't be coming home?

Marsha raced forward. She didn't make it three steps before she stopped. On a sob, she said, "No. They're all too young."

Marcus thought about the boy who'd been his helper all day. He'd prattled on and on about his sisters and how it was his job to look out for them.

He'd laughed and said that Missy and Heather looked more like twins than him and Missy. How could he ever live with knowing this boy would never see either sister again?

Behind them, a door slammed against the wall. Two little girls, who looked enough alike to be twins stepped into the room holding hands. One had long, straight black hair. While the other had the rare golden brown, with curls hanging in rings around her head. Her eyes danced with barely suppressed mischievousness. The golden beauty waved a hand in front of her face and exclaimed, "Whew. Do not go in there."

Marsha flipped around. With a loud, cry she ran across the room and scooped both girls into her arms. Kissing their heads, she said, "I was so scared. I didn't know where you were. I thought…"

The girl with curls tried to wiggle out of her mother's arms. Stuck in place, she said, "Mommy, Missy just had to go—"

The other girl clamped a hand over her sister's mouth and said, "That's a bad word."

Wiggling her curls back and forth, the girl who must have been Heather, said, "Poop is not a bad word."

Turning back to Marcus, Marsha laughed, then said, "Thank you. From the bottom of my heart, thank you."

Serenity heard a mechanical rumble coming from behind them as the garage door opened. A moment later, the shifters charged forward. Shouts of joy mingled with bubbling laughter rang around them. Men and women of all ages knelt while young children ran into their arms.

Ducking away from her defenders, Serenity strode toward the dark shadows of the huge garage. A large double door stood open at the far end of a hall. Slowing her steps, Serenity dreaded what she knew awaited her.

Inside, several women stood together with Marcus and Gage in the center. Women she'd met since arriving, along with others she didn't know, were huddled together. Each woman had one thing in common. They were all grieving.

All had come in hopes of finding their child but there were some whose arms remained empty.

Gage and Marcus's rigid stance and hollow expressions spoke of the helplessness they felt. She knew they would each grieve in their own way, and in their own time. More than anything she wanted to go to Marcus. To hold him and to offer him comfort. But she also knew there were no words. Nothing could ever take away the pain and horror of what happened.

In a corner on the other end of the room, Scarlett sat with a dozen young toddlers. The children were huddled together. And all were crying. Scarlett turned her pleading gaze toward Serenity.

Scarlett took a step toward her best friend. And then she was running. Stumbling into her arms, she clung to her like her life depended on it. And she wasn't certain if she could ever let go. She wasn't sure how much time passed, but eventually she felt someone tugging on her shirt. Stepping back, she stared down at a little girl who couldn't have been much older than two.

Unable to release her friend, Scarlett clung to Serenity. While leaning into her, she explained, "They're the ones whose parents didn't make it. Either one or both were killed. If one…"

"Like Henry's mate," Serenity offered.

"Like Beth," Scarlett muttered. "It was before I was born, but I've seen it with others. Most of the time it's the older ones. But sometimes…"

Serenity patted Scarlett's back then stepped away. Then kneeling beside the young girl, she held her arms out. Her heart broke for these children. She knew all had been given the promise that their parents were coming.

It was something that never should've been done. Even she knew that not all wolves had survived those thirty years. She'd seen a few tufts of fur and bones here and there. But not nearly enough to be the parents of so many children. Looking back at Scarlett, she asked, "What are we going to do? They need someone…"

Scarlett looked at the women still standing in the garage. "We'll get them outside. Maybe an aunt or uncle…or even a grandparent will take them. If not…" She gave a sad smile. "If not, maybe some of those..." She nodded toward the small group of grieving mothers. "There's nothing that can replace the child they lost. But maybe giving them another to love will lessen the pain. At least a little."

Serenity watched her friend walk away. A few moments later, she returned with some of the women. A few were from the Kenneally Pack, others from Whitebark Stand. Each child found themselves in the arms of someone. The weeping mothers, no longer concerned with their own grief, focused their attention on the children. Before long, all the mothers who'd lost their children were offering comfort to a child who'd lost their parents.

Chapter Forty-Four

Sitting in front of the roaring fire, Serenity snuggled closer to Marcus. Three times he'd promised it was the last snow of the season. Until it snowed again, and he repeated the same promise. She didn't care. They still had more than enough wood to carry them well into spring.

It'd taken the combined effort of both packs four months just to get the homes in Whitebark Stand livable. There were still many upgrades that needed to be done, but nothing that couldn't wait. The land lines had been kept in each house while they slowly transitioned to cell phones. It seemed most families still preferred to use their corded phones. She knew the leap into technology would be more of a slow crawl with this pack.

Serenity didn't mind. In fact, she kind of liked the slower pace of the old ways. Somehow, the advances that were meant to make life simpler, only complicated it.

Instead of sitting in the house texting their friends, they preferred to visit them in person. Bicycles were tuned, tires replaced, and the streets were filled with children racing up and down hills.

When the snows began, it was board games, puzzles, and snowball fights. She was amazed to learn that television was a rare thing up here as well. Because of where they were located, nobody had ever bothered with trying to find an antenna that could get reception. Still, she'd never gotten bored.

The pack never blamed her for what her family had done. Instead, they continued to express their gratitude.

As for the orphans? Those who hadn't had relatives to take them in found homes with the parents who'd lost their babies in the attack. In fact, they were expecting their newest member any day now. Surprisingly…or maybe not so surprisingly, the first couple to announce their pregnancy was Marsha and Stan.

Kissing the top of Serenity's head, Marcus said, "So…I was thinking—"

Twisting around, she put a finger against his lips. Shaking her head, she said, "Not yet. There's still so much to be done."

Sighing, Marcus said nothing for a few minutes. Then, standing, he tossed another log on the fire and left the room.

Serenity continued to stare into the glowing, red embers for a few minutes before she went looking for him. She found him shoveling snow off the deck. After grabbing a blanket, she stepped into the crisp morning air. While swirling a finger through the snow-covered banister, she said, "It'll be Easter pretty soon. Will we have an Easter egg hunt?"

Marcus stopped shoveling and turned around. With both hands still gripping the shovel, he said, “You’re kidding, right?”

Serenity turned toward him. Surprised, she replied, “Why would I kid about that?”

Laughing he said, “We’re wolves. You can’t hide anything from us, much less delicious, hard-boiled eggs.”

“Oh. Well. What do you do for Easter?”

Marcus dropped the shovel, walked over, and put a cold hand on the back of her neck. After she yelped, he kissed her nose, then said, “We go to church.”

Serenity looped an arm around his neck then dropped a handful of snow down the back of his shirt.

The snowball fight that followed lasted late into the afternoon. After bringing it off the deck, they were soon joined by several children. By the time the last snowball was thrown, the entire pack had joined in. It might have lasted longer, except Marsha’s baby decided it seemed like as good a time as any to make its appearance.

Running up to change clothes, Marcus asked, “Are you going to call him, or should I?”

After pulling on her shoes, she said, “I’ll call him.”

Two hours later, they were sitting in the waiting room when David rushed in. He tossed his coat on the back of a chair then yelled, “Am I too late?”

A nurse looked up from the station across the hall. "Are you David?" When he nodded, she said, "This way."

The long night stretched into morning. Serenity and Marcus fell asleep after the third time David had come out to tell them it wouldn't be long.

After a nudge from Marcus, Serenity sat up. Standing in front of them, wearing the biggest smile she'd ever seen, was her cousin.

While shuffling from foot to foot, David said, "Are you ready to go see him?"

They followed him down the hall to a large room filled with bassinets. Most of them held sleeping babies. Some had a pink topped card, others blue. Pointing to the second row back, he said, "There he is."

Pressing her face against the glass, Serenity read the card above a tiny golden-haired baby boy. "David Allister Hancock." Without looking back, she said, "I guess Allister didn't make it."

A voice called out from behind them. "Are you kidding me? I've been camping in the parking lot for two weeks. I can't tell you how many times security tried to run me off."

***

Sitting on the loveseat in front of the fire, Marcus couldn't stop thinking about Marsha's baby. He looked at his mate, imagining what their own baby would look like. Would he or she have his dark hair and grey eyes? Or would the baby take after her. Or…

Serenity snuggled closer, kissed his chin, then said, “Do you think our baby will have red hair?

***

Taking out his phone, a bleeding and dying Luka made one last phone call.

Before you go…

Before you get go, I would also like to invite you to visit my website where you can get updates on upcoming books, plus links to my other books.
https://www.marycooknovels.com
Please sign up for my newsletter. In it you will find information on new and upcoming books, plus much more!
https://mailchi.mp/c94b61528cd5/marys-books
I would love to hear from you, to contact me you may email me at:
Lynndaniels1986@gmail.com
Please sign up for my newsletter. In it you will find information on new and upcoming books, plus much more!
https://mailchi.mp/c94b61528cd5/marys-books
I can be found hanging out on Facebook:
https://www.facebook.com/horrorfantasyandthrillers
Or join my Facebook group:
https://www.facebook.com/groups/320682151933041
You can follow me on Bookbub:
https://www.bookbub.com/authors/mary-cook-5f9f5b12-3910-4942-ba99-3a976444852e

I can be found on Goodreads at:
https://www.goodreads.com/author/show/19216394.Mary_Cook
If you're interested in becoming an Advanced Reader Copy reader for me, I'm always looking for new ones:
https://booksprout.co/author/26425/m-l-cook

Acknowledgements

I would especially like to thank my friend Cynthia Haack. Always there when I need you. You lift me up when I'm feeling down. You also don't pull any punches, and for that I'll be eternally grateful.

Many thanks to my cover designer and editor, Lisa Miller, Got You Covered.

A special thanks go to my beta readers. Nora Edington, Robie Moore, and Cynthia Haack.

My thanks go to my most loyal fans. Those who offer words of encouragement when writing becomes difficult. Especially my daughter, Jannette, who has become my number one fan. It seems I've just finished publishing one book, when she's on the phone demanding another.

About the Author:

Mary (M.L.) Cook lives in a tiny apartment in Indiana. When she's not writing, she can be found chasing a very active toddler and trying desperately to entertain a tween, while their parents work. In other words, grandchildren.

However, since she is retired (old), she has hours and hours to write. Worlds come alive. Characters stand over her shoulder. Sometimes they wake her at night. All of them want to have their stories written.

No matter how she thinks the story should go, it goes according to how the character decides it should.

They all write their own stories.

Made in the USA
Columbia, SC
05 August 2022

64325423R00204